[illegible] McAuley joine[illegible] n [illegible]d went on to [illegible]ecome a [illegible] er for [illegible]ight, *Panorama* and *File on* [illegible]. She has a[illegible] produced and directed television documentaries f[illegible]r ITV and Channel 4 and written and p[illegible]ented programmes for BBC Radio. Her previous novels are *Singing Bird*, *Meeting Point* and *Finding Home*.

Also by Roisin McAuley

Meeting Point
Singing Bird
Finding Home

FRENCH SECRETS

Roisin McAuley

1879 21721

SPHERE

First published in Great Britain in 2011 by Sphere
This paperback edition published in 2012 by Sphere
Reprinted 2012

Copyright © Roisin McAuley 2011

The moral right of the author has been asserted.

All characters and events in this publication, other than those clearly in the public domain, are fictitious and any resemblance to real persons, living or dead, is purely coincidental.

All rights reserved.
No part of this publication may be reproduced, stored in a retrieval system, or transmitted, in any form or by any means, without the prior permission in writing of the publisher, nor be otherwise circulated in any form of binding or cover other than that in which it is published and without a similar condition including this condition being imposed on the subsequent purchaser.

A CIP catalogue record for this book is available from the British Library.

ISBN 978-0-7515-3860-1

Typeset in Bembo by Palimpsest Book Production Limited,
Falkirk, Stirlingshire
Printed and bound in Great Britain by
Clays Ltd, St Ives plc

Papers used by Sphere are from well-managed forests and other responsible sources.

MIX
Paper from
responsible sources
FSC® C104740

Sphere
An imprint of
Little, Brown Book Group
100 Victoria Embankment
London EC4Y 0DY

An Hachette UK Company
www.hachette.co.uk

www.littlebrown.co.uk

To Richard

This is a work of fiction and any resemblance to actual persons, alive or dead, is purely coincidental. However, Atalante strongly resembles an inhabitant of Château Sentout, Tabanac, in Entre Deux Mers.

PROLOGUE

1944

Black night. The moon framed in the skylight. A young man and a young woman in a narrow bed. They cannot speak each other's tongue, only the language of lips and limbs. A kiss here, a hand there. Yes. Yes. In any case, it is dangerous to talk. Sound travels. They hear the nerve-jangling rumble of trucks. German soldiers. No one else is allowed on the road after curfew. They lie like statues. The rumble grows louder, peaks, passes, dies away. They turn to each other again.

1

Melanie, 1994

Crisp, zesty, mouth-watering. Light in body but full in flavour. Hints of honeyed sweetness in the finish.

I've led an accidental kind of life right from the start. I should have been born in a tepee. My mom was living in a commune in Marin County at the time. She intended a natural delivery using only evening primrose and tinctures of black cohosh – 'known as squawroot', she told my appalled grandparents – to relieve pain. She was carrying a placard – 'Bombs Kill Babies' – on an anti-Vietnam War march in San Francisco when she went into labour. Before she knew it, she was in an ambulance careering to the nearest emergency room.

The second unintended event in my life was being left in the care of my grandparents, Bill and Dorothy McKitterick. Mom didn't mean to leave me permanently. It just turned out that way. A friend of a friend offered her a job in Washington, DC. Mom thought it was Washington *State*, which would have been fine because she could have commuted. We were all living in Portland, Oregon, at the time.

I don't remember my father. I was only ten months old when he failed to return from the Woodstock Festival in August 1969. He wrote, *Sorry, Babe*, on the back of a three-day ticket and posted it to Mom with a hundred dollars. I watched the film of the Festival a half a dozen times at least in the hope of spotting him.

I have a photograph of Mom and Dad at their wedding on a headland near Mendocino. Barefooted, flowers in their hair. Dad's dark hair longer and curlier than Mom's blonde bob. They were darling. Dad has his arm around Mom. They are smiling. They look blissed out. Happy hippies.

I can see Mom's bump in the photograph. She has her hand on it. On me, I guess. They had a naming ceremony for me – Sky Melanie Moonbeam Star – at Cuffy's Cove a month later.

The marriage lasted a year. Dad lasted three more years. Killed by honesty, his friend Cloudy told me when I got around to tracking down the other members of The Saddlemen, the band Dad played with before he absconded. They cut one record for an independent label. Eighteen mournful songs about cowboys and coalminers. None of them had that kind of background. They were all city boys, the sons of businessmen and lawyers. Mom lost touch with them after Dad died in a road accident. Just like his parents, Mom said.

But Dad's was a different sort of accident. 'His pills were cut with other stuff,' Cloudy told me. 'He got used to doubling up. His dealer was busted, so he got himself a new dealer. Turns out the new dealer was honest. Your dad didn't know that. He doubled up. Overdosed.' Cloudy stared at the grey carpet in his office all the time he was telling me this. When he finally raised his head and met my gaze he said, 'You've got Larry's eyes. I hope you don't have his luck.'

Cloudy is a lawyer in Los Angeles. I never met the other two members of the band. One of them is a session man in Nashville; mostly in work, Cloudy said. The other is a dentist in San Diego. I exchange Christmas cards with Cloudy. He is the only connection I have on my father's side.

I have one photograph of my dad and me. I am sitting on his knee, my arms just managing to stretch around the tummy of a toffee-coloured teddy bear. Dad's arms easily encompass both me and the bear.

The photograph sits on a shelf in the studio apartment I rent in Monterey, not far from the winery where I work weekends. I run the wine club and organise group tastings. Weekdays I live on campus at UC Davis. I drive to Monterey on Thursday or Friday, depending on classes. If I leave my apartment at five thirty on Monday morning, I can be back on campus by nine.

UC Davis was accidental too. I intended to be a teacher like my grandmother. The summer after graduation, I got a job as a harvest intern for a winery in the Carmel Valley. I fell in love with the landscape. The California hills reminded me of my teddy bear. Soft, brown, rounded. I felt I could lay my head on them.

My boss, Vincent Briamonte, owner of Carmel Valley Cottontail Winery, promoted me to the tasting room. I had a good palate, he said, and I explained things clearly to the customers. That October, Vincent offered me a job with time off to study viticulture and oenology. That's how I came to enrol at UC Davis instead of Chapman.

I've never really felt part of a family. Not like my friend Stephanie who has three sisters and a brother, or my boss Vincent who is half Italian and has a battalion of nieces, nephews and cousins. My friend, Linda, has a stepfather and two half-sisters but they all grew up together. I'm sixteen years older than my half-brother and half-sister and I don't see them often.

I had a stepbrother for a while. Mom was briefly married to a pharmaceuticals expert called Hank, who was divorced and had a son, Austin, from a previous marriage. Austin lived with his mother. I only met him once.

When Hank was posted to Singapore, Mom went too. They left me with Mom's parents because I'd started pre-school in Portland and it seemed like the best thing to do. I called my grandmother Grammy and my grandfather Poppa. They called me Melanie. Which is what I started calling myself, although Mom went on calling me Moonbeam for a while and Sky is on my first school certificate.

I overheard Grammy talking on the telephone to Uncle Bobby. I can still picture the black receiver in Grammy's hand; hear the squawking coming through the earpiece, Grammy saying, 'It's been a big shock for Ingrid. I guess she'll stay with us for a while.' I thought she meant Mom was coming home. I quivered with excitement. Grammy saw me and scooped me up in her arms. 'That's you I was talking about, Melanie. You're going to be staying with us for another while. Isn't that great?' It was just after Mom and Hank split up.

Mom stayed in Singapore after her divorce from Hank. She had a secure job with Citibank. Grammy said Mom wouldn't get anything like the same salary back home. I saw Mom once a year at Christmas and I got a letter from her every month. I still do. I keep them in a pink folder I made in grade school.

I was fifteen years old and attending high school in Portland when Mom wrote me she was getting married to a lawyer she met at a conference. His firm was based in Atlanta so she would be returning with him to the United States. I wrote back that I was pleased for her. I could tell from little remarks in her letters that she'd been lonely since Hank left.

I was Mom's bridesmaid when she married Ivor Kitchov at the Church of the Holy Redeemer in Atlanta. The twins – my half-brother Nicky and my half-sister Alex – were born a year later. They have blonde hair and skin that looks dusted with gold. They are like smaller versions of Mom and Ivor. I have the same dark curls as my dad. You wouldn't think I was related to them at all.

2

At the beginning of May, I flew up to Portland for my grandfather's seventy-fifth birthday.

'How've you been, Poppa?' I slung my suitcase on the back seat of the car and slid into the front beside him.

'All the better for seeing you, Melanie. But I miss your Grammy. I guess I take each day as it comes.'

Poppa looked a whole lot perkier than the last time I saw him. His skin had a better colour, like he had been in the fresh air.

'Are you eating properly, Poppa? Getting exercise? Playing a little golf, maybe?'

Poppa hardly left the house the winter after Grammy died. He hardly played golf the following spring and summer. But he ventured out again in the fall. He spent Christmas with Uncle Bobby and Maya in Phoenix. I'd noticed him sounding stronger and more cheerful with every call since then.

At Easter, he'd begun dating a widow from Spokane called May Louise. He met her on a golf course the weekend of his annual Florida get-together with a couple of old wartime buddies. She was in her sixties but looked and dressed a lot younger.

I teased him about her. 'You're such a player, Poppa.'

'I don't know why May Louise pays any attention to an old crock like me,' he said.

But I saw the sparkle in his eyes.

He opened a bottle of wine. No tremor in his hand when he poured. Eyes bright, looking out at the world again. His golf shoes were in the porch – another good sign.

I relaxed, raised my glass. 'Here's to you.'

Poppa introduced me to wine. He acquired a taste for it in France, during the war. He baled out of his fighter plane when it was attacked in the skies over Bordeaux. He spent two months hiding from the Germans before the Resistance smuggled him over the Pyrenees to Spain. He got back to England a month after that. Grammy thought he was dead. She got a letter saying he was missing in action, believed killed. She even got her widow's pension.

She liked to tell the story of Poppa's miraculous return from the dead. 'He turned up on Bobby's birthday. Same day as the letter saying he was alive. Matter of fact, he got there before the mailman. He came walking up the driveway like he'd only been away five minutes.' Grammy always put her hand on her heart at this point in the narrative. 'I was at the top of the stairs, by the small window on the landing. I saw him looking up at me with a smile on his face you could see from a mile off. Well, my heart gave such a leap I thought it would jump out of my ribcage. It was beating fit to burst.'

On the tenth of March every year, Poppa opened a bottle

of red Bordeaux. 'Why today, Poppa?' I asked him when he judged me old enough to be allowed a glass of wine.

'Why today, Poppa? It's not Uncle Bobby's birthday. It's not the day you came home.'

'I'm remembering the day they found me in the forest with my legs shot up. I was cold as ice. Soon as they got me to the house they gave me wine to warm me up, deaden the pain.' He raised his glass in a silent toast.

I imagined him, weak with relief, shivering from the cold, feeling the alcohol warm his throat and trickle through to his bones, sharing a smile with his rescuers. A moment to remember. A reason to celebrate.

Once, after he had come to my school to talk about the war, I asked him if he ever got in touch with his rescuers again. 'I didn't know the family name,' he said. 'They never told me in case I got picked up by the Gestapo. Only one man in the local Resistance spoke any English. He drove the truck that took me to the Spanish border.'

'Wouldn't you like to see them again, Poppa?'

I remembered a trace of regret in his face as he shook his head. 'It was a lifetime ago, Melanie. It's history now,' he said.

Uncle Bobby and Maya flew up from Phoenix for Poppa's birthday dinner. Mom and Ivor arrived from Atlanta. Ivor had booked a new restaurant. He always knew the good places to eat.

Everybody was in high spirits.

'You don't look a day over sixty, Bill. You still have plenty of hair. Not like your son.' Maya ran her hand over Uncle Bobby's shining head. 'My darling husband.'

'Bobby takes after his grandpa Svenson,' Poppa said. 'Bald from the time he was forty. The McKittericks all kept their hair. I've got the McKitterick gene.'

'I wonder where the communist gene comes from,' Ivor said. 'Ingrid told me both sides of the family were lifelong Republicans. Wouldn't have married her otherwise.'

Mom said, 'That's a joke, right?'

'Dad's not a communist,' said Bobby. 'He's just a bit left of the Democrats.'

'That's a communist,' Ivor said.

'No politics, OK?' said Mom. 'Let's just accept that some people don't agree.'

'Too right. You all ready to order?' Ivor signalled to a waiter.

While we all studied the menu, he took a wine guide from his inside jacket pocket. Ivor was a devotee of the wine critic Robert Parker and rarely bought anything to which Parker had awarded less than ninety points out of a hundred. Now he perused the wine list, consulted the guide. This took quite a time. The leather-bound list was the size of a telephone book.

He handed it to me. 'I'm thinking the William Selyem Pinot Noir.'

I was being asked to concur, not disagree, but I thought the mark-up was way too much.

'How about something from Oregon?' I pointed to a Pinot Noir that looked good value for money.

Ivor whisked the wine list from me and snapped it shut. 'I don't think so. The William Selyem.'

'Fine by me.' I shrugged.

Poppa caught my eye and winked.

After dinner, Ivor called for the bill. He waved away our thanks. 'Nice we could all be here for the big occasion.'

Mom left the table. Ivor turned to me.

'Ingrid and I would like to see more of you now that your grandmother has passed away.'

'I still can't believe she's gone,' I said.

'Maybe now you'll get to know your mom better.'

I glanced at Poppa. Bobby and Maya were showing him photographs of their schnauzer, Montgomery. I didn't think they could hear us.

'Dorothy held on to you,' Ivor said. 'Stopped you seeing Ingrid.'

'I don't believe so,' I said. 'Grammy always wanted us to get along.'

It occurred to me that I had lived with my grandmother longer than my mother had. I had probably been closer to her than Mom had been. I had never lived with my mother. Not since I was a baby, anyway.

'You might have more time for us now,' Ivor said.

'Like, I need to spend time with Poppa as well. He misses Grammy too.'

'He's a fine-looking man,' Ivor said. 'Your mother has the same good bone structure. He'll probably marry again. Pity about his politics. But that won't bother a lot of women.'

'Excuse me.' I stood up. 'I need to go to the bathroom.'

Mom was sitting on a stool, re-applying her lipstick.

'You used to be a radical, Mom. You were a flower child. Ivor is so right-wing.'

Mom blotted her lips and stood her lipstick on the dressing table. It looked like a pink torpedo. 'Who says I agree with him?'

'You don't disagree.'

'I just don't argue with him.' Mom met my gaze in the mirror. 'You know, Melanie, there's more to life than politics.

Ivor is a good man. He works hard. He gives time and money to charity. My life with him is,' she paused, 'real.'

'Your life with my dad wasn't real? Is that what you're saying? Mom?'

She spun round to face me. 'I was eighteen. Younger than you are now, Melanie. I didn't know beans.'

'Did you get married so my dad could avoid the draft? I read a lot of people got married around that time for the same reason. They didn't want to go to Vietnam.'

Mom sighed. 'What put all this in your mind, Melanie?'

'I went to see one of Dad's old friends a month back. Cloudy Moncreef.'

Mom turned back to the dressing table. I watched in the mirror as she picked up the torpedo, retracted the pink tip, replaced the gold top. She acted like it was important to be careful about this.

'Can I ask why you did that?'

'I wanted to know stuff,' I said. 'Stuff you didn't tell me. Why did you lie to me about the way Dad died?'

Mom stood up and faced me.

'I did not lie to you, Melanie.'

'You said it was a car accident.'

'I said it was an accident. He was in a car.'

'I asked you how it happened and you said you didn't exactly know.'

'That's true,' said Mom. 'They were on their way to Nashville. When they got there, they found Larry was unconscious. They thought he was asleep. They took him to the ER. But it was too late.'

'He took an overdose. You knew that, Mom. Am I right? You knew and you didn't tell me.'

'You were four years old, Melanie.'

'I asked you about him again,' I said. 'I was at high school. You told me the same thing.'

'Your dad took drugs, Melanie. In the end, they killed him. Yes, it's true. Is that what you want me to say?'

I took a deep breath and asked the question that was really on my mind. A question I had wanted to ask for a long time. 'Did you love my dad?'

Mom was silent for a little while. She looked down at her hands before lifting her head to look me straight in the eyes.

'I loved him,' she said quietly.

I gripped my purse and thought about the photograph I kept inside it. Mom and Dad smiling. Dad's dark hair longer and curlier than Mom's blonde bob. Mom's hair blowing in the wind.

She didn't look any older than she did then. Still slim. Still blonde. Still smiling. Just shinier. Richer.

Mom said, 'It was a long time ago.' She turned back to the mirror and smoothed her hair. She picked up her purse and clicked it shut. 'A lifetime ago.' Her tone became brisk. 'We better get back and join the others.'

She linked arms with me. We went back to the table.

3

Mom, Ivor, Bobby and Maya headed back the next day. Mom said Nicky was in a school play.

'*Hiawatha*. He's the lead. We absolutely have to attend.'

'Naturally,' I said.

Ivor gave me a look.

'I remember the Christmas I came back from Singapore and you were in the school pantomime,' said Mom. '*Jack and the Beanstalk*. You were darling. You tripped on your robe halfway across the stage and the bucket flew through the air.'

'I was looking for you in the audience,' I said.

'Your grandfather stood up in the front row and caught it. Wasn't that just amazing?' Mom laughed. 'Fortunately it wasn't full of milk. The audience loved it. They thought you'd done it deliberately.'

'We were a great double act.' Poppa put his arm around my shoulders. 'Isn't that right, Melanie?'

Bobby said he and Montgomery were going to be a double act at the Maricopa County Dog Show.

'He's certain sure to win a rosette. At least,' said Maya. 'We'd best get moving. Takes a day to get him ready.'

Vincent had given me the weekend off. I went with Poppa to lay flowers on Grammy's grave.

'Fifty-two years together. Except for the war.' Poppa got down on one knee to lay a dozen white lilies at the foot of the black marble cross. He was a little stiff getting to his feet. He stood for a moment with his head bowed.

I stooped to put down my own posy of pink honeysuckle and roses.

Greta May McKitterick,
Beloved daughter. Born March 1947. Died October 1947.
Dorothy Kirsten Svenson McKitterick,
Devoted wife, mother, grandmother. Born 1921. Died 1992.

I glanced up at Poppa. He looked stricken.

'She gave up a lot for me,' he said. 'The Svensons had an automobile business. I had no money and no prospects. They thought I wasn't good enough for her.'

'I'm sure you gave up things for Grammy,' I said.

'I guess I did, Melanie,' Poppa said softly. 'I guess I did.'

Later, in the twilight, we sat on the deck at the back of the house I still thought of as home. Wisteria twined around the posts and tumbled from the roof. The yard was bright with tulips, azaleas, cherry blossom. The air was pungent with the scent of mint, rosemary and thyme. We talked about Grammy's green fingers, the way she planted when the moon was waxing and pruned when it waned, her war on crabgrass and dandelions, her habit of adding a little wine to her stews, even though she rarely drank the stuff, having been brought up as a teetotaller.

I put my nose into the glass, smelled blackcurrants and raspberries. 'Cabernet Sauvignon?' I sniffed again. 'Merlot?' I tasted it. Rolled it around my tongue. After nearly two years at UC Davis and Cottontail Winery, the tasting ritual was second nature to me. I swallowed. 'It's a Bordeaux. Maybe four, five years old? The tannins have softened.' I took another sip. 'I like it. How much?'

Poppa smiled. 'You sure know your stuff, Melanie.' He swirled the wine around in his glass. 'Fifteen dollars. Your mom told me last night that Ivor paid near three thousand dollars for a fifty-year-old bottle of wine. Crazy.'

'Three thousand dollars for a fifty-year-old wine? It might be undrinkable,' I said.

'It's not about drinking,' Poppa said. 'It's about owning.'

We sat in companionable silence for a moment, watching stars emerge from the darkening sky.

I thought about Jesse Arguello, who moved like a dancer. Who was the real reason I lived in Monterey.

I met him in the Lake Hotel at Yellowstone when I was bussing tables the summer after I graduated from the University of Oregon. I liked Jesse straightaway because he didn't make a big fuss when I caught my toe on the edge of the carpet in the dining room and knocked over a side table. He gave his assistants thirty per cent of his tips. Most servers gave fifteen to twenty-five, max. Jesse said he was a socialist and believed in sharing.

He let me fool around on his guitar. We liked the same kind of edgy country music. One balmy evening in July there was a jam session by the shores of Yellowstone Lake. One of the other servers had a clawhammer banjo. He and Jesse played 'Didn't Leave Nobody But The Baby'. I fell asleep sitting back to back with Jesse as he sang 'go to sleep, you little baby' and the moon sailed over the mountain ridge beyond the dark water.

We hooked up for the summer. Summer slid into fall. I applied to do my teaching credential at Chapman in Monterey and in the meantime got the intern job that accidentally turned into a career in the wine industry.

Now I said, 'I'm seeing somebody, Poppa. You'd like him. He's a graduate student. Politics and International Affairs. He's working for the Kerry campaign right now. It's keeping him busy. He's out knocking on doors most nights.'

'Sounds good,' Poppa said. 'You think he's the real McCoy?'

I smiled. 'He could be.'

Poppa put down his glass, folded his arms, stretched out his legs and closed his eyes. His head nodded on his chest. I wondered what it would be like to be seventy-five.

'Funny thing.' Poppa opened his eyes.

'What's a funny thing, Poppa?'

'Memory,' he said softly. 'I was trying to remember myself at your age, Melanie.' He was silent for a moment. 'What was I like at twenty-five? Not me, like I am now. But not someone else either.'

'You were married,' I said. 'You had a son. You were in the war. Big grown-up things.'

Poppa nodded slowly. He closed his eyes again. After a while he said, 'The endless tunnel of memory. You can get lost in there.'

4

'I wish I had more memories of my dad,' I said to Jesse.

We were walking barefoot along the beach at Carmel on a Sunday afternoon in June. I couldn't help wondering if my dad and mom had run their toes through the same soft, white sand.

'A bunch of us saw *Woodstock The Director's Cut* last week,' I said. 'An extra forty-five minutes of footage but I still didn't see my dad.'

Jesse squeezed my hand.

'I used to ask Mom for memories,' I said. 'She would tell me about walking along beaches in California but she could never be specific about what time, what beach, what they did.'

Jesse laughed. 'They probably made love in the dunes. They were probably stoned. Your mom wouldn't want to say that to a kid. They were hippies, Melanie. It was the sixties. You know what they say. If you remember them, you weren't there.'

He pointed to a middle-aged couple strolling by the

water's edge. They were both wearing faded blue jeans and red bandanas but they had about them the unmistakable sheen of affluence.

'I bet they were here in the summer of love,' Jesse said. 'Same blue jeans. Just poorer back then.' He paused. 'Probably not really poor. A lot of hippies had rich daddies to go home to.'

'My dad wasn't rich,' I said. 'I never knew his parents. They died in a road accident before I was born. Mom never knew them either.'

Jesse squeezed my hand. 'Sorry, Melanie.'

One of the things that drew me to Jesse, drew us to each other, I suppose, was that he didn't have much of a family either. His parents divorced when he was fifteen. His younger brothers and sisters moved to the East coast with his mom. Jesse opted to stay with his dad. He had some cousins on his dad's side that he hung out with until they moved away to Los Angeles.

We lay in the dunes for a long time that afternoon. I was dozing, enjoying the sun on my face, when I felt Jesse disengage himself and get to his feet. I opened my eyes and smiled up at him. His face was serious.

'We've spent more time together these last months. It's been amazing. Makes being away from you a whole lot harder,' he said.

'It'll be better when term is over.'

'That's the thing.' He squatted down beside me, scooped up a handful of sand, let it trickle through his fingers in a silver stream. 'No rich daddy. I need to work this summer to pay my classes. I'm going back to Yellowstone.'

'Can't you get a job here?'

'Yeah. As a bartender.' He flung the last of the sand away

and wiped his hands against each other. 'The pay's better in Yellowstone. And the tips.'

'And it's more fun?' I sat up, suddenly angry. 'Because I couldn't get to a couple of parties? I work, Jesse. I don't have time.'

'I work too,' he said. 'I just need to earn more money.' He put his hands on my shoulders, steadied me. 'I'll be back in September.'

'Harvest,' I said. 'When I'll be working harder than ever.'

He looked straight into my eyes. 'Maybe I could move in with you. We'd see more of each other that way.'

'When you come back from Yellowstone?'

'I thought maybe now,' he said. 'My classes are finished. I don't need my room in college.' His mouth puckered in a smile. 'My stuff's on the Harley.'

Turned out, Jesse didn't have much stuff. His Gibson guitar, his harmonica and his second-hand laptop computer were all that could be called permanent possessions. Everything else – pants, jeans, shorts, sweatshirts, sneakers, boots, razor, toothbrush – he had packed into a large duffel bag.

I looked around my apartment. Framed photographs, novels, reference books, decanters, and vases on shelves. Pots and pans, dishware, flatware, glasses in cupboards, a food processor. My clothes jostled in the wardrobe. My shoes were stacked in a cupboard by the door.

I looked at Jesse's things laid out neatly on Grammy's patchwork quilt.

'Is this all you have? No photographs? No books?'

'I store photographs on my computer. Any books I want to keep are at my dad's. I use the college library.' He took off his baseball cap and flicked it on to the bed. 'Wherever I lay my hat, that's my home.'

We spent that weekend with Jesse's cousins, Tommy and Mike, their wives and children, at a beach house rental in Santa Barbara. The children – three girls and two boys – were all under the age of seven. We played volleyball, paddled in the surf, threw sticks for two boisterous Labrador retrievers.

In the evening, when the children were asleep, we played cards by candlelight. And when the cousins and their wives began talking about going to bed, Jesse and I went skinny-dipping.

'I wish I'd grown up in a big family,' I said to Jesse as we walked back up the beach in the moonlight.

'Wearing cast-offs, always having to share a room, squabbling over who gets the last cookie in the tin, taking turns on the computer. Better be rich if you want a big family.'

'But you were happy, weren't you, Jesse? Until the divorce.'

'I guess,' he said. 'Nobody murdered anybody.'

We reached the hut. Mike was on the porch smoking a joint. 'There are some things you just can't do when the kids are around,' he said. 'You'll have to make a few changes to your lifestyle when you settle down.'

Jesse took the proffered joint. 'That won't happen for a while yet.'

We left at dawn the next morning. The house was asleep. Before putting on my helmet, I paused for a moment to inhale the cool damp air and listen to the waves crashing on the sand.

'Come on, let's go.' Jesse turned the key. The engine coughed, rumbled. I climbed on the back of the motorbike. Jesse kicked back the stand. I put my arms around him and held on tight.

Jesse left for Yellowstone a week later.

When I next wrote Mom, I mentioned that a friend had been staying with me for a few days and how few possessions he had. *Maybe we all have too much stuff*, I wrote. *Did my dad leave stuff in Portland when he left? Just curious.*

Mom called me. 'Stuff is what keeps you grounded,' she said. 'Your dad didn't leave much behind. Some clothing. I took it to the thrift shop. He took what mattered to him.'

'He didn't take you. He didn't take me.'

'He wanted to take us. I wanted to go. But you had baby measles.'

What if we had all gone to Woodstock? Would my dad have come back to Portland, got a job, become a lawyer like his friend Cloudy? Measles. My fault.

'Don't you go blaming yourself, Melanie,' Mom said. 'Larry wasn't the staying kind. He travelled light. We were always too heavy for him.'

'So what did he take?'

'His Gibson. His hat.' I knew she was smiling from the way her voice changed. The hurt had faded to nostalgia a long time ago. 'A black felt hat with yellow flowers.'

I glanced at Jesse's blue baseball cap on the hook behind the door.

Wherever I lay my hat, that's my home.

5

Not long after Jesse left, my friends from high school, Stephanie and Linda, came to stay. They had finished college and were both working in New York. We had a lazy time catching up, talking about love and work. 'What else is there?' said Stephanie. She was a psychology major.

They both had regular boyfriends back East. Stephanie was dating a friend of one of her cousins. He was keen for her to take a year out and go to Europe with him. He had cousins in Sicily. 'We're thinking we can work our way down through France and Italy. See Florence and Rome on the way. Maybe take a boat to some islands,' she said.

Linda had gotten engaged to a teacher she met at summer camp in her last year at college. We spent some time planning her wedding. She wanted Stephanie and me as bridesmaids. 'Then I can be maid of honour when you guys get married.'

They were gratifyingly curious about Jesse.

'Do you think you're going to marry him?' Stephanie asked.

'We haven't talked about it,' I said. 'He was hardly living with me a week before he took off for Yellowstone.'

'Hard-working,' Linda said. 'That's good. Remember Jerry? Handsomest boy I ever saw. Lazy as sin. I just knew we'd never be happy. Always be poor.'

'Poor doesn't mean unhappy,' I said.

'Makes it a whole lot harder to keep smiling through the hard times.'

'Pete isn't rich,' said Stephanie. 'But you're going to marry him.'

'Pete has a steady job. Like he works hard. We'll have health insurance. He wants us to have a family. But OK, most important, I love him.'

'Pete is like your mom,' said Stephanie. 'Most people marry their mothers. Even girls marry their mothers.'

'So I'm guessing Patrick has dark curly hair and makes wonderful pasta à la Norma,' I said.

Stephanie laughed. 'Actually, he's blond and he can't cook. I'm not talking looks. I'm talking temperament. Both men and women marry partners who have personalities like their mothers. Or they should, if they want to be happy. That's the theory anyhow.'

'So Patrick uses his hands a lot when he talks?'

'That's not what I mean about personality,' said Stephanie. 'Gestures, mannerisms are mostly superficial. Patrick likes people. He's open. He's very hospitable. He's a little bit judgemental. Just like my mom.'

'I get it,' said Linda. 'My mom is real hard-working. She's reserved. But she's also liberal in her views.'

'I didn't see that much of Mom when I was growing up,' I said. 'How does your theory work in that instance?'

'Your grandmother brought you up,' said Stephanie. 'You ought to marry someone like her.'

'Grammy didn't drink alcohol,' I said. 'I'm in the wine industry. I couldn't marry somebody who didn't like wine.'

'It's what your Grammy was like in her soul that counts,' Stephanie said. 'What kind of person she was.'

'She was strong,' I said. 'She was strict, but fair. She had a neat sense of humour. I sometimes felt she was laughing at me, but in a nice way. Know what I mean? She always knew how to do stuff.'

'Is Jesse like that?'

'He likes fair play. He has a neat sense of humour.' I thought for a moment. 'Yeah. I guess he's like Grammy in a lot of ways. I miss him a lot.'

Things were pretty quiet after Linda and Stephanie flew back to New York. I hung out in the evenings with a couple of friends from college who had summer jobs in Monterey. I worked at Cottontail most days.

In the mornings, fog drifted down the valley and floated over the vines. The grapes glistened with moisture; the air was cool and damp. Around midday, the sun dried the valley, lit the hills, and warmed my skin. That's when I would think about Jesse.

One morning at the beginning of August, when we were quiet in the tasting room, I went with Vincent on his daily tour of the vineyard.

'You look miles away,' he said. 'Thinking about that cute boyfriend of yours?'

'Jesse's gone back to Yellowstone for the summer,' I said. 'He needs the money.'

My thoughts drifted to a night by the lake, a full moon,

and the soft twang of a guitar. My belly tightened at the memory.

'Absence makes the heart grow fonder,' Vincent said. 'I felt certain about Louis when he went to France for six months. He had to stand in line to make a telephone call. Longest six months of my life.'

He stood for a moment, as lost in thought as I had been a moment before.

'He'll be back.' Vincent twisted a grape from its stalk, handed it to me. I tested it with my fingers. It gave a little, was beginning to soften. I bit through the skin, my mouth watering as I tasted the rush of juice.

Vincent picked a berry from another bunch, popped it in his mouth. His jaw worked. 'There's a different kind of texture in the seeds,' he announced. 'I think we've got veraison.'

I loved the word. I rolled it around my tongue.

'You're miles away, again,' Vincent said.

'I was thinking there should be a word for the ripening of love,' I said. 'The way veraison means the ripening of grapes.'

'I like that,' said Vincent. 'That's good. That's real good. That's romantic.' He thought for a moment. 'What about loveraison?' He shook his head. 'Doesn't sound right.'

We filled a bag with grapes from different bunches, different rows, took them back to the cellar, crushed them, tested the sugar content. Vincent's taste buds were in good shape. The berries were ripening all right.

A happy buzz ran around the winery when Vincent made the announcement. Veraison. Veraison. The moment when grapes change colour from green to yellow, if they are white wine grapes, from green to pinkish purple if they are red wine grapes.

'Melanie thinks there should be a word for ripening love,' said Vincent.

Louis, a plump man with tender eyes, stopped sweeping the floor and folded his hands over the top of the broom. 'How about amoraison?'

'You're a poet, Louis,' said Vincent fondly. He studied the calendar on the wall behind the tasting counter. 'Looks like we'll start picking earlier than last year.'

Allowing for the vagaries of the Californian weather, we had just over a month in which to get ready for the harvest in mid-to-late September. The cellar workers cleaned the holding tanks and the fermentation tanks. They transferred the wines that were ready for the market from the oak barrels, in which they had been maturing, into holding tanks, ready for bottling.

The Cottontail Winery did not have its own bottling room. It was a big investment. Vincent hired a mobile bottling truck. It backed up the steep slope to the winery one evening in mid-August. A team of Mexican workers, all regulars, arrived in a bus at dawn the following morning.

I loved bottling day. I adored the speed and intensity of it all. The whole team moved like a line of dancers. And when the last drop was in the last bottle and the hoses had been sucked back into the truck and we stood around grinning, Vincent and Louis invited us all to their ranch further up the valley for a barbecue.

Vincent held up a bottle of Cuvée Carolina – named for his mother – the wine of which he was most proud.

'What can I say, folks? I can't do better than quote from the tasting notes written by young Melanie here.' He squinted at the label on the back. 'An opulent chardonnay aged in French oak barrels for twelve months, Cuvée Carolina rewards the taste buds with a complex blend of tropical fruits, hints of vanilla, liquorice and minerality.' He pointed to the glasses and bottles on a long, pine table. 'Help yourselves. Enjoy.'

There was much clinking of glasses and cries of 'Bravo, Vincent.'

A couple of the Mexicans produced an accordion, maracas and a twelve-string guitar from the back of their bus. They sat by the pool, playing and singing traditional ranchero songs with decorative vocal flourishes. Louis tended the barbecue. I took my glass of Cuvée Carolina to the edge of the terrace and stood gazing back down the valley. In the distance, aluminium strips tied to rows of vines to scare away the birds, twinkled like fallen stars. The sun began its slow slide behind the hills. I thought about Jesse. I wondered if he would telephone that night. If I could make my excuses and get back to my apartment in time for his call.

The air was heavy with a sweet, resinous scent from a carpet of pink flowers directly below the terrace. I inhaled deeply.

'Rock roses,' said Vincent. 'Resilient, long-lasting and low-maintenance.'

I started. I hadn't heard him come up behind me.

'They prosper in poor soil. Like the grapevine,' said Vincent. 'And they smell as good as this tastes.' He raised his glass. 'Well done, Melanie.'

'I didn't do anything.'

'You tasted it in barrel. Your opinion is in this glass as well as on the label.' He put a friendly arm on my shoulder. 'You've got what it takes to be a winemaker, Melanie.'

The music seemed to swell. I felt the whole valley could see me glow. I hid my face in my glass.

'I'm serious,' Vincent said. 'Don't underestimate your talents. When you finish at Davis there's a permanent job for you here. Although I think you'll probably be lured away.'

I had begun a muddled sentence of protest and thanks when a shout, heard even over the plangent strings, made us both turn our heads. Louis was beckoning to us, holding his fist to his ear, mouthing something.

'Telephone call for you, Melanie,' he said when we reached him. 'Take it in the den.'

The band was playing the Mexican hat dance. I skipped into the house, picked up the receiver on Vincent's desk.

'Jesse?'

'Melanie, it's Mom.'

Something in her voice made me suddenly cold. I pulled at the window latch to shut out the strumming of the guitar, the happy cries. I don't think I spoke at all while Mom told me Poppa was in the Good Samaritan Hospital and the doctors didn't know if he would pull through.

'Cardiac arrest,' she said. 'They stabilised him. They couldn't fix the problem with stents. Too many blocked arteries. Thank the Lord I was in Seattle at a conference with Ivor. I'm boarding in ten minutes.'

Vincent called the airlines, got me a cab from town. He pushed two hundred dollars into my hand. 'Go straight to the airport. Buy what you need when you get to Portland.' He said a few urgent words in Spanish to the driver and shooed me into the back of the cab.

The driver said nothing until we slowed down at the approach to the airport.

'Your grandfather is a good man?'

'He is a real good man,' I said.

'Then he get well or he go to heaven,' said the driver.

6

I found Mom and Uncle Bobby in the corridor outside the operating theatre. Mom was white-faced, staring at the wall. Bobby had his head in his hands. Poppa's friend, May Louise, was sitting opposite them. Her hair was untidy. She looked like she had gotten dressed in a hurry. She tried to smile at me. Gave up.

I sat down beside Mom. She took my hand.

'What happened?'

Mom gestured at May Louise. 'She was with him.'

'We weren't doing much,' May Louise said. 'Nothing strenuous.'

Bobby raised his head. 'It's not your fault. It's good that you were there so Dad wasn't on his own. You did right to call the ambulance. You probably saved his life.'

'We don't know that yet,' said Mom.

'He's been in there three hours already,' Bobby said. 'That's a good sign. They haven't given up on him.'

The hospital corridor had a busy timelessness. People

came and went. Occasionally a nurse would stop and say, 'You folks all right?'

Finally a doctor in green scrubs pushed through the swing doors. He had safety glasses and a surgical mask around his neck. He looked at Mom, then at May Louise. He hesitated.

'I'm his daughter,' Mom said.

May Louise did a sort of tiptoe shuffle backwards. I saw she was wearing pink mules with feathers. She had matching varnish on her toenails. She muttered something about sending over Poppa's clothes.

The doctor spoke to Mom. He explained what they'd been doing to Poppa. It sounded a lot like plumbing. I got the main message. Poppa was alive. We would get to see him later.

Bobby released his breath in a long sigh. 'I guess we can get some sleep now.'

I checked my watch. It was a quarter after six. I looked around for May Louise, to tell her the news. There was no sign of her. I figured she had slipped out. I had been too tired to notice.

Mom, Bobby and I went back to the house and prowled around in the restless state that comes when your body is tired but your brain is agitated.

Mom opened the refrigerator, looked in cupboards. 'At least there's food.'

'Poppa takes care of himself,' I said. 'He budgets, but he eats healthy stuff.'

'Too many eggs,' Mom said. 'He should only eat two a week.'

'Actually, red meat is the culprit,' said Bobby.

'Poppa plays golf,' I said.

'That's not aerobic,' said Mom. 'Ivor works out.'

'Ivor is in his fifties,' I said. 'Poppa is seventy-five.'

'I bet he didn't check his blood pressure. Ivor gets his blood pressure checked every three months.'

'Give it a rest, Ingrid,' said Bobby.

I made us some French toast and coffee.

'Nice, Melanie,' said Bobby. 'Mom used to make this a lot.'

'With maple syrup?'

'And sugar sprinkles on birthdays,' Mom said.

'I loved her chocolate cake,' Bobby said. 'She gave Maya the recipe but it didn't taste the same. Maya used the exact same flour, the same chocolate, and vanilla sugar not vanilla extract. Still didn't taste the same.'

'Memory is a flavour,' I said.

We got to see Poppa around midday. He was tethered to machines that bleeped and blinked. He looked thin. His eyes were closed, but I knew he heard us come into the room because he raised one hand a few inches.

He opened his eyes, slowly, like he had pennies on his eyelids. He turned his head so he could look at us. His eyes were like the sea on a cloudy day. He smiled.

'I guess I'm not as fit as I thought I was.'

He closed his eyes again.

After that we could all get some sleep.

I woke in the bedroom that had been mine for as long as I could remember. My teddy bear sat on the chair by the bed. My Muppets poster, my school certificates, framed by Grammy, hung on the wall. I had chosen the pink wall-paper. My favourite books stood on the shelves Poppa made for me. Some of my clothes still hung in the closet. Poppa made that too. It had a sliding door and lots of drawers inside. And he made the blue and white doll's house that still stood in a corner of the room. He made the miniature beds, tables, chairs and cots.

Grammy sewed covers for the tiny beds and chairs from scraps of pink and white material left over when she made the drapes for my room. I made a Grammy, Poppa, Mom, Dad and baby from modelling clay.

I got out of bed, knelt on the floor and opened the front of the doll's house. The clay figures had hardened. Heads, arms, legs had fallen off. I couldn't tell which was which. I picked up a head and tried to attach it to a tiny torso. It wouldn't stick.

I heard a knock on the door and got to my feet. Mom stepped into the room. 'It's six o'clock. Bobby has ordered us some pizza.'

She stood for a moment looking at the doll's house.

'I'd forgotten Dad made that,' she said. 'When he gets better, I'll ask him to make a doll's house for Alex.'

'She can have this one,' I said.

'Are you sure, Melanie?'

'Yeah, I'm sure,' I said. 'You can't hold on to things for ever.'

Two days later, a cheerful nurse got Poppa out of bed and taking a few steps. Out of the woods, she said. Practically a new heart. 'You can start dating again.' She gave him a wink.

Poppa winked back. A slow wink, a tired smile. But I felt like cheering.

The nurse helped him back into bed. The machines were gone but he was still attached to a drip.

'Hurts like hell,' he said. 'But I'm alive. Happy to be

here.' He lay back for a moment and closed his eyes. When he opened them again he said, 'I've been doing a lot of thinking. 'There's something I want to tell you. I was going to wait until I got you all together at the same time. Maybe at Thanksgiving. But it won't wait. I've had a wake-up call. The Lord could take me anytime.'

'You're fine, Poppa. Good as new,' said Bobby.

Poppa put his hand up. 'I've made my decision. Now listen to me.' He took a breath. 'Fifty years ago I fathered a child in France.'

Bobby yelped.

Mom said, 'Oh. My. God.'

'I thought that would surprise you,' Poppa said.

7

The hospital room was white and cool. Bars of sunlight fell through the slatted blinds on to the bed. Poppa's face was almost in shadow. His voice faltered at first, but grew stronger as he told us the story.

I already knew most of it. The unimportant bit, as it turned out. When I was small, Poppa had come to our school to talk about his time in the Air Force during the war. He was a pilot in a squadron based in the south of England, flying fighter planes. In February 1944, he was on bomber escort over Bordeaux one night when his Mustang was attacked and disabled. Poppa parachuted to earth but his legs were shot up. He landed awkward and broke his arm as well.

'It was a pitch-black night. We never flew missions when there was a moon. I couldn't see much as I was coming down. I didn't know how bad I was injured. I passed out after I hit the ground.'

When Poppa woke up some time after dawn, he saw he was in a forest clearing, near a wide, gravel track. He could see a hand-made wooden signpost. Hostens 5. He dragged himself into the trees and unbuckled his parachute. He heard a girl's voice singing, and footsteps on the track.

'I got myself up on one elbow, put two fingers in my mouth and whistled. I gave her a fright, I guess. She was carrying a hand saw. She held it in front of her like a gun when she came towards me. I put up my hands. "American. American. No parley voo fransay." I pointed to the sky, pulled a bit of my parachute out from under the leaves. She made signs for me to be quiet and lie down. "*Boche. Boche.*" She threw more leaves over the parachute. She disappeared. About a minute later a truck pulled up. Next thing I heard German voices. Then the girl's voice. Game over, I said to myself. But the truck started up again and drove away. About twenty minutes later the girl came back on a cart with two other women. They bundled up my parachute, lifted me on to the cart, covered me with twigs, took me to their farm.'

An elderly doctor came, fixed up Poppa's legs, put his arm in a sling, helped get him upstairs to an attic room and left without saying a word.

The next day, a young man came to see Poppa. He was small and muscular and had a big nose. He spoke some English. He said he was with the Resistance. He asked Poppa a few questions, checked his identity tag.

He was the only young man Poppa saw. The rest were prisoners or doing forced labour in Germany, or hiding in the forest with the Resistance. The women in the house seemed to do everything. Poppa figured out they were a mother, her daughter and the daughter's mother-in-law who was staying with them because her house was occupied by the Germans.

'We never used names,' Poppa said. 'Just Madame and Mademoiselle. In case I got picked up later and interrogated. I didn't know where I was exactly. There was a strong wind from the Atlantic the night I bailed out. I didn't know how far I drifted before landing. Except I was five kilometres from somewhere called Hostens. I figured that was the nearest town or village.'

Two months later, when Poppa could walk, he was escorted to another safe house about ten miles away, then to another. 'A big guy came with a truckload of logs he was delivering to a factory making pencils. He drove me to the Pyrenees. A guy with a long face and a beard, Basque, name of Felix, led me over the mountains to freedom.'

The school kids always applauded at that point.

'I'll feel grateful all my life to the brave French women who hid me and looked after me,' Poppa added. 'If the Germans had raided their farm and found me, those women would have been shot.'

Now, lying in the hospital bed, Poppa told us what he had never mentioned before. His face brightened when he said her name.

'Amélie. She was nineteen years old. She wrote her name and age on a piece of paper and showed it to me. I saw her nearly every day. She could speak a little English but we communicated by signs mostly. She brought me my food. She changed the dressings on my leg.

Her father was dead. Her brother was in a work camp in Germany. Their house was occupied by the Nazis. Amélie and her mother cycled back to it once a week to work in the vineyard. Amélie said it was about thirty kilometres away.'

Poppa stopped to catch his breath.

'Amélie was brave. When my leg healed, she cycled with me to the next safe house, and the one after that. We passed German soldiers a couple of times but Amélie just waved at them and yelled something back at me in French. The soldiers laughed. I near fell off the bicycle.'

Poppa gave a little shiver. 'Brings it all back.'

He was silent again.

Mom spoke. 'Did she have a boy or a girl?'

'A boy,' Poppa said. 'She called him Dominique. I got a letter from the Air Force in November, nineteen forty-eight, around the time Dad passed away. We'd moved house a few times. The letter went back and forward between departments for a while before it got to me. You were five years old, Bobby. Dorothy was pregnant with you, Ingrid. We'd lost little Greta May the year before.'

He closed his eyes again. None of us spoke.

'The letter was from a guy in the Resistance. The same guy hid me in his truck. He wrote me Amélie had a child and I was the father. But he was going to marry her and bring up my child as his own.'

Bobby stood up and walked over to the window. He widened the slats with his fingers and peered out. 'Still the same old world out there.'

'Not the same in here,' Mom said.

'This is about changing your will, Dad.' Bobby was still peering out the window. 'You want to leave something to this boy.'

'He's not a boy,' said Mom. 'He's fifty years old. If he's still alive.'

Poppa made a weary, dismissive gesture. 'I took care of that a long time ago,' he said. 'I sent money. Twenty-five thousand dollars.'

Bobby let go the blind. It snapped back into place. He turned an astonished face to Poppa.

'I was grateful to them,' Poppa said. 'They saved me from prison camp, or worse. They were going to bring up my child. I had money from the sale of Dad's store. I told Dorothy I lost most of it gambling on stocks and shares.'

'So that's why she took care of all the investments,' said Mom.

'It was the only lie I ever told her,' Poppa said. 'Dorothy wouldn't have understood. Not back then. She was high-minded and good-living. I loved her. I didn't want to lose her. I was a coward. I know that.'

'Twenty-five thousand. That's a whole lot of dollars,' said Bobby. 'A real fortune in today's money, I guess. How did you know it wasn't a scam?'

'I didn't,' said Poppa. 'But that guy helped save my life. I felt sure he would not lie to me.'

'Did you ever try to contact this son, Poppa?' I asked.

He shook his head. 'I promised not to. That was the deal. The guy was going to marry Amélie and bring up Dominique. I had to step away from the plate.'

'So why are you telling us, Dad?' Bobby asked.

'Something I heard made me think one day a Frenchman might show up looking for me. If I'm not around any more, someone else needs to know my side of the story.'

A nurse came into the room and changed the bottle on Poppa's drip. 'Don't you go tiring him out,' she said.

'I think it's the other way around,' Mom said drily.

'That's about it,' Poppa said. 'It's all in a security box in the old roll-top desk in the basement. The key is in one of the drawers.' He closed his eyes.

* * *

We hardly spoke all the way back to the house. Bobby drove Poppa's car into the garage. The door descended silently behind us.

'What now?' Mom said.

'Well,' said Bobby. 'I guess we could open the box.'

8

Poppa was a hoarder. He grew up during the Great Depression and went to school with cardboard in his shoes because it was better to eat than pay to have them fixed, he said. Nothing was thrown out. He had boxes and boxes of stuff in the basement. Ancient tools, books, clothes. The roll-top desk from his father's drugstore.

Bobby pushed up the cover of the desk. Inside were all the ledgers from the drugstore, and an old-fashioned tin cashbox with a handle and lock. The key was in one of the small drawers in the desk, like Poppa said. Bobby carried the box to the pool table and opened it. He took out Poppa's high school and college certificates and yearbooks, his college graduation photograph. Poppa went to Washington State University on the GI Bill. 'Best thing the government ever did for me was pay my way through college,' he used to say. 'Helped me. Helped the economy too.'

Underneath were photographs and postcards held together with a rubber band, Poppa's medals in a plastic envelope, his wartime notebook. He'd shown it to me when I was doing a high school project on the war. There were descriptions of the airbase in England, a dancehall where he'd taught English girls to jitterbug, a trip to London with some pals, a bombing raid. On a slip of paper inside the notebook was a list of comrades who hadn't made it back. It was a long list.

A blue folder lay in the bottom of the box. Bobby opened it and fanned its contents like a hand of cards on the green baize table. A large envelope marked United States Air Force, two lighter-weight envelopes with French stamps, three small photographs, receipts from Bank of Newport and Western Union.

Bobby passed around the photographs. One was a baby in what looked like christening robes. *Dominique* was written on the back in an upright, flowing hand. The second photograph was of a young woman with dark hair and a wide smile standing in front of a gatepost. In the third photograph she had a baby in her arms and a lanky young man stood, arms folded, beside her. On the back was written, in stiffer handwriting, *Amélie, Dominique, Marc.*

Mom picked up the receipt from Western Union. 'Twenty-five thousand dollars. To someone called Marc Petit. Doesn't that mean small in French? He must be the guy in the photograph.'

Bobby took a letter from one of the envelopes. It was written on tissue-thin paper. 'Too hard to read,' Bobby said. 'I guess we know the story already.'

Mom studied the photograph of the baby. 'I wonder what he looks like now. Do you think he'll ever get in contact?'

'Who knows?' Bobby scratched behind his ear. 'Nothing we can do about it.'

'We could try to find him,' I said.

'No we can't,' Mom said sharply. 'Dad promised.'

Bobby put everything back into the folder.

Mom looked around. 'Did you ever see so much stuff? What is Poppa going to do with it all?' Mom had a real tidy house.

Bobby leafed through one of the old ledgers in the desk. 'Times were hard then.' He whistled softly. 'My oh my.' He shook his head. 'April to June nineteen twenty-nine the store made thirty thousand dollars' worth of sales. Same quarter nineteen thirty-two, sales were ten thousand dollars. That's a drop of two thirds. Makes you think.'

Mom examined a grey pinstriped suit she'd pulled out of a steamer trunk. 'Take a look at this. Isn't this just the neatest mend you ever saw?' She showed me a near invisible darn in the sleeve of the jacket.

'A hedge tear darn,' I said. 'Grammy mended my prom dress like that when I caught it on a nail going out on the porch to show it to my friends.'

'Nobody knows how to do this kind of thing any more.' Mom sighed. 'You can't get anybody to do mending. There are no poor people these days. That's what Ivor says.'

Uncle Bobby rolled his eyes. I hid a smile.

Mom said she was going back to Atlanta the following day. She didn't like to leave the twins with the nanny and the housekeeper for longer than a week.

'Mylene and Lateesha are good with the children but they let them stay up late sometimes and eat the wrong things and Ivor is too busy to notice.'

Bobby said he and Maya had entered Montgomery in a State show at the weekend. 'He was first in his class at Maricopa County. I think he could get best of show this time.'

'You can go back now as well, Melanie,' Mom said. 'The visiting nurse will call with Poppa. And May Louise said she would drop by.'

'I can stay a few more days,' I said.

'We'd like to see more of you in Atlanta.'

'I don't have the time off, Mom. I have the winery as well as college.'

'Well, we'll just have to come over to you, Melanie.'

I began rounding up the contents of the tin box. I picked up the stack of photographs and postcards, slipped off the rubber band and looked through them. Poppa in his leather flight jacket, wide-shouldered, smiling; Poppa in the middle of a bunch of airmen lounging around a table; Poppa in front of Buckingham Palace; sepia postcards of Big Ben and the Eiffel Tower. I thought I could make a montage of them and frame it. I could hang it on the wall of my room in Davis, to make it feel more like home.

9

May Louise came by the house with a bunch of dahlias, a roast chicken in aluminium foil and a large white plastic bag. I couldn't help looking at her feet. She wore navy blue loafers that matched her trousers.

Poppa was upstairs with the day nurse who was helping him to shower and get dressed.

'He'll be down in fifteen minutes,' I said. 'He'll be real pleased to see you, May Louise.'

'He said everybody was leaving Friday.' She sounded girlish and awkward.

'I have more time,' I said. 'I have a nice boss where I work and I don't have college until September.'

I looked in the plastic bag. A pair of slacks, a plaid shirt, underwear, laundered and ironed.

'He left them in the apartment.' May Louise's cheeks were bright pink and her chin was up.

'They smell like they've been dried in the fresh air,' I said. 'Nice to be able to do that.'

I put the roast chicken in the refrigerator, arranged the dahlias in a vase and made us some coffee.

'So he told you,' May Louise said.

She was more relaxed now. I thought she was talking about herself and Poppa.

'I never thought life stopped at sixty,' I said. 'I grew up with older parents. Well, grandparents really. But you know what I mean.'

May Louise looked puzzled.

'Lots of people find romance when they're older,' I said.

'I was talking about when they're a whole lot younger,' said May Louise. 'Like when they make mistakes.'

I realised what she meant. 'It was your idea to tell us about France, May Louise. Am I right?'

'Folks need to know these things,' she said. 'Maybe Bill's son will turn up on your doorstep one day. Maybe not. My guess is, sooner or later, there'll be a telephone call or a knock on the door.' She sounded like she knew what she was talking about.

'Did that happen to you?' I asked gently.

'Four years ago. It was somewhat of a shock, I can tell you.'

I waited for her to continue.

'I got pregnant a few months after I got my first job. I was junior secretary in an advertising agency. There was a party to celebrate a big contract. We both had too much to drink. He left the agency before I knew I was pregnant. He was married anyway. I didn't tell my mom. My dad died in the war. We didn't have much money. I gave my son up for adoption. I called him John Michael after my dad.' She took a deep breath. 'They gave him another name. That hurt.'

I wondered what they had called him. Though it didn't matter.

'Howard,' she said. 'They called him Howard. But when he telephoned the first time he said, "I think you know me. I'm John Michael."' Her eyes filled with tears.

'I'll make fresh coffee,' I said. 'Poppa will be down soon.'

'Do you have decaf? I think he should be drinking decaf. That's what they told my husband when he had his cardiac arrest.' She dried her eyes. 'He was thirty-eight years old and expecting his first child. Howard, I mean. I guess I should call him that. It made him want to find his birth parents, he said.'

'I've heard that happens a lot,' I said.

'I couldn't tell him anything about his father. I barely knew his name. Howard was all questions. Every time we met or spoke on the telephone. What kind of man was he? What did he look like? Did he have my sinus problems? Was he good at math? I couldn't answer. He had a nice smile, I said. He liked to laugh. He was a good boss. I didn't say he liked a good time but that was true too. Howard said, I'm almost forty years old and I'm still looking for my daddy. I don't think he liked his adoptive father much.'

'Did your husband know about Howard?'

'He heard me talking on the telephone,' she said.

'A bit of a shock,' I said. 'Hearing it like that.'

'You bet,' said May Louise. 'That's another reason I thought Bill should tell you everything. He was all right about it, my husband I mean. It was a long time ago. We had a good marriage.' She blew her nose. 'Maybe Bill should have told your grandmother.'

I thought about it. 'Grammy had strong views about morality,' I said. 'I think that's why Mom ran away with my dad. I think Grammy always worried I would do the same thing. But she was a lot less strict with me when I started dating.'

I liked chatting to May Louise. She was older than Mom but I felt she heard the same tunes in her head as I did.

'What did your other children think about Howard?' I knew May Louise had a son and a daughter.

'They're OK,' she said. 'Surprised, but OK. They have kids of their own. I guess that made them understand things better.'

I heard the front door closing. Poppa came into the kitchen. 'I feel like getting some sun on my face,' he said. 'I think we could all go out.'

We had the kind of day that Poppa liked. A stroll in the Chinese garden downtown, followed by a visit to Powell's bookstore. Poppa liked to browse.

May Louise and I drifted to the geography section. She looked around. 'Where's Bill?'

'Looking at history books,' I said quietly.

May Louise took down a French atlas. 'What was the name of the village?'

I hesitated. 'Poppa promised not to get in touch.'

'No harm in looking,' said May Louise. 'Aren't you curious? Think of it as homework. Preparation for when he turns up.'

'He might be dead,' I said.

'I prefer happy endings,' said May Louise.

'Hostens,' I said. 'That was the name he saw on the road sign. Poppa said it was near Bordeaux.'

May Louise carried the atlas to a table by the window. 'You look while I find my glasses.'

I searched the index and found Hostens, Gironde. I turned

to the page, traced the co-ordinates with my finger. 'There it is.'

We bent over the page together.

'I wish we had a photograph,' I said.

May Louise picked a guidebook from the shelf and glanced through the index. 'I guess it's too small to be in here.'

I found a map of south-west France and took it to the cash point. I thought I would frame it and hang it on the wall with Poppa's photographs. 'That's where my French uncle lives,' I imagined myself saying.

In the afternoon, May Louise took Poppa for a drive along the Columbia River. I made dinner. Salad, cold chicken with tarragon mayonnaise, a cherry pie I had baked on an earlier visit and put in the freezer.

'You're a good cook, Melanie,' said May Louise. 'This tart is delicious. The shortest road to men's hearts is down their throats. John Quincy Adams.' She winked at me. 'Are you seeing anybody?'

I told her about Jesse. I was thinking how much I wanted to hear his voice. He knew about Poppa's heart attack. He had called straightaway when he got my message. He knew Poppa had come through the operation, but he didn't know about my French uncle. I tried out the phrase in my head. My French uncle. It sounded good.

10

I got back to Monterey in time for the crush, that's what we called the harvest, at Cottontail. We worked from dawn to dusk. I found myself at the sorting table beside a curly-haired Irishman called Brendan. He had a good eye and worked swiftly. I watched him pick out the shrivelled grapes, the leaves, the tiny twigs, as the bunches moved past us on a vibrating roller.

'How come you're so good at this? I don't think they grow grapes in Ireland,' I said.

'I went grape-picking in France when I was a student,' he said. 'At the same chateau every year. I got to do everything. Hand-picking, carrying, sorting. It was back-breaking work, but I loved it. Especially the food and the wine. Only marvellous.'

His hands never stopped moving rhythmically as he talked. 'About forty of us slept in dormitories. Up at seven. Coffee, bread and jam. Picking until half-past nine. Coffee and a snack. A big feed at twelve thirty. Huge pots of stew cooked by Madame. Cheese. Fruit tarts. Back to work, singing. Another big feed in the evening. As much wine as we could drink. Singing and dancing. Fireworks on the last night.'

He conjured up a picture of trestle tables covered with red-and-white checked cloths, grape-pickers in black bandanas, French rock music in the courtyard, guitars and singing in the dormitory.

'I've never been to France,' I said.

'Ah, you'd love it, Melanie.' The roller stopped. Brendan rested his hands on it for a moment. He turned and looked at me. 'You've got eyes like pansies. Do you know that? Of course you do. I'll not be the first man to notice. If you'll come out with me one evening, when the harvest's over, Melanie, I'll tell you all about France.'

'I'm dating someone,' I said.

'Lucky man.'

Brendan told me he had taken a year out from work to go travelling. In Mexico, he had hooked up with a girl from northern California. They had travelled through Central America, Brazil, Argentina, Peru, and the southern United States. She had dumped him, 'Gave me the heave-ho, somewhere near Salinas, just like *Me and Bobby Magee*.' Now he was in Monterey, but his visa was about to expire. He was going back to Ireland.

'I'm footloose and fancy free until then. If you feel like going for a beer, seeing a movie, or just hanging about, give me a call. I'll be around until Christmas.'

We had the best harvest for years. Vincent was so pleased he gave us all a bonus. I telephoned Jesse.

'Lucky Melanie,' he said. 'I have to work extra hours for my bonus. They've asked me to stay until the end of the season.'

'That's practically a month away.' I didn't hide my dismay. 'Don't you have course registration?'

'I did that before I came up.' He sighed. 'I need the money, OK?' His voice softened. 'You sound really bushed.'

'Absolutely. My back hurts, my hands hurt. I can hardly stay upright.'

'If you were here, I could do something about that,' Jesse said.

Right then I decided to spend my bonus flying up to Yellowstone to see him. Wearing Jesse's oversized T-shirt in bed was a miserable substitute for the real thing.

It took me two flights and the best part of a day and I still had to drive sixty miles in a rental car to get to Yellowstone. The trip was going to cost more than my bonus, and more than I intended to admit to Jesse. He sometimes accused me of extravagance.

The sun was low in the sky when I drove into the park. Long shadows fell across the undulating road. A brown bear and her cub scampered across the asphalt and into the wilderness. On vast patches of prairie, bison herds grazed in the dusk. Gradually, pink and purple clouds filled the sky. The air smelled of ozone. The lake, when I reached it, was like black glass. There was a storm coming.

I parked the car outside the staff lodge of the Lake Hotel, sprinted to the door, reached it as a waitress was coming out, pinning her name badge to her jacket. Eileen, Florida. She stopped and looked at me.

'Don't I know you?'

I recognised her as the chief greeter in the hotel restaurant. She was practically an institution.

'It's Melanie, isn't it? Melanie from Oregon. I remember

you. You were Jesse Arguello's squeeze that year. Am I right about that? Where are you in the park this time?'

'I'm a tourist, Eileen,' I said. 'I'm just here for the weekend.'

'You're staying at the hotel, right? Do you want me to put your name down for dinner? Are you travelling with somebody?'

'I'm here to see Jesse.'

She put her arm out, but I was already halfway through the door. 'It's OK. I know what room he's in.'

I stood in the elevator trembling with excitement. It stopped at the fourth floor. The doors slid open. Two heads. One dark, one blonde. Two faces meeting in a kiss. They broke apart. They backed away from me.

'Oh, shit,' said Jesse.

The girl started shouting and hitting Jesse about the head and shoulders with her hands. The elevator door closed. I didn't move. I could hear the blonde screaming at Jesse. I remembered to press the button. The elevator dropped to the ground floor. I got out, went over to the hotel. Eileen from Florida was at the desk outside the restaurant. I waited while she found a table for a Japanese couple, showed them into the restaurant, came back.

'Who is she? How long has it been going on? It's been all summer, hasn't it?'

Eileen sighed. 'Connie from Kansas. She's a busser. They've been at it since July.' She put her arm around me. 'It happens to us all, honey. You get used to it.'

Eileen got me a room in the hotel, made me sit and eat dinner with her when the restaurant had cleared, listened as I poured out my rage and disappointment, told me her life story in return.

Sometime before dawn, I fell into bed and a dreamless

sleep. In the morning I had a quick cup of coffee with Eileen.

'I see it all in my job,' she said. 'Not just with the staff. With the guests as well. Jesse wasn't right for you. He has the soul of a drifter.'

'Wherever I lay my hat, that's my home,' I said sadly.

'You've got him right there,' said Eileen. 'You need someone calm and steady, like my Ron. Someone with his roots in the ground. You can't think about it now. Your head's still full of that dark-eyed snake. But when your head clears, honey, look around.'

11

Louis saw me coming out of the restroom at Cottontail blinking back tears. He steered me into the office. Vincent got to his feet. 'What's up, Melanie?'

'You don't have to say if you don't want to,' said Louis.

I poured the whole story into their sympathetic ears.

'So, you've given two years of your life to a heel,' said Louis. 'We've all met them. Join the club. I'd go so far as to say we have to meet them so we can recognise real quality when it comes along.'

Vincent said, 'You know when you taste one of those big, blowsy, fruity wines? It hits your palate and for a couple of seconds you think, Wow, a real fruit bomb? Remember how the taste vanishes? It doesn't linger. Then you taste another wine. It doesn't give itself up to you straightaway. You have to roll it around your mouth a few times. You have to concentrate to get all the flavours. It has substance. It has structure. It's a different kind of wow. Jesse is a fruit bomb, Melanie. You need a different kind of wow.' He smiled. 'There's not much else I can say except time heals all wounds. Or as my mom used to say, time wounds all heels.'

At least he had made me laugh.

'We all make mistakes and it's very fun making them,' said Louis. He exchanged a glance with Vincent. 'Mostly, anyhow.'

'What about a handsome young winemaker?' said Vincent.

'I'll look around.'

'It can take a long time to find the right person,' said Louis. 'I kissed a lot of frogs. But Vincent was out there waiting for me. You've got time, Melanie. The sun will shine in your yard again.'

They invited me to dinner on the weekend. Louis opened a bottle of Alsatian Riesling. 'My favourite grape variety,' he said. 'It's a little austere on first acquaintance. But it opens up gradually and shows softness, complexity, durability.'

His gaze settled happily on his partner.

'What's your favourite, Vincent?' I asked.

He thought for a moment. 'Merlot. It's rounded, subtle, fruity. It mellows other varieties. Your turn, Melanie. What's your favourite grape variety?'

'I haven't got one yet,' I said.

My friend Stephanie telephoned from New York to say she was definitely going to travel to Europe with her boyfriend. 'It's too good an opportunity for me to miss. Patrick thinks we should get engaged, or even married, first. But I said travelling together would be a good test of our relationship.'

'That's brave,' I said.

'I'm pretty sure Patrick is the true love of my life,' she said. 'I thought it from the moment I met him. But I want to be certain sure. It's a big decision.'

We talked a long time. I told her about my break-up with Jesse. Stephanie didn't bother with platitudes. 'I thought Jesse sounded a lot like your dad,' she said. 'Not the marrying kind. But I didn't want to say anything. You seemed so happy. I'm sorry I was right after all.'

'More fool Jesse,' was Poppa's verdict. He sounded mellow on the telephone. May Louise had been taking good care of him, he said.

I let the baseball cap hang on my door until November. I thought maybe Jesse would come by for it. He never showed. I took the cap to the thrift shop. Then I telephoned Brendan, the curly-haired Irishman who'd worked beside me on the sorting table at harvest time and talked about France. We sat in a bar in Monterey and had a couple of beers. Brendan had dark blue eyes that crinkled when he smiled and the kind of easy manner that invites confidences. I told him about Jesse.

'He's the one who's a fool,' said Brendan. 'Not you.' He looked me straight in the eye. 'You're a great looking girl, Melanie.'

I realised that for the first time in three months I wasn't automatically wondering if Jesse was going to walk into the bar. I felt light as air.

'I'm not working at the winery this weekend,' I said. 'I'm free as a bird.'

That Friday night, Brendan and I got slowly and peacefully drunk together, listened to sad songs, swapped life stories.

On Saturday morning we got up late, walked to Marina beach and launched kites into a pearly sky.

Brendan told me he came from a place where the mountains sweep down to the sea.

'I know that song,' I said. 'Grammy liked Bing Crosby.'

'That's about the mountains of Mourne. I'm talking about the Wicklow Mountains. They're further south. If you come to Ireland, I'll show them to you.'

He talked about the mountains that rose like purple stacks behind the towns, about brown pubs with crooked walls and low ceilings and about some kind of weird old custom they had of dressing up at Christmas and prancing through the streets collecting money for good causes.

But I was greedy to know more about France and the time Brendan worked the harvest near Bordeaux.

'We picked and carried till the sweat ran off us,' he said. 'We worked like peasants and we dined like kings. The wine flowed like water and we sang till we were hoarse.'

I told him about Poppa and the uncle I thought I had in France. 'I could have cousins as well. Dominique would be fifty years old now. He's probably married with kids. Although I guess he could have moved anywhere.'

The wind caught my kite and took it up into the sky. It wanted to fly away. It nearly pulled my arms from my sockets. But I held on to the lines and didn't let it go.

'At the end of the harvest,' said Brendan, 'we presented a bouquet of flowers to the winemaker's wife. It's called the gerbaude. It's a tradition.'

'The winemaker could be a woman,' I said. 'Like me. I'm going to be a winemaker.'

'Then you'll get the flowers,' said Brendan.

The wind dropped. My kite drifted sideways and fell gently to the sand. I thought about Poppa and his parachute floating to earth.

Brendan wanted to buy gifts for his mom and dad. I drove us to Carmel. We strolled in and out of cobbled alleyways, past the gingerbread cottages with crooked roofs and turrets, the hidden courtyards, the little shops, the cypress trees that seemed part of the unreal architecture of the town.

I felt both companionable and melancholy.

'I know this isn't going to last,' I said.

He didn't contradict me.

'I want you to know I don't normally do this, you know? Hook-up just for a weekend.'

'I know it. You're a serious person, Melanie. I like that. It's OK.'

'You know something? I feel OK about it too.'

Brendan caught a bus to San Francisco on the Sunday evening. He was flying back to Ireland the next day. We exchanged addresses, but both of us knew we were unlikely to get in touch with each other. Brendan said he had unfinished business in Ireland. 'I've had my time out,' he said. 'I'm ready to go back.'

I said it was nice for him to feel he had roots somewhere. I wasn't sure where I belonged.

Brendan took both my hands and kissed each of them in turn. 'You're going to find a man who's grounded. Who's sure about himself and sure about you. I just know it. Have faith, Melanie.' He took a parcel from his rucksack and gave it to me.

'A farewell present,' he said.

I stood waving goodbye until his face was just a blur in the back window of the bus.

I sat in my car and opened the parcel. Inside was a set of six square beverage coasters – paintings by the French Impressionists – and a note. *These might inspire you to visit France. I hope you find everything you're looking for. I will remember our weekend together with great fondness. Raise a glass to me sometimes. I'll do the same to you. Brendan.*

That night I dreamed about France. I was walking along a road. It looked a lot like the road leading up to Cottontail. Suddenly, I was following a group of people. They didn't turn around. They kept their backs to me. They were chattering in French. I didn't recognise any words, although I have high school French. I just knew they were French in the way you know things in dreams. They spoke in little trills and exclamations. They sounded excited. I followed them into a vineyard. I touched a leaf and realised it was made of paper. Bits of torn-up dollars, and white paper with typewriting. I pulled off a paper leaf and read, *Château Moonbeam*. The French people had disappeared. Brendan was walking between the vines. He said, 'Isn't that one of the names your daddy gave you?' I looked up and saw a castle in the sky. The sky was clear blue without a cloud. It was full of parachutes with tiny figures dangling from them. Then I wasn't in a vineyard any more. I was in a cobbled yard full of long tables. People at the tables were singing a Mexican song. They still had their backs to me. One of them turned around and said, 'What are you doing here?' I said, 'I belong here.' Then I woke up.

That morning, I asked my course adviser at Davis, Alicia Shaker, about working the harvest in France the following summer. I told myself I wouldn't try to find my French relatives. But it would be nice to find the place where I had connections.

12

I spent Thanksgiving in Atlanta. Ivor and Mom had a neoclassical mansion filled with antiques, a temperature-controlled cellar to house Ivor's collection of fine wines, a yard with striped green lawns, Greek statues and white roses that had no smell.

On the Thursday morning, Ivor showed Poppa and me around his custom-built cellar. It was twice the size of my apartment and held a thousand bottles. It was divided into three sections, each separated by an archway. The first was where Ivor stored wines that were ready for drinking.

'As you see, the racks are subdivided into red, white and sparkling; and further subdivided into wines from Europe, wines from the United States, wines from Latin America, wines from Australia and New Zealand. They are arranged alphabetically.'

Ivor guided us through the archway to the second section.

'This is where I keep wines that need more ageing in the bottle.' He pointed to a large leather-bound book that lay on a lectern in the middle of the room. It looked like the ledger in which great-grandfather McKitterick recorded his earnings from the drugstore.

'I write down every purchase, in date order,' Ivor said. 'I check the book every month so I can move bottles from here into the ready-for-drinking room. This ensures that every bottle is drunk at the optimum time.'

I was mesmerised. I had never seen anything so anal.

'I bet his socks and shirts are colour-coded,' Poppa whispered to me.

Ivor led us into the third room. His chest inflated. He seemed to almost rise off the ground. 'My collection of fine and rare wines,' he said. 'Some of them are a hundred years old.' He paused, reverent. 'They are all top-rated Bordeaux.'

He began explaining the Bordeaux classification system to us. I already knew it, of course. It had been part of my studies at Davis. I opened my mouth. I closed it again. Ivor was clearly intent in showing off his knowledge.

'Bordeaux wines have always been famous,' he began. 'There are thousands of them. The Emperor Louis Napoleon wanted the best ones for the great Paris exhibition of eighteen fifty-five. He ordered the wine brokers to classify them. Pick out the best. They came up with five rankings for the top wines, known as the classified growths, from number one through five. Most of the wines you see here –' Ivor gestured expansively '– are classified. In fact, most of them are first growths, the top rank. I've got one of the biggest collections in the United States. I'm still adding to it.'

Next, Ivor guided us upstairs to see his collection of Romanov memorabilia. He was of white Russian descent, and liked to tell people he was distantly connected to the Romanovs. The Kitchovs supplied furs to the royal court at St Petersburg. That was some kind of link, I supposed.

Alcoves with spotlights were built into the walls of a gallery that ran around the first floor and overlooked the marble-tiled hallway. In these, Ivor displayed his Romanov memorabilia: signed photographs of Tsar Nicholas the Second and Empress Alexandra; a military certificate signed by Peter the Great; a leather-bound copy of *Eugene Onegin* that had been presented to a grand duke; three silver monogrammed cigar boxes; a gold and turquoise Fabergé Easter egg with the crest of Catherine the Great; a small equestrian bronze of Alexander the Third.

The pride of Ivor's collection was a glass decanter that sparkled under a spotlight. It had a ruby stopper the size of a baby's fist.

'It's a real ruby,' said Ivor.

'That would have fed a few starving families,' said Poppa.

'You think Stalin did better, Bill?'

'I won't get into an argument with you on that, Ivor.'

The awkward moment passed.

Ivor pointed out the Romanov insignia, cut into the side of the decanter. 'Can you see? Come a little closer, Melanie, Bill. You see now? Two crowns, an eagle with spread wings and the Tsar's initials. Cyrillic alphabet. It looks like H but it's N for Nicholas. Tsar Nicholas. Murdered by the Bolsheviks.' He dropped his voice in reverence. 'And I just heard a whisper about something way more exciting.' He put his hand on his heart. 'Another relic. A holy relic.' He paused for effect. 'A bottle of the Tsar's favourite wine from the Imperial cellars in St Petersburg. What do you think of that?'

I had no idea what to say. The world of rare wine collectors was a total mystery to me. I couldn't see the point of collecting wines that might never get drunk, or, if they are, might have turned to vinegar.

'This bottle has never been on the market before. It's been in private hands,' said Ivor. 'I intend to outbid any other collectors for it.'

Nicky and Alex came skipping up the stairs. They ran over to where we were standing.

Nicky pointed to the decanter. 'Can I hold it, Dad?'

Ivor shook his head. He allowed Nicky to hold one of the cigar boxes instead.

Nicky opened the silver box and sniffed. 'It smells like toasted marshmallow.'

'You've got a good nose, Nicky,' I said. 'You could be a winemaker.'

'Poppa says peasants make wine,' Nicky said. 'I'm going to be a judge.'

Alex got to hold the Fabergé egg. She cradled it in her hand and stroked it.

'It's beautiful. Would you like to hold it, Melanie?'

I shook my head. I was too afraid of dropping it.

I went down to the kitchen. Mom was arranging flowers in a silver samovar. She took classes in floral design. She looked up and smiled. 'This will be the centrepiece. What do you think, Melanie?'

'It's beautiful.'

'I think it needs a little more greenery.' Mom threaded a skein of ivy through the handles. 'I'll let it trail on the white linen. That should look elegant.' She stood back. 'There.'

'Can I do anything?'

'It's all taken care of, honey.'

Poppa and Ivor were in the den watching golf on television. There was no sign of the twins. I fetched my jacket from the cloakroom and walked towards the front door. Alex came up from the games room in the basement.

'Can I go with you?'

I liked the feeling of her small hand in mine. We walked down the driveway and emerged on to the quiet, leafy road. It wasn't the kind of neighbourhood where cars were parked by the kerb, or were visible from the sidewalk. Most of the houses couldn't be seen from the sidewalk either. I caught glimpses of fairytale turrets and Grecian pillars. Once or twice I heard the thrum of a lawnmower.

Alex chattered happily about school, about her friends, about her Barbie dolls. 'I guess I'm too old to be still playing with them. Dad says I can collect them instead.' She told me her friends thought it cool that she had a big sister who worked in a winery.

'Can I come and visit you there, Melanie?'

'Sure,' I said. 'If Mom and your dad say it's OK.'

'They don't think I'm old enough to do anything.'

A few drops of rain fell from the grey sky. We turned back and started running. We just made it up the driveway and into the house before the downpour.

'You shouldn't have taken Alex out without her raincoat.' Mom went clucking back down the corridor to the kitchen.

Alex squeezed my hand. 'Mom makes a fuss because she had us late. That's what Mylene says. Mylene had her babies when she was sixteen. When are you going to have your babies, Melanie?'

13

Ivor's son from his first marriage, Christos, stood up as I came into the living room before dinner. He was the marketing manager of a cosmetics company based in New York. He had arrived late the previous night after a long day's travel from a conference in Geneva and had spent most of Thanksgiving Day in bed. I was meeting him for the first time. He had not been at Mom and Ivor's wedding.

'I'm delighted to meet you, Melanie.' Christos shook my hand. 'Shame it's taken so long.' He had dark hair and smiled a lot. I guessed he resembled his mother more than Ivor. I liked him right away.

'I just know you two will get along,' Mom said.

Mom and Ivor's next-door neighbours, Jane and Harvey Kolber, arrived with a pumpkin pie and chocolate truffles.

Ivor mixed cocktails. Nicky and Alex passed around Mom's homemade cheese straws, stuffed mushrooms and tiny buckwheat pancakes adorned with a dab of caviar and sour cream.

'Harvey and I would like to thank you for having us over on this special family day,' said Jane.

'If you can't be with your family, at least you can be with your neighbours,' said Mom.

'First time I've been here for Thanksgiving,' Christos said quietly to me. 'I always used to spend it with my mom.'

'This is only the second time for me,' I said.

Ivor came over and put his arm around Christos. 'What do you think of my handsome son?'

I wanted to say he must be like his mother. I bit my tongue instead and smiled in a lopsided way.

'Our son is working in the Philippines,' said Jane. 'Our daughter is in London.'

'Young people do so much travelling these days,' said Harvey. 'Have you done much travelling, Melanie?'

'Not outside the United States,' I said. 'But I'm hoping to travel to Europe next year.'

'Alex and I have been to Europe,' said Nicky. 'To England. We're going to France at Christmas.'

'Our daughter is doing a lot of travelling in Europe,' said Jane. 'Last week, she went on a train from London to Paris. Through a tunnel under the sea. Isn't that just amazing?'

At six o'clock, we sat down at the long table in the vaulted dining room.

A silver tureen of pumpkin soup sat steaming on the sideboard. Mom ladled it into bowls. Alex and Nicky ferried these to the table. When Mom and the twins were seated, we all joined hands and bowed our heads as Mom recited the Thanksgiving prayer.

'For each new morning with its light,
For rest and shelter of the night,
For health and food,
For love and friends,
For everything Thy goodness sends.'

'Isn't it nice to think that all over our country, people are doing the same thing,' said Jane Kolber. 'Don't you just love Thanksgiving?'

'I bless the day that brought my parents to these shores,' Ivor said solemnly. 'They got out just before the communists banned emigration. They were lucky.'

Mom wheeled in the feast on a hostess trolley. Alex stood beside her and recited the menu.

'Roast turkey; two kinds of stuffing – lemon, herbs and sausage meat,' pause, 'apricots, raisins and couscous. Sweet potato, roast potato, green beans, gravy. Cranberry sauce, bread sauce. Chicory and blood orange salad.'

There was a chorus of appreciation. Alex blushed and sat down.

Ivor got to his feet and tapped his wine glass with a spoon.

'We're going to drink a special bottle of wine, folks. It was buried in a vineyard in France more than fifty years ago, to hide it from the occupying Nazis. It's a privilege to be able to drink it. I'm sure you'll all agree. You especially, Bill. Everybody knows the story of your wartime escape.'

We all applauded. Poppa looked embarrassed.

'Ingrid told us all about it,' said Jane. 'So exciting. Don't you think it would make a great movie? I can see Tom Hanks playing Bill.' She paused. 'Do we know any French actresses?'

'Isabelle Huppert, Juliette Binoche,' I said.

'Catherine Deneuve, Fanny Ardant,' said Christos.

We exchanged smiles.

'It ought to be a big name,' said Jane. 'I bet Meryl Streep can do French.'

'I'm going to speak French right now,' Ivor said. 'Two words. Château Latour. Plus one American word. Enjoy.' He moved around the table pouring wine for the seven adults. Mom poured red grape juice for Nicky and Alex.

Ivor took his seat beside me and filled his own glass.

'I won't say what I paid for this,' he said quietly, 'but your mom and I could have stayed for a week in the Waldorf Astoria for the same money.'

'Or bought a dozen cases of Cottontail's finest Pinot Noir.' I liked to give Vincent's wines a mention when the opportunity arose.

'You're missing the point, Melanie.' Ivor picked up his glass. 'This is one of the world's greatest wines. It has refinement, elegance, intensity.' He sniffed the wine. 'Fifty-six years old, but it still has that blackcurrant, cedar and spice perfume so typical of the Medoc.'

We both put our noses into our glasses. I saw Nicky and Alex nudge each other and giggle. They put their noses into their own glasses and sniffed. I winked at them.

I was surprised by the fruitiness of the wine.

'Remarkably fresh. I can't believe it's more than fifty years old,' I said.

'In all your fancy oenology classes,' said Ivor smugly, 'I bet they never give you anything this good to taste. You can't really know wine until you taste the great vintages. These wines have structure, Melanie. They are made to last.'

We moved to the lounge after dinner. Christos seated

himself beside me on the sofa. 'So you study wine,' he said. 'What did you think of Dad's choice?'

'I don't know anything about rare old wines. It tasted good to me. I thought it might be too oxidised by now.'

'Wouldn't matter to Dad if it was,' Christos said. 'He's a collector. That's what turns him on. I just like drinking the stuff. As long as it tickles my palate, it's fine by me.'

'You got the right idea there.' I returned his smile.

'We had a psychologist lecture us when I was doing my masters,' said Christos. 'He gave us three red wines to taste. He told us they were between five and eight dollars a bottle. We had to write down what we thought about them. Use any adjectives you like, he said. The next lesson he did exactly the same, except this time he told us the wines were between thirty and forty dollars a bottle. The third lesson, he showed us our notes. We all thought the first wines were nice enough to drink, but flat and uninteresting overall. We thought the second wines were complex, rich and packed with flavour.' Christos paused. 'They were exactly the same ten-dollar wines. He'd changed the prices, and our preconceptions. That was the point of the experiment. Perceptive expectation. It's why I often advise our product managers to price up, not down. A lot of people think more expensive is better. My dad is one of them. I guess he didn't have a lot of stuff growing up.'

We both glanced at Ivor. The twins were entwined around him. He was beaming with pride.

'He's got a lot of stuff now,' I said. 'Did you mind your dad and mom splitting up?'

'What do you think?'

'I think I asked a dumb question.'

We shared wry smiles.

'No child wants his parents to split up,' said Christos. 'Mom was unhappy for a long time. She's a whole lot better now she's married again. My stepfather is a nice guy. He's in sports medicine. What about you, Melanie? What age were you when your parents divorced?'

'They didn't divorce,' I said. 'My dad took off when I was ten months old. Then he died.'

'I'm sorry to hear that.' Christos put a sympathetic hand on my arm.

Mom was chatting to Jane and Harvey. All three of them turned their heads and smiled in our direction.

'Your mom is real keen for us to get along,' Christos said. 'I'd like that too. But I want to be upfront with you, Melanie. I'm dating someone back in New York. Her name is Catherine. She's special.'

I liked his honesty. We exchanged telephone numbers and email addresses. Christos promised to call up if he was ever near Monterey. 'It's nice to have a sister, if I can call you that.'

'Sure thing,' I said.

'I had real hopes for you two,' Mom said to me later. 'It's a pity he has a steady girlfriend.'

I didn't mind. I seemed to have acquired an uncle and a brother in the space of a few weeks. It was all right by me.

14

I asked Vincent if he knew any French wine growers. 'I thought maybe I could go to France in between finishing my studies and starting work. If that's OK with you?'

'Good idea, Melanie. Louis has second cousins in Alsace.'

'What about Bordeaux, Vincent? Do you know anybody there?'

He shook his head. 'I've only been there once,' he said.

I told him about the fifty-six-year-old bottle of Bordeaux I'd tasted at Thanksgiving.

'Château Latour. That's a big name,' he said. 'A first-growth Bordeaux. Top category. I guess you know all that.'

'Ivor explained it all. In some detail,' I said. 'But I already learned it in college.'

A day or so later Louis and Vincent came to find me in a rare quiet moment in the tasting room.

'I asked one of my friends who imports Bordeaux about Latour. He looked it up,' Louis said. 'It was a nineteen thirty-eight magnum, wasn't it? You drank a magnum at Thanksgiving?' He glanced at Vincent.

'There's no record of any magnums of nineteen thirty-eight Latour ever coming on the market,' Vincent said.

I was taken aback for a moment. Then I recalled that the bottles had been hidden.

'There wouldn't be a record because the bottles were buried when the Germans invaded France in nineteen forty-one. That's why it never came on the market.' I told them the history of the wine, and about Poppa's wartime experience. They looked relieved.

'That is so thrilling,' said Louis. 'Escape from the Nazis. Buried treasure.'

'Ivor gave Poppa a bottle of nineteen thirty Sauternes. Château d'Yquem,' I said. 'I get to taste it over the holidays.'

'The finest white wine in the world. In a league of its own.' Louis quivered with excitement. 'Lucky you.'

'We are so envious,' said Vincent. 'Happy drinking, Melanie.'

The Cottontail tasting room was busy right up to the moment Vincent put the 'Closed until Wednesday December 28th' sign on the door and said, 'Merry Christmas, Melanie.'

I looked around for Louis but there was no sign of him. He caught up with me when I was about to get into my car.

'I was on the telephone.' He was out of breath. 'Did you say you were going to drink a bottle of nineteen thirty Sauternes? Château d'Yquem?'

'I'll have some help, Louis. There'll be six of us.'

He was hopping from one foot to the other. He looked agitated.

'Are you all right, Louis? Is something bothering you?'

'Are you positive it's d'Yquem nineteen thirty?'

I thought for a moment. Yes. I had a clear memory of

Ivor saying, 'This is the greatest sweet white wine in the world,' of Poppa showing me the bottle, 'That's the year May Louise was born. We'll open it on her birthday.'

'I'm positive,' I said. 'May Louise has a birthday on December twenty-seven. She was born in nineteen thirty. It's a surprise for her.'

'It'll be a surprise all right.' Louis hesitated. He looked like he was bursting to say something.

'Is there something else?' I was still holding open the car door.

'I'm dying to know what it tastes like,' Louis said.

I laughed. 'Me too. Merry Christmas, Louis.'

May Louise was staying in Poppa's house over the holidays. It felt a little strange at first, seeing her in the kitchen making pumpkin pie, brining the turkey; the two of us laying the table. But she was easy company and a light presence.

She had brought a Christmas tree. I found the tree-skirt Grammy made – green corduroy with silver bells, golden apples and red robins embroidered around the hem. I stood looking at it clutched in my hand.

'I'm guessing your grandmother made that,' said May Louise. 'It's real neat work. I was never that good with my hands.' She smiled. 'You just go ahead and do things the way you always did them with your grandmother.'

We put the Christmas candle in the window. We baked cinnamon cookies and made eggnog. May Louise held a chair steady while I stood on it to attach the long-serving angel to the top of the tree.

'Your grandmother is in a place where there is no pain, no jealousy, just love,' she said.

Mom telephoned from the French Alps on Christmas morning. 'Ivor always says it's not proper Christmas until January seven but we all celebrate today anyhow. We'll celebrate Orthodox Christmas too, of course. It's just heavenly here in the snow. What's the weather with you guys?'

'Wet,' I said. 'Grey sky. Cloud on the mountains.'

'No surprise there,' Mom said. 'We've got blue skies, sunshine, powdery snow. We're having a wonderful time. Ivor has gotten to meet the person selling the Romanov bottle. He's so excited. We heard the whole story. So historic. It was presented to the Tsar on a state visit to France. It has the Tsar's initials and the Romanov crest engraved on it. We met up with the nice Englishman who's selling it. He told us they put fake leaves on the trees in the Champs-Elysées for the Tsar's visit. Can you imagine? A loyal servant of the Tsar rescued the bottle from the communists. Don't you think that's romantic, Melanie? It's like something out of a book. We had dinner with him and his girlfriend. I don't know how she manages to stay so thin. They both have that cute English upper-class accent. Like in *The Madness of King George*? We saw it in Atlanta before we left. You should go see it, Melanie. It's very historical.'

May Louise's son, Bute, and his wife, Betty, drove up from Oregon City for May Louise's birthday dinner. They were all smiles and cheerfulness.

'Mom's been on her own for five years,' Betty whispered to me. 'It's such a relief to us that she's met someone nice. We didn't get along with her last beau. He had no sense of humour.'

I had made a pineapple cake. When we finished dinner, I carried the cake to the table and lit the gold candle on top. Poppa poured the Sauternes. May Louise twinkled brighter than the lights on the Christmas tree.

'That is just the nicest wine I have ever tasted,' she said. 'I can't believe it's as old as I am. You're the expert, Melanie. What do you think?'

'Tastes pretty young to me.'

May Louise glowed even brighter.

I had a couple of hours the next morning before I needed to go to the airport. I went down to the basement and switched on the lights over the pool table. The metal security box was still sitting on the green baize. I opened the envelope from the Air Force and took out the typewritten letter. It was covered with office stamps and initials. I guessed it had travelled through many departments and a few wrong addresses before finding its way to Poppa. It was brief and to the point.

The enclosed letter is addressed to Lieutenant William McKitterick Thirty-third Squadron United States Air Force. If you are not the person for whom it is intended you are required to return it forthwith to the address above. The date was 9 June 1947.

I picked up one of the envelopes that had French stamps. It was addressed simply to Bill McKitterick, United States Air Force. I wasn't surprised it had taken a long time to reach Poppa. Inside the envelope was a letter, typewritten, on tissue-thin paper. The metal keys had cut through the paper in places. It was difficult to read. It took me a moment to realise it was mostly in English.

La Mairie,
Astignac
Juin 16/1945
Cher Monsieur McKitterick,

I write for Mademoiselle Amélie [unclear]. *You are the father of her* [paper torn] *Dominique. A beautiful baby that is born Mars 10/1945. Here is photographies. Everything goes well* [illegible] *Amélie will be my wife. She want only for you to know.*

Please to believe the assurance of my [indecipherable] *salutations,*

Marc Petit, Mayor Astignac

The second French-stamped envelope contained a typewritten letter, also indecipherable where the typewriter keys had torn the fragile paper. It was dated 15 August 1947.

Dear Monsieur McKitterick,

We thank you for the money. I give you assurance to be good father to Dominique and also [illegible words] *to Amélie. For you also it must be a promise not to contact.* [?] *this* [unclear] *Dominique is my child. I am her father. He is an easy baby. Please not to contact. That is better for all.*

Please [illegible] *expression of my best sentiments.*

Marc Petit, Mayor Astignac

From the stilted language and the mixed-up pronouns, I guessed he had written in French and then laboriously translated his letter into English.

I looked again at the receipts from Bank of Newport and Western Union. The payment office was Bordeaux. The payee was Marc Petit. So Amélie had married the mayor of some town or village called Astignac. Well, I said to myself, at least my lost uncle had a good start in life.

15

Louis sought me out when I returned to the tasting room on the first weekend after the holidays. 'So how was it?'

'Hey, we had a fun time. Poppa and May Louise were like teenagers. Bute and Betty are nice people. We all got along fine. My pineapple cake looked pretty. Everyone praised my cooking.'

'How was the Château d'Yquem?'

'Yummy. Vanilla, honey, roses, burnt sugar. It didn't taste like it was sixty-four years old.'

'That's no surprise,' said Louis. 'It wasn't.'

At first I didn't take in what he'd said. 'Come again?'

'It was a fake.' Louis looked embarrassed. 'I was emailing the guy who told me about the magnums of Latour. I mentioned the nineteen thirty d'Yquem. My friend keeps a database of all this stuff. He telephoned me. They didn't make d'Yquem in nineteen thirty. The vintage wasn't good enough. It was bottled as generic Sauternes.' He made a little helpless gesture. 'Sorry, Melanie.'

I sat down on the nearest chair.

'I didn't say anything before the holiday because I didn't want to spoil the birthday party.'

'That's some spoiler,' I said. 'What do I do now? What do I say to Poppa? What do I say to Ivor?'

'I had to tell you,' Louis said. 'Vincent and I talked about it. We both thought it was the right thing to do.'

My brain was racing. I remembered Mom's telephone call. Hadn't she said Ivor had met the person selling the Romanov bottle? What if it was the same person who sold him the Château d'Yquem?'

'I have to speak to Ivor,' I said. 'I think he's about to spend a fortune on another fake.'

Louis ushered me to the telephone in his office. I gestured for him to stay. He hovered anxiously while I spoke to Mom.

'Melanie? What's happened? Is it Dad?'

'Poppa's fine,' I said. 'Nobody's sick. Nobody died.'

'You're pregnant.'

'No, Mom. I'm not pregnant.'

'So why have I been summoned from the dinner table?'

I told her about the Sauternes and my worry that Ivor's precious Romanov bottle might be a fraud as well. I heard her deep sigh. 'Hold on,' she said. 'You better speak to Ivor.'

While I waited, I imagined Ivor's gratitude. His realisation that I knew stuff. That I, too, could talk about fine wines and their classifications.

'I knew already.' Ivor's laugh boomed in my ear. He told me the Sauternes was one of his earliest purchases. 'I realised it was a fake twenty years ago when I got invited to a private tasting at the chateau. Nineteen thirty wasn't on the list of vintages. They didn't bottle that year. It was too late to do anything about it. I couldn't track down the guy who sold it to me. I learned my lesson. Now I only buy from dealers I know and trust.'

'You knew it was a fake and you gave it to Poppa for May Louise?'

'Why not? You told us she was thrilled. She liked it. You liked it. Everybody liked it.'

'Did you tell Poppa it was a fake?'

'I'm the only person who needs to know that, Melanie.'

'Your Romanov bottle could be a fake as well.'

'It's genuine, all right. It's got provenance. You didn't notice anything about the label on the Sauternes, did you? Did you check the cork? No. Because you don't know a goddamned thing about rare wines.' There was a pause. I could hear Mom's voice in the background. I thought she was probably telling Ivor to calm down. He spoke more slowly now. 'I know about corks and labels and bottles. I can tell a fake from the real thing. I'm a good judge of character. I've met this guy. He has an office in London. I've met his girlfriend. I've spoken to his secretary. Thank you for your concern, Melanie. It was a kind thought. But if you'll excuse me, my dinner is getting cold.'

I put down the telephone. 'Ivor knew the Sauternes was a fake.'

Louis raised an eyebrow.

'Ivor always knows everything.' I felt flat. 'He's positive this bottle he wants to buy is the real deal. It's got provenance.' I took a deep breath. 'You know something, Louis? I almost wanted it to be a fake.'

Louis said nothing.

'Ivor is so goddamn sure of himself. He's constantly putting me down.'

Louis put his arm around my shoulder. 'You did the right thing, Melanie.'

I thought for a day or two about whether I should tell Poppa. In the end, I just asked myself what Poppa would do in the same circumstances. Then I picked up the telephone and told him the bottle of Château d'Yquem was a fake.

'At least we enjoyed drinking it,' Poppa said. 'Maybe it doesn't matter if you don't have the real McCoy as long as you think you have it. Do you agree, Melanie?'

'Wow, that's a big question, Poppa.'

'Except for people,' he said. 'It matters when it's people. Knowing when they're genuine. When they're the real thing.'

'Are you going to tell May Louise?'

'I'm done keeping secrets,' he said.

He called me a day later. 'May Louise told me she isn't nineteen thirty vintage either.' He laughed. 'Hell, I don't care what age she is. Too late if I did.' He paused. 'I asked her to marry me.'

I was half expecting it, but his announcement still caught me by surprise.

'Are you happy for me, Melanie?'

I liked May Louise. She was not at all like Grammy in personality. Grammy had been strong like a tree. May Louise was light and air. But they had one characteristic in common, a fundamental kindness.

'I'm happy for you, Poppa. It's wonderful news.'

'We're not spring chickens, either of us. No point in hanging around to do this. Time marches on.'

Mom and Ivor offered to host Poppa's wedding to May Louise on the same weekend as Ivor's sixtieth birthday party. May Louise was briefly tempted by the idea of being married in a rose garden with Greek statues, an orchestra and a jazz band, but decided against it.

'It would take away from both ceremonies and add nothing to either,' she told me on the telephone. 'Your mom has been planning Ivor's party for months. Bill and I plan on going to it as a married couple.' She laughed. 'That way we can sleep together in the house and not shock anybody.'

Poppa came on the line and said he didn't want any more time and money spent on him.

'You have work and college, Melanie. Bobby and Maya have booked and paid deposit on a two-week vacation in Europe. Betty has most of her days off allocated already. May Louise and I are planning on something quiet. No fuss. We've got the rest of our lives to party.'

Mom called me a couple of days later. 'I was worried it was maybe a bit soon for Dad to be getting married again, but Ivor says men don't manage so well on their own. Dad has been on his own for over two years now.'

'May Louise is good for Poppa,' I said. 'He laughs a lot when she's around.'

'They might move to Arizona,' Mom said. 'Her daughter lives in Prescott.'

'Her son and his wife live in Oregon City.'

'A daughter-in-law isn't the same as a daughter,' said Mom. 'But I guess that could be an option.'

I had gotten used to May Louise in Poppa's house. It hadn't occurred to me that he would move. A gust of sadness swept over me. I felt suddenly bereft.

'Has Poppa said anything?'

'Not yet. But we think he'll sell up and buy something with May Louise.'

I thought about my room with the pink wallpaper. The yard with its bright flowers. The mountains in the distance. Mom was still talking.

'Ivor's uncle Gus married again. He sold his house and moved in with his new wife. She had a nice garden and it was near the golf course. Gus hated it. He kept thinking about her previous husband. They were much happier when they moved to Florida. But I don't know if it's a good idea for old people to move away from their friends. Of course, women have more friends than men, isn't that always the way? Melanie?'

'Sorry, Mom. I was thinking I still have stuff in Poppa's house.'

'Ivor says you should buy a place of your own. Invest in property. Prices are going up real fast. We can help you with the deposit.'

'I haven't finished college, Mom. I don't have a full-time job. I don't even know where I'll be living.'

'You told me Vincent had offered you a job.'

'I might do some travelling first. Maybe go to France and pick some grapes.'

'You're not going looking for that French family, are you, Melanie? Poppa promised not to get in touch.'

'I'm just interested in Bordeaux, Mom.'

'You should speak to Ivor. He's been to Bordeaux. He knows all about it. He's been to all the chateaux.'

The thought came into my head that I would like nothing better than to prove Ivor wrong about something.

16

Honor

Ripe and well-rounded red berry flavours. Acidity balanced with a hint of sweetness. Harmonious. Drink now or keep for the long term.

When we were young we sang in the kitchen, my sister, my brother and I. We sang as we cleared the table, washed up, put the dishes away and swept the floor. We did all the housework because Mum was crippled with arthritis. That phrase is frowned on nowadays but it's what people said then. Often it was no more than a clichéd way of complaining about a bit of stiffness in the joints – 'Och, I'm crippled with arthritis' – said with a resigned smile by people who had full use of their limbs and could run for a bus if they had to. But for Mum it was literally true. She was in a wheelchair from the age of thirty-five.

We sang with her as we waltzed around the kitchen. Anything and everything. Songs from the hit parade, from musicals, from operettas. The latter we'd learned from Mum and Dad who had met at an audition for the Bray

Light Opera Society. '*The Bohemian Girl*. Terrible plot but great tunes,' Dad used to say. 'I Dreamt I Dwelt in Marble Halls' was one of his favourites. Tommy sang soprano until his voice broke. I took the soprano part when Tommy turned into a light baritone. Kathleen was always a contralto. I wished I had been a contralto. So much richer, I felt.

Our little barbershop trio broke up when Dad died and Kathleen got a summer job as a waitress in America. She came back to do her final exams. She still comes back to Ireland every two years. But from the day and hour she met Seamus Breslin, her heart was in America. He was working in the same restaurant in Baltimore. They married as soon as he finished college.

Tommy went to Westport to train with a firm of accountants. I went to University College Dublin. I graduated without much idea of what I wanted to do. My friend Diarmuid Keenan had graduated two years ahead of me and become an actor. He told me there was a job going with a travelling theatre company which performed plays in schools – Shakespeare, Sheridan, Shaw and any other writers who were in the exam curriculum for secondary schools; *The Happy Prince* by Oscar Wilde for primary schools. I still know it off by heart.

We travelled in a converted bus, squashed beside the costumes and the props. If the school wasn't too far from Dublin, we drove back the same day. If we were up in Donegal or down in Kerry, we slept in bed and breakfasts, or on the bus. It was fun but exhausting. We never knew from year to year if our funding from the Arts Council would be renewed. Actors came and went. Directors came and went. I was the only constant. I was actor, stage manager and costume designer. If the plays were too long, I abridged them. I did all the paperwork. I also drove the bus.

I shared a flat near Leeson Street with two friends from college, Mona Cassidy and Sinead Kelly, who had jobs in the Bank of Ireland. I went back to Ballybreen on the bus most weekends. Mona sometimes came as well. She was from County Monaghan and didn't often go home at weekends. Mum enjoyed Mona's visits. She loved the laughter and the gossip.

Tommy got a job in Bray and married his childhood sweetheart, Nessa. They bought a house only half a mile away from Mum. Which meant I could leave Ireland and the Carousel Theatre Company to look for work in London.

On my last night in Dublin, Mona said, 'We'll go for a farewell drink in Donaghy's.'

We joined the crush at the bar. I was tired and cross. Apprehension, I supposed.

'It's a bit crowded in here,' said Sinead. 'Away and see if there's a table in the back room, Honor.'

I opened the door. The room was dark. I began to retreat. An arm came out from behind the door and pulled me into the room. The lights went on. All eight members of Carousel, most of my Dublin friends and a few from Ballybreen as well clapped and laughed at my surprise. We drank and sang songs until dawn. I nearly didn't get on the plane.

I arrived in London knowing only three people in the entire city. Two of Mum's cousins lived in Ealing, and Diarmuid Keenan had a flat in the Barbican. He had moved to London five years earlier and was getting plenty of work on stage and in television.

Diarmuid was one of my oldest friends. We'd been drifting in and out of each other's lives since we built sandcastles together on the beach at Brittas Bay in the school holidays. Diarmuid gave me my first proper kiss, but spoiled the moment by recoiling and saying, 'Ugh, peppermint toothpaste.' I shouted, 'I hate you, Diarmuid Keenan.' I was thirteen. Diarmuid didn't come to Brittas Bay for two summers after that. We met again when I went to college. We even went out together for a couple of terms, but found that we got on better when we went back to being just good friends. I started using peppermint toothpaste again.

I wouldn't hear from Diarmuid for months, then he would telephone, or turn up, and we would resume our easy acquaintance as though only days had intervened. When I moved to London, Diarmuid persuaded his agent, Eddie Nugent, to take me on. At first, I was cast in enough productions to make me think I might build a successful career. Directors eyed me up at auditions. I usually got at least a small part. After three years, I realised I was always the saucy maid or the buxom wench. The terms were interchangeable. Once, I overheard a director talking about me. I was in his flat and he was on the telephone in the room next door.

'When you first meet Honor she has presence,' he said. 'But put her on stage and she disappears into herself. All that softness turns to cement.'

After that, I knew acting would always be something I did in the gaps between other jobs.

Diarmuid worked more than rested. If you saw him walking down the street you'd think he was all legs and arms and awkwardness, but on stage he was all grace and fluency. He was thirty-six and still playing twenty-year-olds.

He telephoned one wet Saturday in April. I was sitting

by the window in my flat in Woolwich, watching raindrops pitting the canal. Wondering where my next job was coming from.

'How's things?' Diarmuid was his usual breezy self.

'It's been raining all week. I feel like I'm in Noah's ark. Only I've no Noah and no animals. Not even a cat.'

'No room to swing one.'

'You're a great one for saying the right thing, Diarmuid.'

'I've a friend who needs a couple of people for a trade fair next month,' he said. 'Three days' work. Easy money. That'll cheer you up.'

'What makes you think I need cheering up?'

'You always need cheering up these days.'

When he telephoned that wet weekend, he had just been murdered in the third episode of a television detective series. He was waiting to hear if he'd got a part in a touring production of *The Real Thing*. The job at the trade fair was a fill-in.

'Four hundred and eighty pounds,' he said. 'Twenty pounds an hour.' Pause. 'Each.'

This was more than the hourly rate for script reading, waitressing, walk-on parts in television soaps, and small, but at least speaking, roles in fringe theatre productions.

'Go on. Say yes. It'll be great crack,' he said. 'I'll owe you a favour. Cross my heart and hope to die.'

It was our solemn oath when we were children. Diarmuid could always cajole me into a smile.

'It beats watching the rain and waiting for Eddie Nugent to call,' I said.

Four weeks later, I was squeezed into a swimsuit made from some kind of reddish-brown, scratchy material. I wore brown furry ears, brown tights, a red velvet tail and bracelets of plastic walnuts.

Diarmuid was wearing a romper suit of the same rough material but with a longer red tail. He carried a squirrel head under his arm. We were both on rollerblades.

The costumes were Katy Irvine's idea. She worked for an advertising company handling the account for a group of French wine producers. Diarmuid had met her at a party, they'd been going out together for a few weeks. She had big brown eyes and was as glossy and high stepping as a racehorse.

'I don't see what squirrels have to do with wine,' I said.

'Exactly,' said Katy. 'You'll attract attention.'

'Especially with that cleavage,' said Diarmuid.

I made a face at him.

Katy steered us towards a dark-haired man briskly lining up bottles of wine beneath a red, white and blue tricolour, the size of a bedspread. 'Now, Monsieur, what do you think?'

'They will certainly be noticed.' He smiled. 'The *mouche* on Madame is unusual.'

A fly! I shuddered and flicked at myself with my fingers.

'A moment, please.' He pulled a dictionary from his briefcase, thumbed through the pages, looked up at me and touched his cheek with a finger. 'The beauty spot.' He smiled. 'The finishing touch?'

'It's my own,' I said.

'Then you will always be noticed, Madame.'

I glided into the Grand Hall with a smile on my face.

It was laid out in blocks, like an American town. Rows of stands, some the size of a small supermarket, ran at right angles to each other. The roof seemed as high as the sky. Diarmuid and I skated up and down the busy, temporary streets, carrying trays of plastic goblets filled with red and white wine.

I noticed a big man, with the shoulders of a rugby player, strolling from stall to stall, shaking hands, chatting. He had blond hair that curled on the back of his neck. He looked confident. Every time I glided past him, he caught my eye and smiled. At the end of the afternoon, I skated towards him as though pulled by an invisible string. A waiter stepped out from behind a stall. I spun on my blades to avoid him, and almost fell over. The big man grabbed my arm with one hand and steadied my tray with the other.

'Thank you. I was nearly road kill.'

He laughed, took a glass from my tray, eyeing me while he filled his mouth with red wine, sucked in his cheeks and moved his jaw. He swallowed.

'Could be worse,' he pronounced.

He put the glass back on the tray. 'My name is Hugo Lancaster and I'd like to kiss your beauty spot,' he said.

The whole arena seemed to light up.

Hugo waited while I changed out of the ridiculous squirrel suit. He ushered me into a waiting taxi and transported me from the bright airy vastness of the exhibition centre to a hot, dimly lit restaurant.

I sat opposite him at a crowded, boisterous table. Bottles of champagne arrived with astonishing frequency. Hugo regaled the company with round after round of anecdotes sprinkled with witticisms.

I wasn't listening because Hugo's hand was on my knee, and then on my thigh. He was making little stroking, rippling movements with his fingers, and all my nerves were jumping, and I wanted to move and I didn't want to move, and I had to keep a bright face and look interested in his stories while all the time I was conscious only of his touch on my bare skin and my face blazing.

When we finally got up from the table, Hugo behaved with great circumspection. He threaded his arm through mine in a proprietorial way and escorted me through Berkeley Square, Conduit Street, Oxford Circus, Mortimer Street to his flat in Fitzrovia.

The sky was cloudy and traffic roared past. It seemed to me that people turned to look at us, and a tune was dancing in my head. 'People Will Say We're in Love.'

17

Hugo took me on little trips. He would telephone and say he was delivering wine to one or two addresses on the south coast, or in Hampshire or Berkshire or Buckinghamshire, and would I come with him? 'Where are we going?' I would ask, and Hugo would always reply, 'It's a surprise.' Sometimes he would add, thrillingly, 'Bring a toothbrush.'

His customers lived in lovely places. We sailed through the South Downs, the Chilterns, Salisbury Plain, the Vale of Kent. We dined in country pubs with window boxes and beer gardens, or in restaurants by the Thames.

I danced to the rhythm of Hugo's life.

He divided his time between England and France. He had a flat in London and a house twenty miles from Bordeaux. His London flat – above a cheese shop near Fitzroy Square – doubled as an office. Lancaster Direct Wines Limited was engraved on a postcard-sized brass plate on the door to the street. Hugo ran the business from two boxy rooms, directly above the shop. A kitchen and bathroom were on the same floor. Hugo's bedroom and bathroom and tiny sitting room were on the floor above.

He stood me in front of a great map of the wine regions of France that hung on his office wall and showed me where he lived when he was in France.

'Here's the Gironde.' He pointed to a wide estuary north of Bordeaux. 'Two big tidal rivers flow into it. The Dordogne.' He traced a blue line from the south-east. 'And the Garonne.' His finger now followed a blue line north to Bordeaux. 'I live between the two rivers. In Entre Deux Mers. About here.' He stabbed a point south of Bordeaux and east of the Garonne. 'Chateau Le Rossignol. About two miles from Astignac. That's my nearest village. Too small to be on the map. But it's got a butcher, a baker and a chemist. There's a supermarket a couple of miles further on. And a market every Wednesday. I moved in a year ago,' he said. 'It's not awfully big. Nothing like the chateaux in the Loire. Somebody else owns the vineyard. Sorry I haven't a photo to show you.' All said in his offhand, understated English way.

I imagined a house with turrets, crenellations, perhaps a dovecote. A smaller version of houses and castles I remembered from illustrations in fairy tales and Walt Disney films.

When Hugo was in London I stayed in his flat from time to time, but never saw the two young men he referred to as his sales team, Jason and Freddy. He was always talking to one or other of them on the phone.

'Business is all about keeping in touch,' he told me. 'Staying ahead of the game.'

Patricia, a thin, sixtyish woman with a dry smile and an air of never having been surprised by anything, came two days a week to send out invoices, deal with accounts and queries. I passed her on the stairs occasionally. Once, about six weeks after I met Hugo, I got up late – Hugo had a breakfast meeting in the city – and wandered downstairs to the kitchen.

Patricia was making herself a cup of tea. She coloured.

'The kettle in the office has packed up,' she said.

'I'll join you,' I said. 'If you don't mind the dressing gown.'

Perhaps it was the informality of the occasion, but Patricia became quite chatty as we drank our tea. She told me she had worked for Hugo for three years.

'I worked for his uncle Walter before that. He set up the company. Hugo was a dentist when I first met him. He took over the business when Walter retired.'

I set down my mug of tea in surprise.

'Hugo was a dentist?' I couldn't imagine that big, leonine figure in a white coat, with a lamp on his forehead, wielding a drill. I was more used to seeing him with a glass in his paw. Although I never, ever saw Hugo drink too much.

'One of the secrets of selling wine,' he told me, 'is to stay more sober than the people one is selling to.' A wink, followed by a wide smile. 'Caveat emptor, and all that.'

'I didn't know Hugo was a dentist,' I said now to Patricia. 'He's never mentioned it.'

'I don't think he liked it much,' said Patricia. 'He prefers being a wine merchant. He's better at it than Walter. More of a showman.'

'I got the impression he'd taken over the business from his father,' I said.

'Oh, no,' said Patricia. 'His uncle Walter was the wine merchant. Hugo's father was a dentist as well.'

'Did you know all the family, then?' I was curious. Hugo didn't talk much about his relations. I knew only that his father was dead and that his parents had divorced when Hugo was a teenager. His mother had remarried and was now living in Scotland. Hugo said he didn't visit much because Scotland was too cold.

'Not many of them to know,' said Patricia. 'There was only Walter and Reggie. I was at school with Walter's wife, Angela. They went to live in Spain when Walter retired. I think it was because of Reggie's heart attack. Pulling teeth one day, dead the next. He was only sixty-five.'

We sat in respectful silence for a moment. Patricia stood up.

'You've lasted longer than the others.' The words jumped out of her mouth. She looked as though she wanted to call them back.

That evening, as Hugo and I walked hand in hand through Soho Square, I tentatively asked him about his previous girlfriends. He stopped, turned me around to face him. His expression was serious.

'Am I the only man in your life right now?'

I nodded.

'You've had other lovers, right?'

I nodded again.

'I don't want to know about them, sweetie. Let's not go there, OK? No names, no pack drill. Your past is your past. I don't want to know about it. My past is my past. You are the only woman in my life. I am the only man in yours. Let's just enjoy what's ours, eh?'

We had only known each other a few months. It was sensible to wait and see how we got on.

I had no angst with Hugo. We had fun together.

He always had some adventure to recount. How he had

encountered the most wonderful cheese maker. 'Almost made me think about selling cheese as well as wine, but one headache is enough, eh?' How he had met a wine grower who buried a cow horn full of manure at the full moon to make his vines grow strong. 'His wine's pretty good, actually.'

Every bottle had a story, told with fluency and dancing eyes. Usually, we were invited into the client's house. I listened, transfixed, as he recited the history of rare wines he had traced, found, bought, kept 'for connoisseurs'. He would always leave with an order for more.

I knew nothing at that time about appellations, classifications, the mystery of 'terroir'. Wine was a foreign language to me. But I loved the vocabulary – bouquet, aroma, hints of raspberries, fruitiness, nectar, honey, cedar, vanilla, oak – and the stories.

Hugo announced to a spellbound client – a banker who had just had a cellar installed in his house near Henley-on-Thames – that he had sourced some fine wines from the nineteen thirties. A French family had buried them in a field. 'To hide them from the Germans. The Germans were keen on wine from Bordeaux. They occupied lots of chateaux. The owners hid the contents of their cellars. This lot have been hidden since the war. Been there since the Occupation. These are top stuff. They're not only first-growth clarets from a great year, they're living history. I've got four dozen.'

The banker begged to buy a case. Hugo allowed him to buy two bottles. The banker wanted to know more about the family who owned the wines. Hugo said they had insisted on anonymity.

'I want to know more about them as well,' I said to

Hugo as we drove away. 'What happened to the person who buried the wine? How come it got forgotten? How did it get discovered again?'

Hugo put a finger to his lips. 'I can't tell you,' he said. 'A promise is a promise.'

Once, when we were dining in a hotel in the Cotswolds, we had a brief conversation with a shiny American family – father, younger wife, two children – at the next table. The father told us he was a lawyer. He had come over for a conference and was taking a holiday at the same time. He loved England.

The next morning, when I was coming out of the hotel, I saw him chatting with Hugo in the car park. They were nodding, laughing, patting each other on the back. They exchanged business cards.

Hugo has beguiled him, I thought fondly.

'You'd charm the daisies from the grass,' I said when I reached the car.

Hugo laughed and nibbled my ear. He held the door open for me. I loved his old-fashioned courtesy.

'Turns out he's a bit of a wine connoisseur.' Hugo eased himself behind the wheel. He sat for a moment, lost in thought. 'Russian background. Collects Romanov memorabilia.' He patted my knee. 'I might have just the thing for him, sweetie.'

He switched on the engine, thrust the car into gear, and drove off singing,

'*Yankee Doodle went to town, a-riding on a pony,*
Stuck a feather in his cap, and called it macaroni.'

18

At the end of July, Hugo took me to lunch at our favourite restaurant on the banks of the Thames near Goring. He had booked a table on the terrace, a foot from the water's edge. A single white cloud hung motionless in a blue sky. A flotilla of swans sailed serenely past the little boats moored by the riverbank. The water lazily lapped the shore.

Hugo ordered a bottle of champagne. He took my hand, kissed it, held it to his cheek. 'Come back with me to Astignac.'

'I could do with a break,' I said.

'That's not what I meant.'

My heart turned a neat somersault.

'I want us to be together, sweetie. I want you always there when I come home.'

I took a deep breath. 'Are you proposing to me, Hugo?'

'I'm not ready to make the big commitment. Not yet,' Hugo said.

'A little balloon of excitement inside me slowly deflated. I kept my voice steady.

'Does that mean you might make a commitment some time in the future?'

'Of course,' said Hugo. 'I just think we should live together first.'

Two swans flew, honking, along the river. They beat the air with their wings as they lost height. They hopped across the water before subsiding gracefully on the surface. The animals went into the Ark two by two. Was it true that swans mated for life? Hugo wasn't ready for a big commitment but that didn't rule out some kind of declaration in the future. I was spending more and more time in his flat. When he was in France and I was in Woolwich, I felt boxed in, restless, eager for him to return.

A motor launch came phut phut phutting towards the jetty.

Six men disembarked with much laughter and back-slapping. One of them wore a white linen suit. The restaurant manager bustled to greet him.

'Wayne Costello, property developer,' Hugo whispered. 'Fabulously rich. He's just bought a thousand-acre estate in Hampshire. I've met him a few times.' Hugo waved at the man in the white suit and got a nod in response.

'He collects wine and football clubs.' Hugo kept his voice low. 'He loves to show off. I've just sold him a bottle of Château Margaux for a vertical tasting. Every year from eighteen ninety-five to nineteen twenty-five.' Hugo's smile widened. He raised his glass. 'And that, my sweet, is why we can afford to sit here drinking champagne.' He leaned towards me. 'I heard Wayne was looking for a bottle of nineteen twenty-one to complete the sequence. I supplied it. *Et voilà!* Two thousand pounds.'

I nearly choked on my champagne. I had less than that in my savings account.

'I'm poor,' I said. 'I need to work.'

'You're not working at the moment, sweetie. You haven't any jobs in the pipeline.'

'That's not true,' I said. 'Eddie has put me up as a reader for a new company making recordings of books on cassette. It's run by a friend of his. They're the next big thing, he says. Books on tape.'

Hugo looked unconvinced.

'I miss you when you're away, Hugo,' I said. 'I love it when we're together. But I need more time to think.'

I got a call from Eddie the next morning. 'Sorry, darling. They want a well-known name. Sells more audio-books, apparently. Not good news for you, I'm afraid. I can't say I'm surprised. But,' he paused, 'here's your consolation prize. My friend needs someone to abridge *Silas Marner*. The guy supposed to be doing it fell off a ladder and broke both his wrists. You've got a degree in English, haven't you? You could do it. I'll only take five per cent.'

Disappointment silenced me.

'Tell you what,' said Eddie's voice in my ear, 'I'll waive my commission on this one.'

I telephoned Diarmuid.

'I've never known Eddie do that before. He must feel sorry for you,' he said.

'Thanks, old friend. That makes me feel terrific.'

I telephoned Hugo.

'Pays peanuts,' he said.

'Pays my rent.'

'Why rent in London when you can live with me in France for free?'

I looked around my minuscule flat. Grey walls, grey

carpet, grey curtains, grey sky beyond the window, grey water below. Hugo was like an explosion of colour in my life.

'I've made up my mind,' I said. 'I'll come and live with you in Astignac.'

19

Not counting a couple of blurry weekends in Paris with a theatre director I had a fling with, and a day trip to Calais with Diarmuid to buy wine for my thirtieth birthday party, I hadn't been in France for any length of time since the year before I did my Leaving Certificate. The nuns organised an exchange with two convent schools, one in Paris and the other in Normandy. They decided to split up friends who were known to make mischief together. My best friend, Madeline, got Paris. Well, the outskirts of Paris. At least she could go into the city on the train. I got rural Normandy. It snowed. It rained. The wind blew constantly. It was a two-mile walk in dismal weather to a small town with one café. I was reminded of it when I read *Madame Bovary*.

Hugo laughed when I told him about the school trip. I didn't tell him about my weekends in Paris. 'No names, no pack drill,' he had said.

I flew home to Ireland to tell my mother I was moving to France. I felt I had to make that kind of announcement in person.

My mother pursed her lips and said, 'Why buy a cow when you get free milk?'

I telephoned my sister in Baltimore. She gasped with excitement. 'Is he going to marry you?'

'I don't know, Kathleen.'

'You're taking a bit of a chance,' she said.

My brother, Tommy, promised to come out and visit me. 'If you're still there in a year's time.'

'And why wouldn't I be there?'

'The six-month expiry date,' Tommy said. 'All your fellas seem to have one.'

'This one's different.'

Tommy began singing 'Some Day My Prince Will Come'.

I joined in automatically. 'He's out there waiting for me,' I sang. 'Some day, some day.'

But a tiny voice in my brain was still asking, 'Is Hugo the real thing?'

Mum softened after I had been home for a few days. She asked me to fetch a suitcase from the top of the wardrobe in the spare room. 'It's been up there for I don't know how long. Ever since I've been in this contraption anyway. We didn't go away much after that.'

I carried the red suitcase to the kitchen table.

'Open it,' said Mum.

There was another, smaller suitcase inside. Both cases were lined with pink, silky material. They looked as though they had never been used.

'I took them on my honeymoon,' Mum said. 'You can take them to France.'

'It's not a honeymoon,' I said unsteadily.

Mum was suddenly girlish. 'You might take them on honeymoon yet.'

I knelt down to give her a hug. 'Thanks, Mum.'

She stroked my hair. 'Times change. They're all moving in with each other these days. Maybe it's a good thing. Maybe not.' She sighed. 'I don't know.' Her voice fell away. We stayed in a silent embrace.

'Times change,' Mum repeated quietly, 'but human nature is still the same. People value what's hard to get.' She moved her hand to tap me on the shoulder. I looked up at her. 'Don't undervalue yourself, Honor.'

She shook herself into her usual briskness. 'Now. Let's get you organised.'

I packed the bits and pieces I wanted to take to France into Mum's honeymoon suitcases and flew back to London. Hugo met me at the airport. We stopped at my flat to pick up another suitcase, my portable typewriter and three boxes of books. All my worldly goods.

I loved London but I wasn't sorry to leave. I didn't own a flat. I couldn't afford one. Every time I looked, the prices had gone up. My last acting job, a minor role in three episodes of *The Bill*, had earned me enough, just, to eat and pay the rent for three months. I could write more easily in Astignac. There would be fewer distractions. This was the beginning of a new life, I told myself. Of course I was doing the right thing. I had no reason to fret. No reason at all.

We stood on the deck of the ferry as it approached Caen in the pink light of dawn. Hugo put his arm around me. He squeezed my shoulders. 'We are going to be happy together,' he said. 'Welcome to France.'

We rattled up the gangway. I rolled down the car window and turned my face to the morning sun. We sped through a much prettier Normandy than I remembered. It was the beginning of August. All of France was on holiday. Every town and village was *en fête*. I felt excited, optimistic and in love.

We arrived at Le Rossignol after dark. The headlights picked out important-looking wrought-iron gates and an imposing, two-storeyed building with steps up to a majestic front door, narrow, balconied windows and, at the far end, a turret with a tiled, pointed roof.

I gasped with admiration. I clapped my hands. Hugo got out and opened the gates. We rolled down the short driveway, swept around the side of the house and parked beside the gable wall. I realised the building was only one room deep. The wide facade was exactly that. A facade.

Hugo switched off the engine. The lights died.

'Around here,' he said, 'things are not always what they seem.'

20

Hugo unlocked and pushed open the carved wooden door. He took my hand and tugged me over the threshold into the dark hallway. He switched on the lights. The interior was charming. High ceilings, chandeliers, carved wood panels – 'boiseries', Hugo called them – on either side of an imposing stone fireplace; a marble staircase that was a little too big for the house.

I was in a mood to love Le Rossignol.

It stood on an escarpment three hundred feet above the valley of the Garonne. The river was about a mile away, as the crow flies. The house fronted on to one of a network of roads that criss-crossed a hilly plateau. At the back was a garden with apple and plum trees, old roses and a spreading chestnut tree. Beyond the garden, the land sloped gently towards the river in a series of small, vine-covered hills. To the right of the house was a low limestone cliff, about twenty feet high, the white stone glimpsed behind a curtain of ivy.

In our first hot week together at Le Rossignol, Hugo

was on holiday. We drove to the coast. We toiled up the highest sand dune in Europe and looked back over the vast expanse of pine forest we had crossed to get to our sandy hilltop. We sauntered hand in hand through Bordeaux, past eighteenth-century merchants' houses of pale buttery limestone.

We lazed in the garden. I liked to contemplate the house, with its yellow-stone walls, its blue shutters echoing the sky. And when that sky was a cloudless dome, Hugo's house seemed to me like a ship riding the crest of a wave in a green sea of vineyards.

I say Hugo's house, because that's how I thought of it. If, at the beginning, when I skipped around and about it with cries of delight and thought it could be my home, Hugo, for all his generosity – pulling a wad of notes from his pocket, 'Buy whatever you need for the kitchen' – reminded me that it was not.

'I have money, Hugo. I'll share the cost of furnishing,' I said, at the same time thinking it would probably eat up all my meagre savings. The house had barely any furniture beyond a large mahogany bed and a television.

'We'll share expenses. Food and so on.' Hugo kissed my forehead. 'But it's my house and I'll pay for the furniture.'

'I want to pay my share, Hugo.'

He put his hand up to silence my protests. 'It's going to cost a bit. Let's wait and see how we rub along before plunging into debt together. Eh?'

'Are you having to borrow to pay for all this, Hugo?'

'Only joking.' He opened his wallet. 'See? Lots of cash.'

We bought a sofa and armchairs, a bookcase, lamps, a coffee table, a wardrobe, another television – for Hugo, who liked to watch sport. I liked to watch drama. Otherwise, our tastes were similar. We had a brief, good-tempered disagreement over the shape of the dining table. I think round tables are more convivial. Hugo thought a rectangle better suited the shape of the large, stone-flagged room that ran along the back of the house. We compromised on a rectangular table with side flaps that turned it into a circle.

Diarmuid and Katy stayed overnight with us on their way to Biarritz. In the morning, we visited a wine chateau on the outskirts of Bordeaux. The chateau was the grand fairytale building I had once imagined Le Rossignol to be. It had turrets and mansard roofs. It was wide and deep, yet seemed light and airy. Hugo said it had been built in the sixteenth century. Its wine had been a favourite of Charles the Second and was mentioned in Pepys's diaries.

The winery, by contrast, was startlingly modern and clinically clean. We wore obligatory green paper coats and slippers as the guide showed us the ceiling-high stainless-steel tanks filled with fermenting wine, the steel ladders, the control panels with lights and dials. Two men in white coats with clipboards padded silently around, like doctors in a clinic.

In low-ceilinged cellars, heady with the scent of wine, lines of oak barrels lay on their sides in rows that stretched as far as I could see.

'In eighteen fifty-five there was a huge exhibition in Paris,' said Hugo. 'The Emperor Louis Napoleon asked the Bordeaux wine brokers to rank the wines in order of importance. Sensible businessmen, they didn't bother trying to taste thousands of wines. They looked at their records over the previous fifty years and worked out which wines always sold for the highest prices. Then they put them into five classes, known as grands crus. Premier cru was the top class. The rankings still exist and still pretty much determine prices.'

We watched robotic arms gripping, slapping labels on bottles moving briskly along a conveyor belt.

'Most of this wine was bought when it was still in the barrel,' said Hugo. He pointed to the bottle swivelling on the labelling machine. 'A licence to print money,' he said. 'That bottle will double, triple, quadruple in price when it reaches the market. It might never be drunk. It's an investment.'

At the end of the line, a team of white-coated women hand-wrapped the bottles and packed them in wooden cases.

'Each case is already worth a thousand pounds,' whispered Hugo. We had been watching for five minutes. By Hugo's calculation, ten thousand pounds had just sailed past under our noses.

Diarmuid whistled. Katy stared at the bottles sailing towards the packers.

'Investment wines,' said Hugo. 'That's where I make my money.'

We drove to Cap Ferret, a thin arm of land shielding a vast expanse of water from the Atlantic. Small villages of tightly packed wooden houses, painted blue and white, dotted the sheltered side of the peninsula. The land was so flat, it seemed to melt into the bay. Blue and white boats rested on the water. Low waves crept to the shore a few feet from the restaurant where we lunched on crab and langoustines. There wasn't a cloud in the sky.

'When did the world fall in love with wine?' said Diarmuid. 'When I was growing up, we hardly saw the stuff at all. Weddings, maybe. And Christmas. But the only drink in the house was a bottle of whiskey for when the parish priest or the doctor called. It started to change when I was at college and the girls all drank white wine instead of lager and lime. Do you remember, Honor?'

'I do. And fine and sophisticated we thought ourselves.' My mind roamed happily over our shared past.

'When John Huston directed *The Dead*, the James Joyce short story,' said Diarmuid, 'he filmed wine on the table for the Christmas Party. But it's Guinness in the story. It's Guinness they drink with the goose. The wine of Ireland.' He paused. 'But Houston knew his audience wouldn't believe the Misses Morkan were middle class if they saw them drinking Guinness at a dinner party. He changed the truth to convey the truth.'

'Joyce would have loved that,' I said.

'Everybody drinks wine these days,' said Katy.

'And spouts bloody piffle about it,' Diarmuid groaned. 'Sorry, Hugo. I just mean they don't know what they're drinking half the time.'

'Quite so,' said Hugo. 'It's a frightful minefield. Which is why people like me exist to do your buying for you.' He topped up Diarmuid's glass. 'Take a good sniff before you taste. What does it remind you of?'

'Alcohol,' said Diarmuid.

Hugo ignored the joke. 'You shouldn't be able to smell alcohol. Not if it's a well-made wine. And this is a well-made wine. Can you really smell alcohol?'

Diarmuid shook his head.

'So what do you smell?'

'Fruit?'

'Take another sniff. What kind of fruit?'

Diarmuid sniffed again. 'Grapefruit?'

Hugo nodded approvingly. 'Typical scent of Sauvignon Blanc. You're drinking Sauvignon, blended with a little Semillon. Classic white Bordeaux.'

For a moment I thought Hugo was about to deliver the well-rehearsed sales speech I had heard a dozen times. But he said no more. He leaned back in his chair and tilted his panama over his face.

That was the thing about Hugo, I reflected. He was never predictable. I liked that.

'It's delicious, whatever it is.' Katy held out her glass for a refill.

'That's a nice watch,' I said.

'Don't you just love it? I made Diarmuid buy it for me. He was a bit reluctant.'

Diarmuid looked embarrassed. Katy made a face at him. She turned her wrist to display the logo on the clasp. 'Guess how much.'

'It looks expensive,' I said. 'I have no idea.'

Hugo raised his hat from his face and leaned over to peer at Katy's watch. 'Ten pounds. Or fifty francs or five deutschmarks or not a lot of whatever currency they have in the place where you bought it.' He sat back with a complacent smile.

'What makes you think it's a fake?'

Hugo stretched across the table, lifted Katy's wrist and with a deft movement of his other hand, loosened the watch, slid it over her fingers and opened his hand like a conjuror to reveal the watch now lying on his palm.

'It's not a bad fake, as fakes go,' he said. 'Not bad at all. But there's not enough attention to detail. That's where cheap counterfeiters go wrong. The sapphire on the winder is the wrong shade of blue.'

He took Katy's hand, slid the watch back on to her wrist and re-fastened the clasp.

'I thought it was a good fake,' said Katy, with surprise.

'There are fakes and fakes,' Hugo said. 'A good one is a work of genius. Take Han van Meegeren, for example. He painted Vermeers that fooled the experts.'

'And the people who bought them were happy,' said Katy. 'What did it matter if they weren't the real thing?'

'It matters,' said Diarmuid. 'You wanted that watch. You knew it was a fake. I bought it for you. That's one thing. But suppose I bought you a watch and I told you it cost me a fortune, it's the real thing, but it's a good fake that fools you?'

'I'd be seriously pissed off,' Katy said.

'Exactly,' said Diarmuid.

'But you wouldn't be pissed off in that instance,' said Hugo. 'You wouldn't know it's counterfeit. You would love it. Like the buyers of Mr van Meegeren loved their Vermeers.'

'I'd be jolly furious if I found out,' said Katy.

'But if you didn't find out?'

Katy tilted her head, considered the question. 'What one doesn't know can't hurt.' She smiled lazily. 'I don't know. It's too complicated.'

'It's complicated all right,' said Diarmuid. He had a black look on his face. I wondered if he thought Hugo had been flirting with Katy. There was a hint of tension in the air.

'Where does the value reside? In the thing itself? Or in our idea of it?' I said quickly. 'Did you read that story in the newspapers a while back about the painting that was discovered to be by Leonardo da Vinci? Everybody thought it was by some minor artist. So, one day there's a painting by Giuseppe di Bloggi, and it's worth a bit of money, but not that much. The next day it's by Leonardo da Vinci and it's worth millions. But it's the same painting.'

'At least it's not a fake,' said Diarmuid. 'Nobody tried to fool anybody.'

'Nobody tried to fool me with my watch,' said Katy. 'I know it's a fake. I don't mind. I love it.' She blew a kiss at Diarmuid.

He smiled back at her. The tension seemed to have eased.

We walked the half-mile or so to the ocean side of the peninsula, struggled up the sand dunes, watched the Atlantic waves rear up and throw themselves endlessly on the shore. Hugo and Katy collapsed on a bench. Diarmuid and I strolled along the boardwalk above the beach.

'When we were at college, a gold watch was the prelude to an engagement ring,' I said.

'It's not a real watch. It doesn't count. Katy thinks it's a huge joke.' He paused. 'She's beautiful, isn't she? High maintenance but great fun.'

'Is she the real thing, Diarmuid?'

'Maybe. I don't know.' He stopped. 'She was flirting with Hugo.'

'Hugo flirts with everybody,' I said. 'It doesn't mean anything. Don't worry.'

'I'm not worried.'

We stood for a moment and watched two surfers in the curve of a giant wave, unbalance, fall in, get back on their boards and paddle back out again.

Diarmuid said, 'What about you, Honor? Is Hugo the real thing?'

I hesitated.

Hugo came up behind me. 'Time to drive back, if we want to avoid the traffic.'

Just before Diarmuid and Katy had to turn south for Biarritz, we stopped by the side of the road to say our goodbyes. I found a moment to whisper in Diarmuid's ear, 'I want it to be the real thing this time.'

Diarmuid kissed my cheek. 'Good luck,' he whispered.

He and Katy got back into their car. I stood, waving, until it disappeared into the distance.

21

About a week later some of Hugo's friends came to lunch at Le Rossignol. One of them, Jerry Giff, was a graphic artist who had a studio near Bergerac. He designed and printed the brochures for Hugo's business. The others were friends and their wives from Hugo's student days, who had bought holiday homes in the Dordogne. Robert and his wife Sarah were bankers. Duncan was a city lawyer. He and his wife, Emily, brought their sturdy fifteen-month-old son Arthur.

'Nice to see you again,' Sarah said to me.

I had no recollection of ever having met her.

She laughed. 'You were with Hugo, in Le Caprice. You'd been at a wine fair, I think. I'm not surprised you don't remember us. Hugo was monopolising you. But we remember you.'

'Don't worry,' said Emily. 'You didn't dance on the table or pass out or do anything frightfully silly. It's just that you were new to the group. It's easy to remember newcomers. We are such a crowd, I'm not surprised you don't remember any of us.'

It was late-August hot, with barely a breeze, and cooler inside the house than out. Hugo opened the French windows. We sat looking out on a landscape so still it could have been painted. There was not a soul in sight.

'It's the quietest time in the vineyards, before the vendange, the harvest,' said Hugo. 'No more spraying. All the work is done. It's up to the sun, now.'

I passed around a plate of tiny squares of toast smeared with foie gras.

Hugo poured honey-coloured wine. 'Swirl it around a bit. Put your nose into the glass. Smell it. Then taste it.'

We all put our noses into our glasses and sniffed. I smelled honey and caramel and, maybe, a hint of orange blossom. I tasted burnt sugar and something delicate I couldn't name that lingered on the tongue.

There was a litany of appreciation from around the table.

Jerry said, 'This is one of the wines on your list, isn't it, Hugo?'

Hugo nodded. 'Cerons. Perfect with foie gras.'

I slipped away to bring the rest of the food to the table. It was the first time Hugo and I had entertained as a couple. I felt on parade.

I had poached a fat brown trout, pushed butter and fresh chopped tarragon under the skin of a chicken, and cooked it in a pot with a generous splash of white wine. I served the trout and chicken cold with a sorrel sauce for the trout and a tarragon sauce for the chicken.

I didn't relax until Hugo brought in the cheeseboard and whispered in my ear, 'Well done.'

I felt I had passed an exam.

Jerry patted his stomach and requested a break before tackling the peach tart from the patisserie.

Emily smeared sun-block cream on Arthur, and fixed a white cotton hat on his head. He staggered around the garden like a tiny drunk. Emily, Sarah and I followed his meanderings. The men stayed at the table and talked sport.

'It's another language.' Sarah laughed. 'Sometimes, I can't understand a word they're saying, when we're all standing around after a meeting.'

Emily murmured, 'I wish I could say that. I'm just a housewife.'

Sarah said quickly, 'You're not allowed to say that.' After a pause, she added, 'I wish I was just a housewife with a family.'

We sat on the garden wall while Arthur investigated a watering can.

'Duncan thinks you're awfully good for Hugo,' Emily said. 'It's time he settled down.'

'If you feed him as well as you've just fed us, he's a jolly lucky man,' said Sarah. 'Robert's lucky if he gets a lamb chop and a pudding from Waitrose.'

When we returned to the table the men were talking about money.

'I shorted some oil stocks just before the price fell,' Duncan said.

'Good call,' said Robert.

Jerry said, 'I'll get those brochures I've just printed, in case I forget.' He ambled off.

Hugo opened another bottle of honey-coloured wine.

Robert squinted at the label. He whistled. 'Château d'Yquem. You're a great host, Hugo. You do your friends proud.' A pause. 'What does a bottle of d'Yquem go for these days?'

'You can't ask your host the price of the bottle of wine he puts in front of you.'

'Go on, Hugo. We're old friends. Serious question.'

'Depends on the year and the availability.' Hugo concentrated on pouring a small quantity of wine into each glass.

Jerry returned with a brochure for Lancaster Direct Wines, 'I've marked what you're drinking.' He handed the brochure to Sarah.

'Good Lord,' she said. 'I could buy a lot of handbags for that. Or a small car.'

'I was thinking about putting some of my bonus into wine futures,' said Duncan. 'Prices for top-class growths have risen year on year.'

'I don't deal in wine futures,' said Hugo. 'I deal in wine past.'

He had everyone's attention.

'I sell wines that have proved their worth. Old wines. Wines with a history. Wines like the one we're about to taste.'

Hugo's fingers played up and down the side of the glass. He looked into the distance for a moment, as though deciding how much to say.

'The French don't do credit like we do,' he began. 'If they need cash in a hurry, they go to Crédit Municipal. It's a sort of respectable pawnshop run by the local councils. It'll give you a twelve-month loan equivalent to half what you pawn. Does a jolly nice trade in family heirlooms for hard-up aristocrats.' He paused. 'But it won't take wine in pawn.' He tapped his glass. 'Even wine like this.' He paused again. 'Which is where I come in.'

Sarah spoke first. 'You mean you loaned somebody money against this bottle of wine?'

Hugo smiled.

'You loaned him a few hundred pounds?'

Hugo sniffed the wine. 'Honey, almonds, orange blossom, caramel.'

'I assume he didn't repay you, which is why we're drinking it,' said Robert.

Hugo was enjoying the guessing game. He took a sip. Licked his lips. He almost purred. I stroked his back.

'Was it just one bottle? Was it just a few hundred quid?' Duncan tried to sound casual.

'Let's just say I acquired the wine in a private arrangement between gentlemen.' Hugo grinned. 'He got cash. I got my hands on some terrific wines at a very attractive price. The sort that don't come on the market often.' He took another sip. 'This wine will still be drinking well in ten, twenty, fifty years. The price will keep going up.'

'How much are you selling it for?'

'You haven't even tasted it, Duncan.' A note of anxiety in Emily's voice made Arthur cry.

Duncan dipped a finger in the wine. 'This will soothe him.'

'More,' demanded Arthur.

Hugo laughed. 'We'd better drink it before Arthur scoffs the lot. You're on holiday, Duncan. Switch off your brain.' He cut into the tart. 'Pudding everybody?'

I sat discussing London house prices with the others. I felt a sham because I didn't own any houses and they owned two each. I said as much, quietly, to Emily.

'You'll have a house if you marry Hugo,' she whispered back. She gave my arm a quick squeeze.

Robert emerged through the French windows. 'Nice place you've got here, Hugo. I've just been having a mooch around.' He dropped into a seat beside his wife. 'You'll never believe it, Sarah.' He grinned. 'Hugo has kept a lot of stuff from the old days. I thought he couldn't wait to get out of dentistry.'

'Nostalgia,' said Duncan. 'Hugo's a sentimentalist.'

'That's one way of putting it,' said Robert. 'He had quite a reputation at Bart's. He always had some girl stashed away.'

'At least one, I heard,' said Duncan. 'He played his cards close. I don't think they ever knew about each other.'

'He's settled down now, of course,' Emily said quickly.

'I wonder how much of this vintage wine he's got stashed away.' Duncan looked to me for an answer.

Hugo never took me with him when he was buying wine for Lancaster Direct. 'Nice to have you around when I'm doing deliveries, darling,' he had said to me shortly after we met, 'but not when I'm negotiating.' As always, he had softened his words with a kiss.

'I don't know much about Hugo's business,' I told Duncan. 'Honestly. I have no idea what he's got in the cellar.'

Duncan looked disappointed. Later, when I was clearing away the coffee cups, I found him in the kitchen, writing a cheque. He looked up and grinned. 'I won't try to squeeze anything more into the car today. Hugo will bring the wine with him when he's in London next week.'

I felt a sense of anticlimax when we waved them goodbye. They had brought with them a whiff of the buzz and bustle of London, and now they were taking it away again.

I stood in the gateway, looking back at Le Rossignol, its face darkened in the shadow of the evening sun.

22

Budburst. The moment when the vine erupts into flower, promising fruit. Budburst. That's what I had with Hugo. Budburst, again and again and again. That summer, I wakened with the sun in the morning and lay for a time listening to Hugo's contented snore before wrapping myself around him and going back to sleep.

When I finally got up, I usually flung open the shutters and inhaled the perfumed air the way Hugo inhaled wine. Lavender, roses, pine, wild garlic.

'I can smell the figs,' I said to Hugo one morning when we both stood by the window. A thrush sang vigorously in an apple tree.

'*That's the wise thrush; he sings each song twice over,*
Lest you should think he never could recapture,
The first fine careless rapture,' I recited.

Hugo and I turned, smiling, to each other.

But the telephone rang. Hugo disengaged himself and disappeared up the stairs into his office in the attic.

I brought him coffee and a slice of baguette with butter and jam.

He was sitting at his desk, with his back to me, holding the receiver to his ear with one hand and jotting down notes with the other. I set the tray on top of a filing cabinet.

Hugo might have looked untidy with his shaggy haircut and unbuttoned shirt, but his office was the opposite. His desktop was uncluttered. Drawers and pigeonholes were neatly labelled. Reference books marched systematically across the shelves under the eaves.

I glanced around. A birthday card from me was displayed on the desktop, beside a photograph of me in a bubble bath, only my head visible above a sea of white foam. The walls were festooned with photographs. Hugo and me laughing, snapped by Diarmuid at a pub on the river; Hugo in the rugby team; Hugo with a cricket bat; Hugo with a tennis racket; Hugo on a golf course; Hugo raising a glass to the camera; Hugo aged about seven, I supposed, eyes blazing with excitement, standing beside a snowman about twice as high as himself. He had the same impish grin in all the photographs. I felt a sudden rush of affection. I kissed the nape of his neck. He jumped. Spun round in his chair.

'I didn't hear you come in.'

'I've brought you breakfast.'

He pulled me on to his knee. 'You spoil me.'

'I love you, Hugo.'

'Me too, sweetie.' He hugged me closer. 'Me too.'

Once or twice a week, Hugo made excursions to winemakers or to Jerry Giff's studio in Bergerac. Sometimes

Jerry would drive over to Le Rossignol. He and Hugo would retreat upstairs to the office for hours on end. I would hear faint laughter drifting down the stairs, or loud and inventive swearing about France Telecom, or the television blaring. The roar of a crowd, the high-pitched excitement of a commentator. A lull. Then a buzzing sound. The distant hum of motor racing, I supposed.

By mid-September, around Le Rossignol, the grapes hung heavy on the vines. The leaves turned to pink, red, copper, gold. Hugo loaded up the estate car with boxes of wine from the cellar, and left for London. 'They'll start harvesting soon,' he said. 'Everybody will be too busy to see me. It's a good time to go back and catch up.'

He was away for three weeks. I had never felt so solitary.

When I was growing up in Ballybreen, I could see horses, sheep and cattle, green fields and purple mountains ablaze with gorse, from my bedroom window. But our house was on the outskirts of the small market town so there were neighbours on either side of us, and it was only a hop and skip to the shops. I wakened to the clanking of a farm gate, the clop of hoof-beats as the horses crossed our neighbour's yard on their way to the field, the clinking of milk bottles on our doorstep.

In London, the street where I had lived was always busy. It was never dark. I needed heavy curtains as well as a roller blind to block out the glare of the street lamp outside my window. The garage and shop at the corner stayed open all night and added noise as well as light. In the morning, the volume rose, as though someone had turned a dial on a giant radio. The air was stale and smelled of diesel fumes.

At Le Rossignol the air was sweet. The nearest house

nestled behind a line of trees about two hundred yards away. Only the moon and stars lit the sky.

Hugo telephoned most evenings. 'Everything OK, sweetie? Missing me?'

'Missing you. Everything OK,' I always replied.

The silent nights unnerved me. During that first week alone in the house, I heard faint creaking noises, as though the house itself was settling down to sleep. Gradually, I began to be more aware of the rasping threep threep threep of the crickets like a pulse in the night, and found it as sleep inducing as counting sheep.

My mornings began with a drive to the boulangerie in Astignac for fresh bread, and, if I was feeling self-indulgent, a chocolate croissant. After breakfast, I carried my typewriter to a wrought-iron table in the shade of a chestnut tree. While the sun shone, I preferred to work outside.

From time to time I stopped tap tapping to rest my eyes on the landscape. There was always a horizon. It was one of the things I liked most about Le Rossignol. I never saw a horizon in London or at home in County Wicklow where we were surrounded by mountains.

I worked until the light seeped from the sky and, in the far distance, a smudged pink line below an indigo sky marked where the land ended and the invisible ocean began. Then I would take a walk along the quiet narrow roads, past the silent vineyards and occasional patches of meadow filled with delicate grasses and pink and purple flowers that seemed to glow in the dusk.

I never met anyone and rarely saw a car. Sometimes, when I passed a house, a frenzy of barking would break out until I reached the end of the fenced garden, then the only sound would be my footsteps once again.

When the weather closed in, as it did for a few days, earth and sky merged in a light grey mist; droplets of rain clung to the leaves of the trees; vaporous, wispy trails drifted through the vines, and lay like gauzy ribbons on the Garonne; the air became damp and still. I retreated indoors until the sun broke through the clouds and established itself again.

I began to notice the regularity of the lives around me. The man who inspected the vines below Le Rossignol in the early morning. The Mobylette that buzzed along the road around nine o'clock. The yellow van that went by, and sometimes stopped to deliver post at Le Rossignol, about an hour later. And when I was having my mid-morning coffee, a large white dog usually trotted past the house towing a petite, dark-haired woman on the end of a leash. If I was in my usual spot under the chestnut tree, she always released a hand to give me a friendly wave before she was yanked forward again.

One morning, I glanced out of an upstairs window and saw a red-haired woman standing at the corner of the garden where a small gate opened on to the road. She seemed to be looking past the house to where the vineyard sloped into the valley.

The next day, I was working in the garden when a sudden feeling of being watched made me look up, and there she was again, still as a statue, holding the handlebars of a black bicycle.

She came to life as I walked towards her. She propped the bicycle against a telegraph pole, took off her sunglasses and energetically shook the hand I held out to her across the gate. She had clear blue eyes, a confident smile and unnaturally red hair of a shade I had only ever seen on Frenchwomen.

'I am sorry. I did not mean to disturb you. I often stop here. I lived in this house until I was twelve years old.'

She spoke correct, hesitant English.

'The father of my grandfather built this house. His wife gave it the name Le Rossignol because a nightingale sang on her wedding night.'

I was charmed by the story. 'Were they happy here?'

'It was a long time ago. Who can know a marriage?' She smiled. 'But for me it was a happy house.'

'Were you sad to leave it?'

'Of course. But we had no choice. There was a big frost. A frost so terrible . . .' she paused to search for words, her hands chopped the air. 'The vines broke. They died.' She shook her head in remembered disbelief. 'Nearly forty years ago, but we still talk about it.' She replaced her sunglasses.

I shielded my eyes and followed her gaze through the dappled shade of the chestnut tree down the curves of baked earth between the vines, heavy with fruit, to the bushy trees in the cleft of the valley. I couldn't imagine all that fecundity shrivelled by frost.

'And then came three wet summers and three bad harvests. We were ruined. We sold the house and the vineyard. We moved to Bordeaux.'

'You cycled here from Bordeaux!' It was a good twenty miles.

She laughed. 'Not so far as Bordeaux. I visit with my brother. He lives eight kilometres from here, near Polignac.'

'Far enough on a bicycle,' I said. 'Plenty of hills.'

'Perhaps. But my mother cycled thirty kilometres to here, once a week, in the war. I make a shorter journey.'

She saw my confusion. 'Le Rossignol was occupied by the Germans. My father was a prisoner of war. My mother and grandmother went to live in Les Landes. But every week they cycled to the vineyard here.'

It suddenly occurred to me that they might have hidden wine from the Germans.

'During the war,' I said, 'did your family hide things?'

'Of course. The best china, for example. But the Germans were officers. They didn't break anything.'

I was going to ask her about wine and the war, when the large white dog and the small dark woman came towards us like a moving tug-of-war.

'Christine!' In a blur of continuous movement the owner of the bicycle bounded forward, seized the collar of the dog, brought it to a halt, embraced the dog-owner, kissed her on both cheeks, and turned back to me with a broad smile on her face.

After that, it was introductions all around. The bicycle owner, Madame Barron, was a cousin of the dog-owner, Madame Ragulin. The dog was called Atalante.

'*Une Chienne des Pyrénées*,' said Madame Barron.

'My husband loved Atalante.' Madame Ragulin sighed. 'Atalante loved my husband.'

She crouched to ruffle the shaggy fur of the panting dog. I saw that '*Qui M'aime Aime Mon Chien*' was printed across the back of her over-large T-shirt.

There followed a flurry of French conversation. I gathered that Madame Ragulin had been recently widowed. I murmured condolences. Madame Barron embraced her cousin again. I hunkered down beside Atalante. She regarded me through pink-rimmed, golden eyes.

I stood up. Madame Barron and Madame Ragulin shook my hand in farewell. Atalante lumbered forward. Madame Ragulin was jerked into movement. They proceeded up the road. Madame Barron wheeling her bicycle. The white dog leading the way.

23

The grape harvest began suddenly. One moment the vineyards lay silent in the sunlight. The next moment, tall yellow tractors were crawling up and down the parallel rows of vines, shaking bunches of grapes into a giant mechanical maw. The hum of the harvesters started up in the early morning, paused for an hour or two in the middle of the day, and continued long into the night.

I had imagined grape-pickers in red bandanas with baskets on their backs, but after my initial disappointment, I became fascinated by the machines. I even got up in the night to stand at the bedroom window and watch the giant harvesters with their glaring lights, like huge alien insects with enormous eyes eating whole acres of vines.

The roads all around were busy with machinery. The constant rumble reminded me of harvest time at home in County Wicklow and induced a faint melancholy feeling. Some part of me was yearning for the comfort of the known.

When I felt those ripples of anxiety, I would bend my head to my book and absorb myself again in *Silas Marner*.

One morning, I clambered into the ancient Renault to drive to the boulangerie. The key wouldn't turn in the ignition. After several futile attempts, I gave up, breakfasted on the remains of the previous day's baguette, and settled down to work.

A few hours later, when my concentration began to flag, I decided to try starting the Renault again. It sparked into life. I drove it straight to the garage on the outskirts of Astignac, and found it was closed.

I got out of the car and looked around. There was not a soul to be seen. In the distance, I could see steel shutters on the boulangerie and the pharmacie.

A thin-faced woman emerged from a single-storey house beside the garage. Her expression was a mixture of exasperation and concern. She raised her wrist and tapped her watch.

'*C'est le déjeuner.*' Her tone implied that no civilised person would dream of working between the sacred hours of twelve and two, and that I, too, should be at home eating my lunch. A man came out of the house. Her husband, the garage owner, I assumed. He gestured that I should leave the car and come back later.

I gave them an apologetic wave. They went back into the house.

It was nearly one o'clock in France but not yet noon in London. I walked to the telephone box outside the post office – which was, naturally, closed for lunch – and telephoned Hugo's office in London.

'He's still at the wine auction,' said Patricia, in a tone of voice that assumed I knew all about it.

'Of course,' I said, in a tone that implied I had forgotten, as indeed I might have, because when I was absorbed in work I didn't always hear what Hugo was saying to me. 'I dare say I'll hear all about it later, Patricia.'

'I can tell you now,' she said. 'He got a better price than he expected. He's gone to celebrate.'

I imagined Hugo sitting in the middle of a large, jolly crowd, throwing his head back to drain a glass of champagne.

I was alone in a village in rural France. It looked as though all the inhabitants had been spirited away. There was a café in the square but it was usually full of men in overalls. I didn't feel like joining them. I decided to walk back to Le Rossignol.

After about two miles, I stopped feeling sorry for myself. The sun shone. A cool breeze refreshed the air. My heart lightened, I quickened my step. At the top of the ridge where the road flattened out to snake along the escarpment, I stopped to get my breath back and absorb the stillness of the landscape. The motionless river, the silky poplars on the far side, the water tower rising above them like a white, glistening mushroom, the navy-blue line of the horizon.

A small movement caught my attention. I heard the rumble of a tractor. Three cars swished past me in succession. I felt suddenly energised. I filled my lungs with air and began to sing.

'Val-deri, Val-dera, Val-deri, Vald-era ha-ha-ha-ha-ha- . . .'

A car slowed down and stopped ten yards in front of me. The window slid down. The song died in my throat. I marched on, hot-cheeked.

'*Bonjour!*' A smiling redhead was waving to me, gesturing to me to get into the car. It was Madame Barron, who had once lived at Le Rossignol. I recognised the hair. It seemed churlish to refuse her offer of a lift. I opened the door and eased myself on to the back seat beside her.

The driver was a dark-haired man of about forty. An older woman, with a straight back and silver-blonde hair occupied the front passenger seat. They both turned and regarded me with amused curiosity.

'My mother, Madame Rousseau,' said Madame Barron. 'And my brother, Didier Rousseau.' We all shook hands.

'The car broke down,' I said. 'The garage was closed.'

'Did you have lunch in Astignac?' asked Madame Barron.

'I'll have a sandwich when I get home,' I said.

Madame Barron translated for her mother, who clucked and said something.

'*Manger chaud*,' said Madame Barron. 'My mother says one must eat hot at lunchtime.'

'The English don't eat lunch, Doudou,' said Didier Rousseau. 'They often only have a sandwich.' He threw me a smile over his shoulder. 'I worked in London for five years.'

'Actually, I'm Irish,' I said. 'But I think we just eat sandwiches these days as well.'

I had a sudden memory of running home from school in the middle of the day. A big bowl of steaming potatoes on the table. A beef stew. Or lamb chops. Cabbage. My stomach growled.

Madame Rousseau turned to me from the front seat and wagged her finger. '*Manger chaud*.'

When we drew up at the gates of Le Rossignol I invited them in, but they said they had an appointment.

'Another time, then.' I tried to get out of the car but couldn't open the door. Childproof locks? Didier Rousseau got out and released me. We shook hands again. He bowed slightly, a broad smile on his face.

'I think we have met before,' he said. 'You were dressed as,' he hesitated, '*esquirriel*?'

I had no idea what he meant.

'I translated the *mouche*. The beauty spot. I recognise it.' He was still smiling.

Now I remembered him. The dark hair. The hooked nose. He had been at the wine fair.

'Squirrel.' I scratched myself reflexively. 'I was dressed as a squirrel.'

'I think I know your husband,' he said. 'Monsieur Lancaster.'

'He's not my husband. He's my . . .' I paused to think about what to call Hugo. Partner? Lover?

'Boyfriend? Is that the English word?' He managed to make it sound faintly ridiculous.

'I'm sure the French have a better one,' I said.

He laughed. 'And we have a better word for goodbye. *Au revoir*. Until we meet again.'

They all waved to me as they drove away. I had a skip in my step as I walked to the door. I was making friends at last.

24

Jerry Giff drove over from Bergerac one afternoon with a parcel for Hugo. 'You go right ahead with your work. I'll take this up to the office,' he said.

We had coffee on the terrace. Jerry stretched out his legs, linked his hands behind his head and looked around. 'Nice spot,' he said. 'Forty hectares of vines and cellars to make wine in.'

'I don't think Hugo wants to make wine,' I said. 'Just sell it. He's never even shown an interest in the garden. He thinks flowers grow in shops.'

'We could hire a winemaker,' said Jerry. 'We could hire guys to do all the work. Everything is mechanised these days anyhow. All Hugo would have to do is sell. He's good at that.'

'We? Did you say we?' Jerry had startled me. 'Are you and Hugo thinking of buying a vineyard?'

'It's just an idea we've tossed around,' he said. 'Hugo says the land here is top-notch. The wine sells at a premium.'

'I didn't know Hugo was interested,' I said. 'He's never mentioned it.'

'No point,' Jerry said. 'The owner won't sell. We made an approach, oh, maybe a year or so ago. He's in his late seventies. His wife insisted on living in the city. His son isn't interested in making wine. You'd think the old man would want to cash up and get out. But no.' Jerry stroked his moustache. 'He's a big shot around here. Chateau Le Rossignol is well regarded.'

'He calls it Chateau Le Rossignol even though he doesn't make wine here?'

'He's got a modern winery, all state of the art, stainless steel, temperature controls, on the other side of Astignac.'

'But he doesn't live here.'

'That doesn't matter. He's got the label. He owns the house. He owns the name.'

I stared at him. 'What do you mean, he owns the house? I thought Hugo owned it.'

Jerry looked uncomfortable. 'You should check that out with Hugo.' He stood up. 'Well, I must be getting along.'

When I had closed the door behind him, I rested my back against it. I felt tired and stupid. I realised how little I knew about Hugo's business. I couldn't remember if he had ever claimed to own Le Rossignol, but he had never talked about paying rent either.

He telephoned that evening. 'Hi, sweetie. Everything all right? House not burned down? You haven't run off with the postman?'

'I thought you owned this house,' I said, without preamble. 'I didn't know you were renting it?'

'You never asked.' Hugo sounded surprised.

'I didn't know you and Jerry wanted to buy it and run a vineyard either,' I said.

'It was just an idea we had,' said Hugo. 'I've always wanted to own a vineyard. Nothing came of it.'

'You should have told me you were renting,' I said.

'What does it matter? You live for free.'

'I want to pay my way. I can contribute to the rent.'

'Don't be ridiculous,' said Hugo. 'You haven't any money.'

That was true. I couldn't afford to be proud.

'I'll put a bit extra into the kitty,' I said.

I sat at the table and worked out how much more I could contribute to the upkeep of Le Rossignol. Hugo was handy in the kitchen and often cooked, with flair, but the unspoken bargain was that I was principal cook and housekeeper and Hugo paid the bills.

He kept cash, for buying food and anything needed for the upkeep of the house, in a biscuit tin which sat on top of the refrigerator. I already put the equivalent of fifty pounds a week into the tin. I reckoned I could economise more on food. I was at Le Rossignol on my own almost as often as I was there with Hugo. I would use the telephone as little as possible. I would be assiduous in switching off lights, not filling the electric kettle to the brim when I made myself tea or coffee. I would not buy any new clothes.

The following morning, I didn't touch the cash in the biscuit tin but went instead to the bank in Astignac and changed a traveller's cheque before shopping.

The answerphone was winking when I got back. I had a message from Hugo. 'I'll be home in time for dinner. Crack open the champagne. I can't wait to see you.'

There was no champagne in the house. Hugo had opened a bottle the night before he went away – to console me, he said – and had forgotten to replace it. I took the key to the cellar from a hook behind the kitchen door, and went to fetch another bottle.

The cellar was beside, rather than below the house. It was, properly, a cave in the limestone ridge that ran along the side of the house. The stout wooden door was fitted with a bolt and padlock, although a thief would have to know the cave was there because a curtain of ivy concealed the entrance. It couldn't be seen from the back windows of the house, never mind the road.

I opened the padlock, pushed open the door, groped for the switch. Yellow light flooded a surprisingly high-ceilinged space filled with racks of bottles. The air was fruity and alcoholic, as though wine had been spilled. A row of dusty, empty bottles stood on the ground. No broken glass. The smell must have built up over years. This was where Hugo stored his rare wines. The ones aged between ten and a hundred years old, he'd told me. The wines he imported directly from the producers for resale in England were shipped to a bonded warehouse in London.

I had been to the cellar only twice before – once to call Hugo to the telephone, the second time to announce lunch. I remembered Hugo at the desk in the alcove, turning around, startled. My asking if all the wines in the cellar were worth a queen's ransom. Hugo smiling, reaching for a bottle on the rack beside the desk. 'I keep the bog standard ones here.'

'That's where I go when I need a bottle for the house?'

'You shouldn't need to. I keep us well stocked.'

I remembered looking at a row of bottles beside me. I hadn't been able to see the labels. I had put my hand on a bottle to turn it over.

'Don't touch them, darling,' Hugo had said sharply. 'They're worth a lot of money.'

'I just wanted to see the label,' I said. 'I can't see any labels. How do you know what's where?'

'All systematic,' Hugo said. 'I store them face down so a thief won't know what's worth stealing.'

'Sounds as if they're all worth stealing.'

'Which is why I keep the cellar locked,' said Hugo.

Now I found a champagne bottle on the bog standard rack and carried it carefully back to the house.

I was in the kitchen washing lettuce when Hugo strode through the door, threw his coat over a chair, grabbed me around the waist and waltzed me around the kitchen until I was dizzy. He lifted me off my feet and carried me, shrieking with delight, halfway up the stairs. We scampered, hand in hand the rest of the way and fell on to the bed in a tangle of arms, legs and trousers. We hardly spoke until we lay drowsy and replete.

'I've missed you,' I said.

'Me too, sweetie.' Hugo kissed my bare shoulder, fell back on the pillow, raised two arms to the ceiling and gave a whoop of satisfaction. 'It's been a very good few weeks.'

He told me he had a new client. A steel manufacturer from Shanghai.

'I sold him six magnums of nineteen twenty-one Pétrus,' said Hugo. 'The Chinese adore red wine. Auspicious colour, and all that. It means good luck. They're not interested in any of the great white wines. They love red Bordeaux. They can't get enough of it.' He threw his arm around me and pulled me close. 'Like I can't get enough of you.'

'I wish you didn't have to go away so much, Hugo.'

'You like this house, don't you? I'm getting the money together to buy it. I need to find new clients. It's for us, sweetie.'

'Jerry said you were interested in buying the land as well, Hugo. I didn't know that.'

Hugo stiffened. 'You don't know that,' he said. 'You especially don't know it when you're talking to anybody around here. I like to keep my business private.'

'I don't know that many people,' I said. 'I work most of the time when you're away. But I met someone who used to live here.'

I told him about seeing Madame Barron standing by the gate to the garden. 'This house was occupied by the Germans during the war. Did you know that, Hugo? Her great-grandfather built it. It's her family who hid the wines, isn't it, Hugo? Her cousin came along the road and I didn't get the chance to ask her.'

'Don't.' Something in Hugo's voice made me sit up. I stared at him.

'Don't ask her. She will deny it, anyway.' He sighed. 'You're in rural France, sweetie. There's a lot of rivalry and tittle-tattle. The war is still a sensitive subject. Collaboration, and all that. I do business with a lot of these people. I can't afford to get involved in local gossip. Especially not about who did what during the war.'

'I'm just curious, Hugo. I won't say anything.' I was silent for a moment. 'Was it you who discovered the wine, Hugo? Did you find it here? In the cellar?'

Hugo put his finger to his lips.

'You have to tell them, Hugo. If that family hid the wine, it lawfully belongs to their descendants.'

'It isn't their wine, sweetie. Definitely not. I did not find it here. You are not to speak about it to anybody. Please. Now can we leave it at that?'

He swung his legs to the floor and reached for his trousers, irritation in every movement.

'I didn't say anything to Madame Barron. I won't say a word to anyone.'

Hugo turned to face me. His features relaxed. 'I'm sorry, sweetie. But I know what this place is like. Rumours fly about. Who's buying this. Who's selling that. Best to stay out of it.'

I had roasted a chicken, bought cheese in the market and baked an apple tart. I took the champagne from the fridge, 'Just as you ordered, Hugo.'

He popped the cork, filled our glasses. Then he took a second look at the bottle in his hand.

'Where did you get this?'

'I got it in the cellar. We'd drunk the bottle in the fridge, remember?' I smiled at him but he was lost in thought.

'Did I choose the right bottle?' I said anxiously. 'I took it from where you keep the house wines.'

'Yes, this is fine,' he said absently. He put the bottle on the table and picked up his glass. 'Cheers, sweetie. Nice to be home.'

25

If Hugo noticed that he didn't need to top up the cash in the biscuit tin, he didn't mention it. Neither did I. We settled into a domestic routine. It was now too cold to work outside. My indoor workspace – not grand or ordered enough to be called an office – was a former scullery. It was so small I could touch both walls at the same time. I worked in a jumble of manuscripts, notes stuck to the wall, books in precarious pillars on the floor. But I had a view of rolling vineyards and the wide horizon.

I enjoyed reading and abridging *Silas Marner*. I loved the story of the motherless child brought up by the old man, the metaphor of the stolen gold coins, replaced in his miserly affections by the golden-haired child. My sense of natural justice was placated when the good ended happily and the bad unhappily.

Hugo spent his time between the attic and the cellar. He drove his estate car back to England every third week or so. The Renault was spending more and more time with Monsieur Lanot, the mechanic at the garage in Astignac.

Hugo bought me a pink bicycle on which I explored the narrow roads running up and down the valleys that criss-crossed the low plateau between the rivers Garonne and Dordogne.

I came to realise that the region was replete with houses like Le Rossignol. Nineteenth-century houses, vine-clad, turreted, showing a resplendent face to the world, but often less substantial than they looked. I didn't mind this grandiosity. I thought it added charm to the countryside. And didn't the newly prosperous everywhere in the world, not just in nineteenth-century Bordeaux, try to outdo their neighbours and show off their wealth?

I liked, too, the Victorian Gothic churches with their tall spires crowning every village on the escarpment that ran along the east bank of the Garonne. They reminded me of Irish Catholic churches of the same era, often ugly, reassuringly familiar. Once, cycling down to Astignac on a foggy autumn morning, the church spire, blackened with age, loomed through the mist and for a moment I thought I was back in County Wicklow.

A kind of homesickness overtook me. A yearning for the landscape of which I had been fleetingly reminded, and for the assurance of belonging. I braked, dismounted from my bicycle, and stood shivering in the cold damp air.

There was something timeless in the scene before me. It reminded me of the framed print that hung in the school hall in Ballybreen. *The Angelus* by Millet. Two French peasants, a man and a woman, in a field, facing each other, heads bowed, praying. I remembered the clatter of desks as the whole class stood to recite the angelus at noon. The certainty of it all. Nothing certain now.

I squared my shoulders and got ready to mount the

bicycle again. A man in stout boots and thick gloves emerged from a row of vines and deposited an armful of prunings on the ground. It wasn't until he called out a greeting and came towards me, that I realised it was Didier Rousseau. He nodded at the pile of reddish brown branches.

'We call these sarments. They burn well and make a nice smell.'

I had seen bundles of the same thin sticks advertised for sale at the garage. They were perfect for kindling.

'Just what I need to light the wood-burning stove,' I said. 'It's always going out.'

'Would you like some?'

'Oh, no, thank you.' I didn't want him to think I was looking for something for nothing. 'I'll get some at the garage when I'm in the car.'

'I could tie them to the back of your bicycle. If that doesn't unbalance you too much.'

I smiled and shook my head. 'Thank you but please don't bother.'

I put my foot on the pedal and pushed off. The bike gathered speed and wobbled slightly as I raised one hand in farewell.

That afternoon, a pale sun shone fitfully in a grey sky. Black clouds advanced from the north-west. A sharp wind stripped the trees. Damp brown leaves littered the terrace. The radiators clanked and grunted in their gallant struggle to heat the large sitting room whose flagstones and long French windows I had so admired when I first arrived. I had dreamed of cosy nights by a roaring log fire. Where had that cliché come from? I had never seen a roaring log fire. In those first winter months in Le Rossignol

I coaxed, I bullied, I showered logs with firelighters but never managed to make them roar. They smouldered sullenly and spat back at me.

I opened the iron doors of the fat black stove, pushed some firelighters underneath the blackened logs and applied a match. The firelighters burned brightly for a few minutes but failed to ignite the logs. The room smelled of smoke and paraffin. I went upstairs and pulled on tartan leggings, a pair of Hugo's ski socks, a heavy green Aran jumper and a knitted Fair Isle hat with a bobble and was thus clad when I answered a knock on the front door and found Didier Rousseau on the doorstep with an armful of crimson twigs.

'I'm not always in fancy dress,' I said.

'I've brought these to light your fire.' He was trying not to laugh.

I showed him my sad efforts with the stove.

He poked at the grey and black lumps of wood. He lifted a log from the basket beside the stove, sniffed it. 'Damp. Impossible to make a fire with these. Where did you get them?'

'From the shop at the garage.'

He glanced around the room, picked up three or four logs from the basket, carried them to the nearest radiator and lined them across the top. 'We can leave them here to dry.'

I lifted a couple of logs and put them on another radiator. I was too surprised to speak. I heard the front door open, felt a blast of cold air, heard a car boot being slammed shut, the front door being closed again, footsteps on the flagstones.

'I will show you how to light a fire. With dry wood.' He

transferred an armful of logs to the empty basket, picked up the fireside tongs and shovel and began removing the lifeless logs from the stove. I was torn between indignation and relief. I was clearly redundant. I retired to the kitchen.

I returned, minus the knitted hat, with a pot of coffee and some buttered scones. The twigs were blazing. Cheerful flames curled around the logs. A sweet smokiness now filled the air. The basket was filled with logs. Didier sat back on his heels. He looked pleased with himself.

'Thank you, Monsieur,' I said. 'It makes a big difference to this room.'

'Didier, please. Let us be informal. I am pleased to help.' He settled into the other armchair by the fire.

I poured coffee and proffered the plate of scones.

He bit into one. 'Delicious. One of the things I liked about living in London.'

'It's a great city,' I said. 'Did your wife like living there?'

'Very much,' he said. 'So much that she left me for an Englishman.'

'I'm sorry,' I said lamely.

'A banker.'

'Do you have children?'

He shook his head. 'And you? Do you have children?'

'I don't.'

Although I hardly knew him, I felt relaxed in his presence. It was nearly dark in the room. The light from the fire played on our faces. A log in the fire jumped and spat out a few sparks.

'I was born in this house,' Didier said. 'My mother, my grandfather and my great-grandfather also.'

'Do you mind seeing someone else living here?'

'Anything can happen to a house. It can change shape,

burn down. It is the land that is important.' He stood up and walked to the window. 'We had the best land in the appellation.'

I moved to stand beside him. It was just before sunset. The garden was bathed in pale pink light. On the slopes below, the leaves on the vines seemed to glow.

'The vines face south-west,' said Didier. 'They see the sun all day. The land drains well because it is on a slope. The soil is argilo-calcaire, clay and chalk. The clay gives strength to the grapes. The chalk gives minerality and reflects heat. This house is built with limestone.' He pointed to the ivy-hung ridge that ran along one side of the garden. 'My mother told me all the stone came from there. From natural caves. And when they had excavated the limestone, that's where they made the wine.' He paused. 'Of course, I never saw the caves. I was a baby when we left.'

'Would you like to see them now?'

He looked pleased. I went to get the key. It wasn't on its usual hook behind the kitchen door.

'Hugo must have taken it,' I said, embarrassed. 'I'm sorry. But he should be back soon.'

There was an awkward pause. We returned to our seats by the fire.

'It must have been tough to lose everything,' I said.

He nodded. 'My father found a job in the car industry. We moved to Paris. But we spent our summers with our cousins in Astignac.'

'I've met one of your cousins. Madame Ragulin?'

'Christine.' He smiled.

'I see her on the road most days with her dog.'

'Christine is totally attached to Atalante. Especially since her husband died. Anton was only fifty-four. They had no children. They lived for each other. Anton had no relatives in France. And poor Christine never knew a father. At least Doudou had Papa. My mother married my father when Doudou was very young.'

He sensed my confusion.

'Doudou is my half-sister, Dominique. I still call her Doudou. It was her *petit nom* when I was a child. We have the same mother but different fathers. You met her with Christine. Do you remember? She recognised you when we saw you walking from Astignac.'

The door opened and the lights went on.

'Why are you sitting in the dark?' said Hugo.

'I didn't hear you come in. Didier brought us sarments and dry logs for the fire.'

Didier got to his feet and shook hands with Hugo 'I did not know until recently that you lived here.'

'No reason why you should. You invoice to the London office.' Hugo turned to me. 'I buy wine from Chateau de la Lune.'

'Selling well, I hope?' said Didier.

'Not bad. There's a small niche market for organic wines.'

'Biodynamique.'

'Well, not many people have heard of that,' Hugo said. 'But they understand organic.'

'What's the difference?' I asked.

Before Didier could answer, Hugo said, 'Monsieur Rousseau believes the moon and magic potions produce good wines.'

'You are sceptical,' said Didier. 'I am a Frenchman. I am naturally sceptical. But,' he smiled, 'it works. Come over some time and I will explain everything to you.' I felt his invitation was addressed to me.

'We might do that sometime,' said Hugo. 'Thank you for the logs.'

Didier moved towards the door.

Hugo looked at his watch. 'Will you show Monsieur Rousseau out, sweetie? I have to make a telephone call.'

'So, back to my magic potions,' said Didier as we walked to his car. He pointed to the now dark sky. 'There's a full moon hiding itself somewhere. It makes the vines grow and people think foolish thoughts.' There was a laugh in his voice. He didn't seem to take himself too seriously.

I said as much to Hugo later, when we were having dinner.

'He's a Frenchman,' said Hugo. 'They all take themselves seriously.'

'He's the half-brother of Madame Barron. You remember I said she was born here? Didier was born here as well. They left in the nineteen fifties after a big frost.'

'It put a lot of winemakers out of business,' said Hugo.

'I think he'd like to buy back the vineyard.'

Hugo stopped eating. 'Did he tell you that?'

'It's just an impression I got.'

'What did he say? Tell me exactly what he said.'

'He said how good the land was. That's all.'

'What else? Did he say anything else?'

'Not much.' I thought about our conversation. 'He didn't seem that attached to the house. He just said the land was the best in the area.'

'Did you tell him I was interested in buying it?'

'Of course not,' I said. 'You asked me not to say anything.'

Hugo seemed content. He took up his knife and fork again.

'The owner won't sell to Didier Rousseau,' he said. 'Marc

Petit won't sell. There's bad blood there. Or so I've been told.'

'I thought you didn't get involved in local gossip.'

Hugo grinned. He was relaxed again. 'Fair point. But Monsieur Petit, despite his name, is a big man around here. I can't avoid hearing stuff about him.'

'Why is there bad blood between him and Didier Rousseau?'

'I don't know and I don't care,' said Hugo. 'Maybe nobody knows. It's like *Jean de Florette* around here. Feuds go on for generations. I stay out of it. You should too.'

'One of our neighbours at home hasn't spoken to his brother for twenty years because of a six acre field,' I said.

'You'll know what I mean, then,' said Hugo.

26

I was shopping at the market in Astignac about a week later when I saw Didier Rousseau emerge from the Mairie. He returned my wave and came across to where I was hesitating over an array of cheeses, most of which I had never seen before. He greeted the cheese seller, pointed at the display, said something too rapidly for me to follow, and before I knew it, he had paid for and handed to me three neatly wrapped parcels of cheese. 'All delicious, I assure you.'

He brushed away my attempt to repay him. 'You can buy me a coffee instead.'

I thought we would walk to the café on the square, but he steered me down a side street towards the river. Did I know about the tidal bore on the Garonne, the mascaret? I didn't. Would I like to see it?

We joined a small crowd on the riverbank. A line of surfers stood waist deep in the water about fifty metres downstream. The river was brown and fast flowing.

'Now you will see the power of the moon,' said Didier.

'It pulls the sea into the estuary at high tide. The river flows against it and makes a wave. Mascaret, from the Gascon, *boeuf tacheté*. The leaping cow.'

A curving, frothy wave about four feet high came up behind the surfers. They stood on their boards and rode the wave until one by one they fell in. The wave swept serenely past us. It was followed by another, and another, each one smaller than the last, until only a faint swell remained.

The surfers waded out of the water and climbed into cars parked near the riverbank.

'Now they will race the mascaret upstream and surf it again,' Didier said.

'And fall off again,' I said.

'But of course. That is part of the fun.'

We walked back to the café on the square. Didier told me he had come to Astignac to deposit documents at the Mairie. He had just bought four hectares of land further along the road that ran past Le Rossignol. 'We were going to look at it that day we passed you singing on the road.'

'Like an idiot,' I said.

'Not at all. It was charming. My mother said that. And she decides everything in our family.'

We drank coffee and talked about London and Dublin, where Didier had spent one or two weekends during his time in England. A small man with a big nose pulled out a chair beside Didier, said something quick and cheerful, and sat down. He looked to be about seventy. I recognised him as the mayor of Astignac, Jean-Jacques Marly. His face was still on election posters around the village. The waiter brought him a coffee. Didier introduced me.

Monsieur Marly seemed to know that I lived at Le Rossignol.

'A beautiful property. Your mother still speaks of it, Didier. Everything goes well with her?'

We chatted for a few minutes in a mixture of French and English.

'My regards to Madame Rousseau,' the mayor said. He disposed of his coffee in two swallows, patted Didier on the back, shook my hand and left.

'I think he would like to marry my mother,' Didier said.

'Does she feel the same way?'

'She doesn't want to marry again,' Didier said. 'She still misses Papa.'

He told me his father had died five years earlier from a heart attack. 'That is when I decided to stop being a banker. Papa often spoke about retiring and becoming a winemaker again. I bought Chateau de la Lune four years ago. Maman is pleased. She likes Paris but she loves to visit me here.'

He allowed me to pay for the coffee. We went on chatting in an easy way as we walked to where our cars were parked. We shook hands. Didier repeated his invitation to visit Chateau de la Lune. I thought I might take him up on it.

The year was declining into shorter days. My first five months in France had gone by in a flash. I brushed away the melancholy that came with the sense of time speeding up, by counting my achievements. I had finished the abridgement of *Silas Marner*, checked the manuscript, and retyped a dozen or so pages. I had posted it to Telltapes – the audiobooks company. My French had improved, thanks to Christine Ragulin with whom I was now on first-name terms. She worked from home, translating English novels into French and sometimes telephoned or called in to ask about an unfamiliar English expression. Because my French had improved, I could now chat with the shopkeepers and the girls on the checkout counter at the supermarket. I was beginning to feel part of the community. And I went with Hugo to my first village event.

It was the first year of the Christmas market in Bordeaux. The shops in Astignac complained that they were losing business. The mayor had announced a one-day Christmas market in the village to encourage local commerce.

About a dozen stalls, selling hot wine, crêpes, tiny cakes made with rum and vanilla, foie gras and every imaginable kind of duck product, lined the square. The plane trees were decked with coloured lights. A giant inflatable Santa lay flat as a sheet on two wooden pallets in the centre of the square, surrounded by rows of excited children. A small band – one accordion, two cornets, two guitars and a small drum – played 'Jingle Bells'. It seemed to me that the whole village had turned out. I caught a glimpse of Didier and returned his wave. Jean-Jacques Marly asked for volunteers to take turns inflating Santa Claus. He affixed a foot pump to the inert red and white shape. A tall man came forward out of the audience.

'That's Marc Petit,' said Hugo quietly.

'Monsieur Petit,' cried the mayor, clapping his hands.

The crowd took up the applause. I glanced at Didier. His hands were in his pockets. When I next looked for him, he had disappeared.

Hugo and I sat outside the café, drinking hot wine and watching the firemen tie the air-filled Santa to the tower. The child in me was enchanted. The adult in me was wondering if Hugo was going to come home with me for Christmas. Tommy and Nessa had invited both of us.

'We should have replied by now,' I said. 'They'll be needing to order the turkey. We need to book our flights.'

Hugo looked uncomfortable. 'Listen, sweetie. I'm not sure I can come. I'm really busy.'

'You'll be in London,' I said. 'You could easily pop over.'

'I'll be here,' he said. 'I've got lots to do here. Jerry has asked us over to his place for Christmas. He's having a few other people as well.'

I thought about Christmas in Jerry's house. We had gone there for dinner a few times. There'd be the usual group of expats exchanging moans about French bureaucracy, saying how much they missed Marmite and curry, dancing to Duran Duran and Dire Straits. All friendly, predictable fun. But I wanted the friendliness and predictability of home.

'I don't make a big thing of Christmas,' Hugo said. 'A crowd of us usually go to Val d'Isère for the skiing. Duncan and Emily and Robert and Sarah are going. You liked them. Why don't you come with us?'

'You said you'd come to Ireland.'

'I said I might go.'

'I'd love you to meet my family, Hugo.'

'I will, sweetie. I will. But just not at Christmas, OK?'

'New Year, then,' I said. 'You could come for New Year.'

Hugo put his mouth to my ear. 'Let's keep our voices down. People are looking at us.' He sat back. 'I'm driving to Val d'Isère. I can't leave the car there and fly to Dublin. It's much easier if you can come skiing as well. We'll have lots of fun. We can see your family another time. I promise.' He waved at someone in the crowd. 'I'll be back in a minute.' He loped across the square. I warmed my hands on the wine glass and watched Hugo and Marc Petit pumping hands, slapping each other on the back.

If I was honest with myself, I was more relieved than

disappointed by Hugo's decision not to come to Ballybreen. I could imagine Mum and my sister-in-law dropping well-intentioned hints about weddings, Hugo smoothly flicking them away. My brother repeating his joke about six-month sell-by dates. Well, it was seven months almost to the day since I met Hugo, and we were still together. So much for Tommy's jokes.

The next day, Hugo went to Jersey for a vertical tasting. Although I knew it meant tasting bottles of the same wine in a sequence of different years, the expression always made me imagine people drinking standing up. 'But the amount of wine you get through, you must all be horizontal,' I had observed to Hugo.

'We taste and spit out, sweetie.'

'Eighteen ninety-six to nineteen twenty-six. Thirty years? That's a lot of spitting. I bet a fair bit trickles down your throat.'

He laughed. 'We'll do our own horizontal tasting when I get back. I promise.'

Patricia telephoned minutes after Hugo's estate car pulled out of the driveway.

'You've just missed him,' I told her. 'He's on his way to the airport.'

'Is that Honor?' She sounded surprised. 'I thought you were going to Jersey with Hugo.'

'It's not my kind of thing,' I said. 'Can I take a message?'

'Those Russians telephoned again. And Vladimir Mirsov wants to speak to Hugo before the weekend. I could leave a message on his desk but I don't think he's coming here this trip. There isn't enough time between flights.' She paused. 'You take care now, Honor. Nice talking to you.'

It was a day for telephone calls.

Diarmuid rang. 'I'm still on tour. We're in Bolton this week. Good audiences but bugger all to do after the show except drink and play poker.' His tone was resigned, philosophical. 'It beats being on the dole. Did you get my postcard?'

'What postcard?'

'About New Year. Will you be over?'

'I will. Tommy invited us for Christmas but Hugo will be away skiing. He's not coming home with me.'

'It's scary for a man to meet a woman's family for the first time,' said Diarmuid. 'It's a bit of a statement, and all that.'

'It's a bit of a statement living with me. Is that not the case?'

'It could be,' said Diarmuid.

'Why do I attract men who don't want to get married?'

'Maybe he's biding his time.'

'Like you, Diarmuid? You've been biding your time for years.'

'You need to meet the right person.'

'You mean Hugo's not the right person for me?'

'Well, maybe you're not . . .' Diarmuid's voice grew faint.

'Maybe what? What did you say?'

'Sorry, Honor. I was just saying goodbye to Katy. She says hello and goodbye to you.'

'And the same to her. What were you saying before that?'

'I can't remember. So will you be in Finnegan's on Stephen's Day?'

'Amn't I always?'

'I'll be seeing you, so,' said Diarmuid. 'Happy Christmas, Honor.'

No sooner had I hung up, than the telephone rang again. It was my friend and former flatmate, Mona Cassidy.

'I've great news for you, Honor,' she said. 'David proposed to me yesterday.'

David had been going out with Mona since before I left Dublin for London.

'We're going to buy the ring tomorrow,' she said.

'Congratulations, Mona,' I said. 'When is the wedding?'

'August bank holiday Monday. We picked the date ages ago.'

'How did you pick the date when he hadn't proposed?'

'We decided we'd get married the time I moved in with him. We've been saving up for it since then. You have to book hotels wild far in advance. David always said he'd propose to me when he had the money for the ring.'

'Did he go down on one knee?'

'He did,' she said. 'Right in the middle of the restaurant. We were in La Stampa. All the waiters whistled. The manager gave us a complimentary bottle of champagne.' She paused to draw breath. 'I've a favour to ask. Would you and Tommy ever sing at the wedding?'

I telephoned Tommy and told him about Mona's request.

'Of course I'll sing,' he said.

'She wants "O Perfect Love" in the church, and "Ain't Nothing Like the Real Thing" at the reception. Apart from that we can choose what we like.'

'Have you any ideas?'

'"Là Ci Darem La Mano".' I automatically began to sing.

'There we'll be hand in hand, dear.
There you will say, I do.
Look, it is right at hand, dear;
Let's go from here, me and you.'

Tommy didn't join in. I stopped. 'Don't you think that's a beautiful duet?'

'It's beautiful all right, but it's not suitable. Don Giovanni is tempting Zerlina to be unfaithful on her wedding day.'

'But it's a great tune. And not that many people will know the plot.'

'I'll look out a few alternatives,' said Tommy. 'We can talk about it when you're home.'

I told him I would be coming on my own. He made no comment.

I telephoned Mum.

'It'll be nice to be all together at Christmas,' she said. 'Don't be going and spending any money on a present for me. I have more than I need.'

But of course I went into Bordeaux to see if I could buy her something special. I was in a department store handing over money for a soft pink cashmere scarf, when I glanced sideways and saw at a counter, no more than twenty feet away, a man with his back to me, hand outstretched dangling a necklace of glossy red beads for the inspection of a small girl with a flushed, excited face and a smiling blonde woman in a fur coat. I distinctly heard the word, 'Papa.'

The man turned to select another necklace from the stand. Dark hair falling on the forehead, slightly hooked nose, mouth curved in a smile. The unmistakable features of Didier Rousseau. I stared at him. He looked straight past me. I might as well have been invisible. I snatched my parcel and my change from the startled saleswoman, muttered an apology and blundered through the shoppers to the exit.

Didier Rousseau had seemed open, honest, friendly. It

seemed instead he was just another married man pretending to be single.

You thought you had an admirer, Honor Brady, I said to myself. He flattered you and flirted with you and you enjoyed it. A bit of you thought a rival might make Hugo come up to the mark. Idiot. I berated myself all the way back to Le Rossignol.

27

I was still aggrieved when Hugo arrived back from Jersey. He burst into the kitchen, smiling, rubbing his hands together.

'Fantastic tasting,' he said. 'Well worth the trip. He had only one year missing. Nineteen twenty-one. And I supplied it. What do you think of that?'

'Great,' I said sourly.

Hugo dropped his overnight bag on the floor. 'What's wrong, sweetie?'

'You're never here. I'm lonely.' The words were out before I could stop them.

'Get out and meet some people. Join something.'

'Join what?'

'Oh, I don't know. Some women's group.'

'Don't be ridiculous. Anyway, I've been working.'

'You never talk about your work.'

'Neither do you, Hugo. You come back, go straight up to the office, or fling yourself into an armchair.'

'I fling myself at you first, sweetie.'

I wasn't in the mood for cajolement. 'You go up to your office. You watch whatever sport you can find on television. You sit down at the table. Eat. Drink. Behave like a caveman. And you tell me bugger all about your business. So when Patricia rings up about some Russians I've no idea what she's talking about.'

Hugo paused in the act of taking off his overcoat. 'What Russians?'

'I was going to tell you. They rang your office. And Vladimir something needs to speak to you urgently.'

'What time is it?'

'See what I mean?' I cried. 'You're going to go straight up to your office to call him and you'll be on the phone for ages and I'll be down here going mad with no one to talk to.'

'It's too late to call him,' said Hugo.

'So talk to me instead,' I said. 'Who's Vladimir? What does he want?'

Hugo stood for a moment, regarding me. Then he said, 'OK. Put on a coat and come with me. I'm going to show you something.'

I whisked my jacket from the hallstand and followed Hugo through the back door and up the path to the cellar. It was dusk. The road was quiet. Even so, Hugo glanced around quickly before pushing aside the curtain of ivy, undoing the padlock and opening the heavy door.

We stepped into the dark. Hugo flicked a switch. Blackness became yellow light. He pulled the door shut behind us. I jumped. He put his hand on my arm. 'You're not claustrophobic, are you?'

'No.' I shivered despite my coat. The cave was cold.

Hugo led me into an alcove, lit by a single, naked light

bulb. He lifted a bottle from one of the racks and held it towards me, like a restaurant waiter presenting a bottle for inspection.

'Look at the label,' he said.

It was faded, and spattered with age and dirt spots, but I could see the black and gold lettering. Château Latour.

'A great wine,' said Hugo. 'But that's not the important bit.' He turned the bottle over and wiped it with his cuff. 'Can you see what's etched into the glass?'

I peered more closely.

'Some kind of crest or coat of arms,' I said. 'It looks like H with squiggly bits on top. Some kind of motif.'

'It looks like H,' said Hugo. 'But it's actually N. It's the Cyrillic alphabet.' He spoke with a kind of suppressed excitement. 'N for Nicholas. Tsar Nicholas the Second. The letter N over a double-headed eagle with crown and sceptre. The Romanov crest.'

I was too astonished to speak.

'This bottle was presented to the Tsar on a state visit to France in eighteen ninety-six. A lot of people would like to own it,' said Hugo. 'Vladimir Mirsov is one of them. He made a pile of money smuggling jeans into the Soviet Union and selling them on the black market. He had the cash to buy up businesses that were privatised. Made even more money. Then there's a weird organisation that wants to restore the monarchy in Russia. They're always on the phone to Patricia. They'd like to get their hands on this.' Hugo stroked the bottle. 'And I've got an American collector interested as well. He's going to be in Val d'Isère at Christmas. That's another reason I'm going. I'm taking this with me. He wants to see it. He's ready to pay top dollar.' Hugo raised the bottle to his lips. 'It's going to make me a lot of money.' He replaced it tenderly on the rack.

'How did you get it, Hugo?'

'It's a great story,' he began. 'Nineteen seventeen. October twenty-fifth, nineteen seventeen, to be precise. A mob storms the Winter Palace in St Petersburg. The Tsar has abdicated but his wine is still in the cellars. Hordes roam the palace. They find the cellars. They break in. They start drinking. They're crazy drunk for weeks. The Bolsheviks try to pipe the wine into the river but the mob just drink it from the gutters. In the end,' said Hugo, 'they declare martial law, break what's left of the bottles. Result? A lot of broken glass and the biggest hangover in history.' Hugo paused. 'But,' another pause, 'there was one poor sod among the looters who was a bit more sober than the rest. He'd been a footman in the palace. He knew his way around. He managed to save a few bottles. He smuggled them out under his coat, apparently. Amazing, don't you think?'

'But how did *you* get the bottle, Hugo?'

'After glasnost and all that,' said Hugo, 'the footman's grandson left Russia and came to France where I met him.'

'How much did you pay for it, Hugo?'

'Privileged information. I'd rather not say. But I paid generously. Enough for the operation, and some more.'

'What operation? Paid whom, Hugo? What happened to the man who'd been the servant in the Winter Palace?'

'I paid his grandson. The old boy himself died in the nineteen fifties. The Revolution didn't do much for him. He worked in the shipyard. He died of cirrhosis. It must have been vodka. He never touched the wine. He was superstitious about it, apparently. He'd been happy in the palace. Well fed. He wouldn't touch the Tsar's wine. He never even told anybody he had it, except his daughter. She told her nephew. He sold the wine to me because his aunt needed the money for an operation.'

'If it was looted . . .' I stopped to think. 'Who would be the rightful owner?'

'Who knows? There are loads of people claiming descent from the Romanovs. Half of them are frauds. The chap who saved this had as good a claim on it as anybody.'

'What is it worth, Hugo? You said it would make you rich.'

'Did I?' Hugo picked an invisible piece of fluff from under a fingernail. He looked up. 'A bottle of Château Lafite that belonged to Thomas Jefferson sold for one hundred and five thousand pounds at Christie's. This could be in the same league.' He rubbed his thumb and forefinger against each other in the universal gesture for money. 'In the end, it's what someone is prepared to pay for it.'

'Someone like Vladimir whatsisname?'

'Maybe,' said Hugo.

'Or the Russians who want to bring back the Tsars?'

'I doubt it. They don't have the money. And they're bonkers.' Hugo shivered. 'I'm getting cold standing here.' He put his hand on my arm. 'Don't say anything about this. It's hush-hush.'

'You've got a lot of valuable stuff.' I looked around.

'Too right.' Hugo stood thinking for a moment. 'Maybe we should get a dog to help keep an eye on the place.'

'You took the key of the cellar, didn't you, Hugo? To stop me coming in here.'

'You'd lost your keys, remember? I didn't want you to lose this one.'

'I didn't lose them, Hugo. I just lost the little doofer from the key ring so I couldn't find them in my bag. You don't trust me.'

'Of course I trust you. It's just that you didn't know everything. Now you do, I trust you to keep quiet.'

He shepherded me to the door. We made our way back to the house.

That evening, Hugo made a fuss of me. 'Because you're leaving tomorrow morning. Because I want you to miss me, that's why.' He gave me an extravagant-looking parcel – a confection of gold wrapping paper and red ribbon. 'You mustn't unwrap it until Christmas morning and you have to promise to think of me.' He opened a bottle of champagne. 'I've put two bottles in your suitcase to take home with you.' He had bought caviar, 'because you won't be scoffing it with me in Val d'Isère.'

We put on extra jumpers and socks and sat out on the terrace eating caviar and drinking champagne. The sky glittered with stars. Hugo held my hand.

'I've been preoccupied, sweetie. I promise things will change. I'll be around more when I've sold the Romanov bottles.'

I heard the plural through a contented haze. 'Bottles? Did you say bottles, Hugo?'

'Oh, yes,' said Hugo. 'There's more where that one came from.'

28

I fell happily into the familiar routine of Christmas in Ballybreen. Last-minute shopping on Christmas Eve. Midnight Mass with Mum, Tommy and Nessa. Bacon and eggs in the kitchen when we got back to the house. Taking Mum breakfast in bed. Walking the dogs on Tiveragh hill while Mum and Nessa cooked Christmas dinner. Opening the presents before we sat down to eat.

Mum stroked her scarf. 'It's gorgeous. But I told you not to be going spending your money on me.'

She watched me undo the red ribbon on the gold parcel to reveal two boxes, one of them was plain white cardboard, the other was red faux leather. I opened the white box and took out a key ring attached to a tiny Coca-Cola bottle. I opened the red box. A gold watch lay coiled around a velvet cushion like a snake.

Mum gasped and clapped her hands.

It wasn't until I was attaching my keys to the ring that I noticed the writing on the Coca-Cola bottle. 'It's the real thing.' No fake watch for me.

Hugo telephoned that evening. I thanked him for the watch.

'I enjoyed the joke,' I said.

'What joke?'

'Coca-Cola. It's the real thing.'

Hugo was a thousand miles away but I heard his laughter as though he was in the room beside me.

Diarmuid remarked on my good spirits when I met him on Stephen's Day.

'I feel great,' I said. 'Great to see you. Great to be here. Where's Katy?' I glanced around Finnegan's.

'She's with her dad in Barbados.' Diarmuid smiled at me. 'To tell the truth, I'd rather be here. Paddy serves the best stout in Ireland. No. In the world.' He raised his glass. 'Look at that creamy head. You could take a spoon to it.'

He was wearing a straw wig and pretty much the same clownish outfit as previous years – a yellow checked shirt, red braces, baggy brown trousers, hobnailed boots. Most of the regulars were in similar gear. I was one of the few conventionally dressed. I preferred to take my place among the spectators when Diarmuid and the other wren boys paraded through the streets playing tin whistles, beating the bodhran, singing, collecting money for charity.

'It's a funny thing.' Diarmuid looked around at the assembly of clowns, Santa Clauses, leprechauns and motley yokels. 'The wren boys used to hunt the wren and tie it to a holly bush. That was the tradition.'

'Parading the poor dead bird.' I shuddered.

'Now it's a fake bird, we do it for charity, and this year it's the Irish Wildlife Trust. Saving the wren from extinction. Irony, eh?'

'And saving the tradition,' I said.

My lunchtime drink with Diarmuid on St Stephen's Day was another tradition. He and his parents usually spent Christmas with relatives near Ballybreen. Diarmuid and his cousins were enthusiastic wren boys. I followed them as they pranced through the streets waving their collecting tins, shouting, '*The wran, the wran, the king of all birds, St Stephen's Day got caught in the furze. Although he is little his family is great. Come out your honour and give us a trate. Hurrah, me boys, Hurrah.*'

Afterwards, when the money was counted and handed over, we all crowded into the pub, and when the laughter and the talk died down and the cousins drifted back to the house, Diarmuid and I went for a walk.

A blustery wind blew bits of paper and empty polystyrene food cartons along the pavement. We put our heads down, funnelling the cold air past our ears, and walked briskly to the beach.

'How's Hugo?' Diarmuid shouted into the wind. 'Is he coming over at all?'

'He's skiing in Val d'Isère.'

Diarmuid put his arm around me and gave my shoulders a quick squeeze in commiseration.

'I might join him after Christmas if I can get a standby flight,' I said.

We walked towards the water's edge.

'That's where you kicked over my sandcastle.'

'What?'

'You ran over to me with your pigtails flying and your face blazing and you jumped on my lovely fort with its turrets and ramparts.' Diarmuid shook his head, all mock sorrow. 'Don't you remember?'

'It was a long time ago,' I said. 'But if you'll accept a late apology, I'm sorry.'

'Doncha know, babe,' he said in a Boston accent, 'love means never having to say you're sorry?'

'That's the dumbest thing I ever heard,' I said. 'And that's a line from a film too.'

We stood smiling at each other, but I felt as though something solid had suddenly slid sideways. I was unsettled for a moment, oddly self-conscious. Like a child again.

'I'm sorry I wrecked it.'

'Me too,' he said.

A wave washed up, inches from our feet. We jumped back. A brown and white terrier ran forward into the speckled surf, yelped, scuttled back. It seemed to have come from nowhere. There was no sign of its owner. Diarmuid picked up a piece of driftwood and hurled it towards the dunes. The terrier dashed after it.

'Hugo and I are thinking about getting a dog,' I said.

'Why don't you just go the whole hog and have a baby?'

'What?' I halted, not sure whether to laugh or remonstrate.

'Your brother Tommy, and Nessa,' said Diarmuid. 'No children. Three dogs.'

'Your cousin Frank, and Eileen. Two children, two dogs.'

'The children came first.' Diarmuid dug at the sand with his heel. 'You're still waiting for your life to begin, Honor. Fish or cut bait.'

I stared at him, hot-faced. 'Hugo has a role in this, you know. There are some things I can't decide on my own. Why am I even discussing this with you?'

I turned my back on him and took a few steps towards the track that led away from the beach. Two boys, only fractionally taller than the red setter and the black Labrador trotting beside them, came running towards me. 'Uncle Muidy, Uncle Muidy! They jumped up and down excitedly while the red setter ran circles around Diarmuid and me and the Labrador truffled in the sand.

Their father, Frank, emerged from the dunes, disentangling two leads. 'These fellas should be on the leash,' he said cheerily. 'And I don't mean the dogs.'

'I was just going back to the house,' I said.

But five-year-old Rory was tugging at my hand. Diarmuid was hoisting three-year-old Oscar up on his shoulder. Frank was marshalling the dogs. I gave in with as good a grace as I could muster. We set off down the long expanse of strand.

I was stiff with rage. 'The whole hog.' What a thing to say. Where had that entire conversation come from? Damn Diarmuid. I glared at his back.

Rory disengaged himself from me and ran to take Diarmuid's hand. Damn Rory. If he hadn't attached himself to me I could have got away. You should be ashamed of yourself, Honor Brady, for cursing a child. What's got into you?

I didn't know whether I was more cross with Diarmuid or with myself. I picked up a pebble and hurled it into the sea. Diarmuid and I were like two people in a boat, I thought. We'd be sailing along nicely, and then a squall would blow up out of nowhere and the boat would nearly capsize.

Thirty yards ahead of me, I saw Diarmuid lower Oscar to the ground and push the two boys towards their father. He hung back and waited for me to catch up.

'Honor, listen. What I really meant was, is Hugo the one?

The real thing? Because if he isn't, you shouldn't be hanging about.'

'For God's sake, Diarmuid,' I hissed. 'Why don't you get another mouth to put your foot into? If you can't say the right thing, just shut up.'

'If that's how you feel,' he said rigidly.

Frank looked around. 'You two all right? I'm taking these lads home.'

'I'm going home myself,' I called out. 'Cheerio, Frank.'

I turned and stomped away. When I looked back, Frank and the children had reached the other end of the street. There was no sign of Diarmuid.

I was coming downstairs for breakfast the following morning when an envelope dropped through Mum's letterbox. I picked it up. It was addressed to me. Inside was a postcard of Brittas Bay. Diarmuid had scrawled, 'Sorry, sorry, sorry' on the back.

I ran outside and caught up with him at the crossroads. 'It's all right,' I said breathlessly. 'I'm sorry too.' My words made a cloud in the frosty air. The wind stung my bare arms.

'Get back inside before you catch your death of cold.' Diarmuid's hands were dug deep into his pockets. He was wearing a red knitted woollen hat and scarf.

'Mammy knitted them for me,' he said, before I could ask. 'Don't laugh.'

'I wouldn't dream of laughing. Your Mammy's a great knitter. Will you be in Mulligan's tonight?'

He shook his head. The red bobble on the hat bounced. 'I'm off back to London today. Frank's taking me to the airport in half an hour. I just didn't want to leave things the way they were.'

He unwound the scarf. 'Put this round you and go home, Honor.' He draped it around my shoulders. 'It looks better on you.'

'What'll your Mammy say?'

'She won't mind me giving it you. She knows I'll get it back.'

He put the red hat on my head. Gave me a little push. 'Go on home now. I'll send you a postcard from Hollywood.'

I was half-turned to go. 'Hollywood?'

'I was going to tell you yesterday. I'm up for a bit part in a western. Playing an Irish cowhand. I probably won't get it.' He tried to sound offhand but I knew he was excited.

'You probably will,' I said. 'You'll be great, Diarmuid. Break a leg.'

'Make sure you don't do the same on the ski slopes. Happy New Year, Honor.' I thought I glimpsed a half smile before he turned, hunched his shoulders and walked away.

29

I borrowed Tommy's car and drove up to Dublin to see Sinead Kelly. We met in Bewley's in Grafton Street to reminisce and gossip over coffee and sticky buns.

Sinead took off her raincoat and hung it on the back of her chair.

'Do you miss Ireland at all? Or are you having such a grand time in the fine weather that you don't think about any of it?'

'It rains in France too,' I said. 'The climate isn't that different where I am. It's a lot warmer in the summer, all right. But it's cold in the winter. And it rains. Are you going to come out and visit me?'

'I might go in the summer,' she said.

She told me she had bought a small house in Clondalkin.

'When Mona moved out of the flat and moved in with David, I thought it was time for me to move on as well. I've given up thinking any man is going to provide for me. I can look after myself.'

'You look happy, Sinead.'

'And why wouldn't I be happy? I like my independence. I have a low mortgage because I work in the bank. I earn good money.'

'What if you were poor?'

'If I was poor I might be looking a bit harder for a man,' she conceded. 'But I'd rather be poor and happy than married to some dull bugger of an accountant. I went out with a man from Wexford for a while. A golf professional. He had no conversation at all. He spent most of his time practising. He didn't do enough practising on me. I hit him into the rough.'

Sinead had a booming laugh. Heads turned. She lowered her voice. 'I'll say one thing for him. He improved my golf swing. I'm playing off sixteen now.'

We chatted for a while about Mona's wedding.

'What about yourself?' said Sinead. 'Any news there? Is your man going to propose one of these days?'

'I hope so,' I said.

'What's he like? I'm dying to meet him. You'll have to bring him to Ireland. Is he going to come to Mona's wedding? That could put the idea of proposing into a man's head. Mind you, it can scare some of them off as well. That's what happened to my cousin, Brendan. He was engaged to a girl he'd known since he was eighteen. Then he was best man for one of his football friends. He was as white as the tablecloth during the reception. The next day he kicked the whole thing into touch. Took off for America. The poor girl cried for a week.' Sinead bit delicately into a bun. 'She's better off without him.'

'Is that what she thinks?' I said.

'Why wouldn't she think that? She's a teacher,' said Sinead. 'Good job, long holidays. Plenty of time for golf.'

'She's a golfer?'

'They'd booked a honeymoon on the Costa de la Luz. She went with a girlfriend instead. They spent ten days learning to play golf at Valderrama. It's only the top course in Spain. Can you imagine? She's playing off twenty-one now.' Sinead winked. 'She does a lot of practising with a new man she met at the club.'

'What happened to your cousin?'

'Brendan's not one to be tied down. I heard he took up with some girl in America but she dumped him. Sauce for the goose. He's supposed to be coming back. What about Hugo? Is he serious? Are you serious?'

'We do a lot of practising,' I said.

Sinead laughed. Heads turned again.

On New Year's Eve, my sister, Kathleen, her husband, Seamus, and their three-year-old son, Conor, arrived in Ballybreen on a surprise visit from Baltimore. They were thinking of coming back to settle in Ireland, they said. Seamus, who was in the restaurant business, had put in an offer to buy a hotel on the outskirts of Dublin.

'Great potential.' He rubbed his hands together. 'We went to a business seminar in Washington. The Celtic Tiger. That's what they're calling it. It's a good time to invest. Besides,' he and Kathleen exchanged a smile, 'we think Ireland is a great place to bring up kids.'

'Kids!' Mum's hands flew up to her cheeks. 'Am I right in thinking . . .?'

'You got it,' said Seamus. 'The baby's due in July. A little brother or sister for Conor.'

Tommy and Nessa clapped. I joined in the general congratulations. I was happy for Kathleen and Seamus but I couldn't help feeling a slight sense of exclusion.

'Our plan is to rent somewhere while the deal is going through,' said Seamus.

'Don't be thinking about renting.' Mum was aflutter with excitement. 'Will you not all stay here until you're ready to move?'

'You'll be next,' Kathleen whispered to me with a smile.

Mum has better hearing than a bat. 'No carts before horses, please,' she said tartly.

Tommy winked at me and gave my shoulder a nudge. He sat down at the piano. 'I think this calls for a tune.'

He ran his fingers along the keys before moving effortlessly into an introduction to 'I'll Take You Home Again, Kathleen'.

'It's not about going home to Ireland,' I said. 'The man who wrote it was an Austrian and his wife was called Jenny.'

Nobody heard me. They were all singing.

I flew to London on a sleety New Year's Day, intending to stay the night in Hugo's flat before travelling on to Bordeaux. London looked deserted. I had arranged to meet Eddie Nugent for a drink but it was Sunday and the pubs were shut, which Eddie said was just as well because he had a hangover. We sat in a café in Soho and drank hot chocolate. Eddie had brought Coco, his cinnamon-coloured labradoodle, whose brown eyes and springy curls were remarkably like his own. She sat quietly by the table, her head resting against Eddie's knee. Rain rattled like rice against the café window.

'Lucky Diarmuid, off to California,' I said.

'He's got a good chance of getting the part,' said Eddie. 'He's got the build and he can ride a horse.'

Coco shook herself and made to get up. 'She's restless.'

Eddie stilled her with his hand. 'It's all the excitement of Christmas. We'll go in a minute, darling.'

'Hugo and I are thinking about getting a dog,' I said.

'Things going well with you two then?'

'Pretty well,' I said.

Eddie gave a nod of satisfaction. 'Good. It's terrible for a pet when a couple splits up. I almost had to go to court to get custody of Coco.' He tickled her ear. 'Leon has visiting rights. He takes her for walks at weekends and whenever I'm away. We were able to agree on that.'

'That's nice,' I said faintly. I didn't know what to say. Eddie, who had never previously talked to me about his private life, had opened up an entire hinterland of hurt.

He patted my hand. 'Don't look so worried, Honor. A dog will bring you closer together.' He paused. 'And console you if you split up.' A pause. 'Providing you get custody.' He gave me a quick smile. 'Only joking.'

He was suddenly brisk. 'They were pleased with the abridgement. You could do this full time, Honor. It's not brilliant pay, but it's a growing market and you've got into it early. I'll be taking a commission on this next one.' He pushed a book towards me. 'Happy New Year.'

'Thanks, Eddie,' I said. 'You've steered me in the right direction.'

His face reddened. 'Only doing my job, Honor.' He adjusted his scarf. Coco got to her feet.

I pulled on my coat and stood up. 'How long were you and Leon together?'

'Ten years.' He shook his head. 'I thought he'd be around for ever. I was wrong.'

* * *

It felt strange staying in the flat without Hugo. I closed the curtains and switched on the electric radiators to make the atmosphere cosier. The bed was made up with fresh white sheets. It looked cold. I hunted for a hot-water bottle. Hugo was as methodical in London as he was in Le Rossignol. I looked first in the bathroom cupboard, then in the cupboard by the kitchen sink. No hot-water bottle. Then I looked in the cupboard above the electric kettle. No hot-water bottle on the first shelf. I stood on a chair to reach the top shelf but found only a box full of old wine labels, all neatly sorted into decades. There were even some from the nineteenth century. I had to smile. Men definitely had a collecting gene, I thought to myself. My brother, Tommy, still had his collection of football cards. Diarmuid had confessed to once having been a stamp collector.

I got down from the chair. At least the exertion had warmed me up. I opened the refrigerator and found eggs, bacon, a carton of orange juice, some tired-looking cheese in a plastic wrapper and a few shrivelled mushrooms. I slipped the headphones of my Walkman over my ears and sang 'My Old Man' along with Joni Mitchell as I cooked myself bacon and eggs. Her words exactly captured my mood that evening. The frying pan looked too big. The bed felt too wide.

Hugo telephoned as I was about to switch off the bedside light.

'Just calling to wish you goodnight,' he said.

'Hugo, how do you manage without a hot-water bottle?'

He laughed. 'You're my hot-water bottle. I'll be waiting for you at the airport tomorrow night. Sweet dreams.'

I fell asleep with a smile on my face.

* * *

I didn't take a proper look at the book I was going to abridge until I was on the train to Gatwick airport the following morning. It was a book I had never come across before. *The Odd Women* by George Gissing. I turned the book over and read the blurb on the back.

A dramatic exploration of the dilemmas facing the single woman at the turn of the century. Set in grimy, fog-ridden London, the novel paints a vivid portrait of the hardships and inequalities in and outside marriage, and of a society whose values are in flux.

So many odd women – no making a pair with them . . . The pessimists call them useless, lost, futile lives.

Terrific. Just what I needed. I put it back in my handbag and opened a magazine instead.

Make this the year you resolve to have a baby.

A well-known obstetrician was advising women to have children before the age of thirty. I was already four years too late. I put aside the magazine and gazed out of the window. Tower blocks, surburbia, more tower blocks, parks, football grounds, Victorian terraces, allotments – all seen through a film of dust. Never an unbroken sweep of countryside. I realised I missed the landscape around Le Rossignol. The beckoning horizon. The big sky.

Did Hugo want children? I had never asked him. The magazine glared up at me. Hugo had given me a gold watch. It signified commitment. Maybe now was the time to ask.

'Why do you keep looking at me, sweetie?' Hugo loaded my suitcase into the boot of the car. 'You haven't taken your eyes off me since you landed. Did I cut myself shaving? Or are you just glad to see me?' He laughed and pulled me close for a kiss.

'I'm looking at you because you look great, Hugo. No cuts. No broken bones. Tanned and healthy. In fine shape altogether. How was Val d'Isère?'

'Oh, the usual crowd. Pity you couldn't join us. You would have enjoyed it.'

'I might join you next year,' I said. 'Did you sell the bottle?'

'A breeze. A happy customer. The mad Russians are a bit put out. But if they show me the money I can produce another bottle.' Hugo closed the boot. 'Let's go.'

I glanced at him from time to time on the journey back to Le Rossignol. He was smiling. Happy. I thought about Hugo and me with a baby in the back of the car. Yes, I could imagine that. Hugo with a baby in his arms or on his knee? That was more difficult.

'About the dog,' I began.

'What dog?'

'Do you remember we talked about getting a dog? I just wondered, Hugo. Is it what we really want?'

'I think it's a good idea,' he said. 'What about a Dobermann?'

'A Dobermann's not very cuddly,' I said, dismayed.

'It's not about cuddliness. It's about barking and sharp teeth. We're talking about a guard dog. A Rottweiler. Monsieur Lanot at the garage had a break-in last year. They took the cashbox and all his tools.'

And so we were deflected into a discussion about the advantages and drawbacks of different dogs. Terriers – not scary enough; poodles – needed too much grooming; Border collies – chased everything on the road.

In the end, a decision was made for us when Christine Ragulin slipped on a patch of black ice and broke her pelvis.

Hugo and I heard Atalante barking furiously. We rushed

out and found Christine, grey faced, whimpering with pain. Hugo dialled the emergency services.

'Don't worry, I'll look after Atalante,' I said, as Christine was stretchered into an ambulance.

We watched it pull away, lights flashing. 'Well,' said Hugo. 'It seems we've got ourselves a dog.'

Atalante uttered a single howl, and regarded us through mournful, marmalade eyes.

30

And then it snowed. The landscape was white as far as the horizon. Soft white flakes tumbled from a dark grey sky and coated the house, the trees, the vines, the distant steeple. I felt I was living in a snow globe.

Hugo grumbled and said he had seen enough snow in Val d'Isère. I was enchanted. I couldn't remember the last time I had made a snowman. Hugo sat by the fire with a hot whiskey and watched me through the French windows. Atalante bounded happily about, knocking off the stick arm of the snowman, refusing to give it back until I offered her a biscuit instead.

She was indefatigable. She dragged Hugo and me, but mostly me, for miles along the roads around Le Rossignol. She was greeted by everyone we met. A horn would toot, a car window would roll down, an arm emerge in a friendly wave. People came out of their houses for a chat. They all knew about Christine's misfortune. Poor Madame Ragulin. Be sure to give her our best wishes. How fortunate that you can take care of Atalante. Sometimes we met them exercising their own, inevitably smaller, dogs. Atalante regarded these with ladylike indifference. Sometimes we were followed by an eager-looking brown and white Dalmatian. Whenever he appeared, Atalante behaved like a slut. Hugo resorted to throwing stones at him.

Hugo said he'd forgotten a dog took so much looking after. It would be easier, and probably cheaper in the long run, to install an alarm, he said.

After a week, the snow melted as quickly as it had come. Hugo set off for a vertical tasting in Berlin. I began my abridgement of *The Odd Women*.

Two days later, Christine came home from the hospital. She had been prescribed complete rest for a further six weeks at least. I took Atalante and her tartan mattress back to the kennel – it was the size of a small shed – in Christine's garden. After that, I went twice a day to take Atalante for a walk.

For the first two weeks after her release from hospital, Christine was marooned in an armchair, instructed to use her crutches only when she needed to walk to the lavatory or move between her chair and the bed in a spare room downstairs. She never complained, although I saw her swallow dozens of painkillers. A nurse came in the morning and at night to help her get dressed and undressed and open the shutters. Dominique Barron came with cheeses and home-cooked meals for the freezer. Madame Klein, the butcher's wife, sent up a beef bourguignon and a confit of duck. Christine's neighbour, Madame Martin from the pharmacie, brought bread and usually made Christine's lunch. On the few occasions when she wasn't able to do so, she telephoned me. I cycled over to Christine's house, transferred one of the many dishes made by Dominique from the freezer to the microwave, tossed a salad, selected a cheese.

My days became as regular as the postman's. I worked for two hours after breakfast; walked Atalante; had lunch; worked some more; walked Atalante again. At night, I came back and closed the shutters on Christine's house.

When I brought Atalante back from our afternoon walks, I laid a tray with blue and gold porcelain teacups from the Imperial factory in St Petersburg, and made tea in a silver samovar.

Christine told me her husband's family had fled from Russia in nineteen seventeen taking only what they could pack into two large trunks. The samovar, the blue and gold tea set, a dozen silver dishes, jewellery, four rugs. She didn't mention wine. I had promised Hugo not to ask. But I pictured the Romanov bottles wrapped in rugs at the bottom of a trunk.

Anton's grandfather sold the rugs, the silver and most of the jewellery, Christine said. One of the rugs – shades of deep blue and gold – lay on the sitting-room floor. One afternoon at the beginning of February, when Christine was finally able to move slowly around the house, she took me upstairs to show me the other rug – shades of pink and grey – on the landing. The door to the bedroom was open. I glimpsed the great mahogany bed with one lonely pillow and I felt lucky to be waking up beside Hugo most mornings and guilty for my recent twinges of discontent.

I scolded myself on the way back to Le Rossignol. You ungrateful girl, Honor Brady. Hardly a girl any more, I automatically added in parenthesis. You're thirty-four. But isn't life good to you? Haven't you all the good things you yearned for when you lived in a poky flat in Woolwich?

When you were run off your feet as a waitress? Are you happy now, Miss Discontented? No. Why?

Well, for one thing, Hugo now seemed to be away all the time. He had been twice to London, twice to Paris and once to Berlin since the beginning of the year. And when Hugo wasn't away, Jerry Giff always seemed to be around. He was easy enough company, but he and Hugo spent most of the day upstairs or in the cellar, and most of the evening drinking whiskey. When I joined them, conversation seemed to dry up. When I gave up and went to bed, I could hear them talking and laughing. I felt excluded.

'You were ages,' I had said to Hugo the previous night when he finally came to bed. 'What were you talking about?'

'Work, getting the brochure right. Maybe eventually having a website. A lot of businesses have them now.' He reached for me, but I was sleepy, disgruntled and disinclined.

When I went downstairs in the morning, I found a note on the kitchen table. *Gone to Bergerac with Jerry. Back late. H.*

It was almost dark by the time I cycled home that afternoon. The house was cold. My tiny study was freezing. I took my work into the sitting room. I had lit the stove at lunchtime with the last of Didier Rousseau's logs and now it was nearly out. I went to the lean-to at the side of the house to look for more logs. They were damp. I carried four of them into the house and lined them up on the radiator.

I made myself a hot whiskey. I still felt cold. I made myself another. I was carrying it through the hallway to the sitting room when there was a knock on the front door. Didier Rousseau was on the doorstep with an armful of logs. I greeted him coolly, stood back ostentatiously to allow him to carry the logs to the basket by the dying fire.

He tipped them into the empty basket. 'Just in time.' He dusted his hands. Smiled at me.

I didn't smile back.

'Is everything all right?' He looked concerned.

'Thank you for the logs,' I said as civilly as I could. I didn't say that I had seen him with wife and child, Christmas shopping in Bordeaux. I did not offer him coffee or a drink.

He looked at the glass of whiskey in my hand.

'You are more pleasant when you are sober.' He went quickly from the room. A moment later I heard a car door slam, the roar of an exhaust.

I felt like crying.

I sat down, picked up my pencil and opened *The Odd Women*.

'But do you know that there are half a million more women than men in this happy country of ours?'

'Half a million!'

Her naive alarm again excited Rhoda to laughter.

'Something like that, they say. So many odd women – no making a pair with them.'

The words swam up at me. I felt the misery of Alice and Virginia Madden living in a boarding house, eating meagre dinners at a table three foot by one foot. Leftovers. Of Monica Madden marrying a man she didn't love to avoid the same fate. Poverty and spinsterhood. One a bleak consequence of the other.

No wonder I was discontented.

31

Diarmuid telephoned one afternoon around the middle of February.

'I'm bored,' he said.

'How can you be bored, Diarmuid? You're in America.'

It was about five o'clock and beginning to get dark. I had just come back to the house and was wondering if I could face another hour or two with *The Odd Women*. I was almost ready to post the abridgement to Telltapes. They had already sent me *Anna Karenina* – my next assignment. And a second audiobook company had commissioned me to abridge *Villette*. I knew I should go back to work, but I welcomed the distraction of Diarmuid's telephone call.

'I've been in a trailer in a canyon all week waiting to deliver thirty-eight words of dialogue,' he said. 'The actor I shared with was on a mobile phone to his agent most of the day when he wasn't asleep. He was friendly enough the rest of the time but he didn't play cards.'

'You're always talking things down, Diarmuid. If it was

me, I'd be dead excited. And don't go telling me it's just a job like it was any old job. I want to hear all about it.'

I was envious, of course. I had long since given up any notion of a full-time acting career, but a trace of regret remained.

'I have one hundred and forty words of dialogue altogether. I'm in six scenes.' Diarmuid paused. 'It's enough to get me second billing.' Now I could hear excitement in his voice.

'I'm an Irish cowboy. I left home with a price on my head. The hero stops, exhausted, at my shack. He has a posse chasing him. Am I going to help him? Or am I going to turn him in? And wouldn't the bounty be enough to bring my sweetheart over from Ireland?'

'And what do you do, Diarmuid?'

'You have to watch the film.'

'Will you invite me to the premiere?'

'It's not big enough to have a London premiere, never mind a Hollywood one,' he said. 'But we'll watch it together.'

'That'll be nice. How's Katy?'

'She came out before the shoot. We had a week on the coast at Carmel. You'd love the scenery, Honor. Big surf, long white beaches, winding valleys, big soft hills, when they're not covered in fog. There's a lot of fog on the coast. We went to a few wineries as well.'

'Hugo is always saying he'd like to add Californian wines to his list.'

There was a pause.

'I suppose you two are doing something tomorrow?' said Diarmuid.

'Tomorrow?' I couldn't think what he meant. Then I remembered it would be Valentine's Day.

'Hugo's in London. But he'll be back tomorrow night. I imagine he's planned something. What about you?'

'I've sent my Valentine.'

'You picked the right time to call,' I said. 'I've just come in from walking the dog.' I was longing to tell Diarmuid about Atalante.

'So you got yourselves a dog.'

'In a manner of speaking.' I began an account of Christine falling on the ice. 'I was expecting an ambulance but the fire brigade arrived.'

Diarmuid interrupted me. 'Tell me another time, Honor. There's someone at the door. Probably room service with my breakfast. I have to go. Sorry.'

I was pleased Diarmuid had telephoned. I thought about our quarrel at Christmas. Had he been drunk? I tried to remember what we had quarrelled about when we broke up all those years earlier, when I was nineteen. Diarmuid had already graduated and was in his first year at the Gaiety Theatre drama school. I had blurred memories of pink taffeta, strappy silver sandals that were agony to dance in, Diarmuid in a dinner jacket, sparkling wine, an argument, shouts, tears. I had walked back to the flat in my bare feet, carrying my high heels. What had upset the boat that time? What had Diarmuid said to me? Was that when he told me I had a fine rump in that particular dress and then tried to make out it was a compliment? Whatever it was, it was the wrong thing, anyway. Fifteen years ago. Time evaporates. Had Diarmuid finally found his match in Katy? He wasn't going to tell Katy she had a fine rump. She was all skin and bones. And nothing seemed to ruffle her. Just as well.

The following morning, I skipped out to meet the postman. He rolled down the window of his van, wished me good day, smiled broadly and handed me a large pink envelope. He had barely driven off when the florists' van arrived with two-dozen red roses.

I waltzed my bouquet back to the house and telephoned Hugo. There was no answer. I tried again at lunchtime.

'He's at a tasting,' Patricia said. 'Did you get your card? And the roses?'

'Did you choose them, Patricia?'

'No,' she said. 'I took the card to the post.' She was a bad liar.

I was in a mood to quarrel when Hugo telephoned from Heathrow to say he had booked a table for dinner at the best local restaurant.

'You're never content,' he said. 'I don't have time to go shopping for cards. Did you want me to forget all about it? What does it matter who orders the flowers? I decided to send them. I'm paying.'

'You're always away, Hugo.'

'And you're never around when I'm at home. You're always walking that damned dog.'

'It was your idea to get a dog, Hugo.'

'It's not our bloody dog,' he said.

We had both calmed down by the time Hugo got to Le Rossignol. We set out for the restaurant in a taxi, determined to enjoy ourselves. I asked about the tasting. Hugo said he had, yet again, supplied a missing bottle in a sequence of years. He asked me about *The Odd Women*. I told him I was more than half way through the abridgement. We drank a lot of champagne and giggled all the way home.

We reached enthusiastically for each other that night. But sometime before dawn I wakened with a racing heart, a tight throat and the feeling I couldn't breathe. I got out of bed, threw open the window and took great gulps of air. My panic subsided. Hugo slumbered on. After a few minutes, I closed the window, went down to the kitchen and drank two glasses of water. I went back upstairs on jelly legs. Hugo woke up.

'What's wrong?'

'I don't feel too well,' I said.

He sat up and switched on the bedside light. 'You're not pregnant, are you?'

'I'm definitely not pregnant.' I watched his face.

'That's a relief.' His mouth relaxed.

'Did you think I would try to get pregnant without telling you?'

'Of course not.'

'So why did you ask?'

'Accidents happen.'

'What would you do if I said I was pregnant, Hugo?'

He scratched his head. 'I don't know. I haven't thought about it.'

'Maybe it's time we thought about it. Do you want children, Hugo?'

He considered the question. Neither of us moved.

'I can imagine being a dad,' he said eventually. 'But not right now. I've got business to finish. Then I'll think about it.'

'And talk about it?'

'I can hear your biological clock ticking.' He held out his arms. 'Come here.'

I got back into bed. Hugo held me tight. 'We'll talk about it. But not at the moment. OK?' He rocked me in his arms.

'OK,' I said.

He disengaged himself, lay down, turned over. I fitted myself against his back. It was how we usually went to sleep. Hugo was soon snoring gently. I was wide awake. I went downstairs again and made tea. I sat at the kitchen table in the grey light of dawn. Hugo had given me the answer I wanted, but I felt strangely flat. Anticlimax, I supposed.

32

Christine was by now able to drive a car and walk for two miles without pain. After a trial period, when we both held on to the dog-lead, she could manage the self-willed Pyrenean mountain dog by herself. But I still walked Atalante three times a week. I had become fond of her, and was secretly relieved that Hugo had decided on an alarm system instead of a dog. I couldn't imagine another creature replacing the majestic Atalante in my affections.

I had become friendly with Dominique Barron, who drove over from Bordeaux to call on Christine once a week. One afternoon in early March, I came back from a walk with Atalante to find that Dominique had brought her mother, Madame Rousseau, as well. I remembered the straight-backed woman in the front seat of the car who had tut-tutted her disapproval of people like me who didn't have the sense to eat a hot lunch.

There was no disapproval in her smile today. She greeted me warmly and I found myself included in an impromptu celebration of Dominique's fiftieth birthday, and in discussions about a party in June to celebrate the twenty-fifth anniversary of her marriage to Michel-Henri Barron.

Christine poured me a glass of champagne. 'We are discussing how many of Tante Amélie's admirers to invite to the party.'

'Maman received two Valentine cards,' said Dominique.

They repeated their remarks in French for Madame Rousseau. She waved away their teasing, but she was pink-cheeked and cheerfully tipsy.

'Maman should marry Monsieur Pommier,' said Dominique. 'He is rich. On the other hand, Monsieur Marly has political power.'

'He has a big nose,' said Christine.

'A big nose never spoiled a handsome horse.'

A car drew up outside the house. I glanced out of the window. A blonde woman in a fur coat, a child with a red necklace and a man with a flop of dark hair and a hooked nose got out and walked towards the front door. They came into the room exclaiming, laughing, kissing cheeks.

I had not seen Didier Rousseau since the afternoon he had delivered logs to Le Rossignol, when I had been rude and he had rebuked me for my supposed drunkenness. What would I do if he pretended not to know me again? If he ignored me, as he had done in Bordeaux? I gripped my glass and tried to merge with the wallpaper.

The blonde looked at me with friendly interest. The child twisted her necklace and hid behind her father's coat. He stepped forward as though he had never seen me before and offered his hand. I stared at it.

'I present to you my cousin Philippe,' said Christine. 'His wife, Anne-Marie, and their daughter, Marie-Christine.' She beamed at the child.

'I think you know my brother,' said Philippe Rousseau.

The resemblance was so strong I still thought he was Didier. It took a moment for me to realise that they were twins.

I was so relieved, I couldn't stop smiling. The rest of the afternoon passed in a cheerful blur and ended in a flurry of cheek kissing and hand shaking.

When the others had gone, Christine sat down beside me. She was in a mood to gossip.

'Marie-Christine is a charming child, don't you think? I hope Didier will marry again. I would like another little cousin.'

'Is there anyone in his life?'

Christine shook her head. 'Not since he divorced Claudine. He works too hard. He has put all his money into Chateau de la Lune. He can't afford a wife. He can't afford a holiday. Claudine thought he was mad. We all thought he was mad. To abandon a good job in banking. Imagine. He had an apartment in Auteuil and a house in Cap Ferret. Now he has only a . . . ? *Comment dites-on délabre?*'

'Dilapidated?'

'Exactly. A dilapidated chateau in Entre Deux Mers. And he runs it according to the principles of some lunatic German educationalist.' Christine threw up her hands. 'Plus, he pays a fortune to Claudine. So. He can't afford to marry. Unless he finds a woman who can work in the vineyard, take no vacation, and believe in the power of the moon.'

'Hard to find,' I said.

'But Tante Amélie will marry again,' said Christine. 'I am sure of it. She was always beautiful.' She picked up a photograph in a silver frame from a table beside the sofa and handed it to me.

'Tante Amélie and Gerard Rousseau on the day of their marriage. I was a flower girl. He was a handsome man, *n'est-ce pas*?'

I looked more closely at the photograph. 'Good Lord, he has a black eye and his arm in a sling.'

'Marc Petit did that,' said Christine. 'He attacked Uncle Gerard. He almost killed him, Maman told me. He was violently enraged because Amélie was his fiancée. Everything was arranged. The Mairie, the church, the curé, the reception. One week before the marriage, Amélie said she could not marry him. She was in love with Gérard Rousseau.'

'That was brave of her,' I said.

'Marc Petit waited for Uncle Gerard outside the café in Astignac. There was a big fight by the river. Uncle Gerard fell into the water. Jean-Jacques Marly came to rescue him. After that, Marc Petit went to Algeria. But life is strange, is it not? The frost destroyed the vineyards. Grandfather had to sell Le Rossignol. Marc Petit returned from Algeria a rich man. He became the owner after all.'

'I saw him at the Christmas market,' I said.

'He does not like any member of our family. He was humiliated when Amélie refused him.'

'It was sad for him to be jilted,' I said. 'But it was the right thing to do.'

We sat admiring the wedding photograph. The slender, dark-haired bride with the big smile, the handsome groom with one black eye and one broken arm, the proud parents, the two little flower girls.

'Who is the other flower girl?'

'That is Dominique. We are almost the same age. Two little girls, each without a father,' said Christine sadly.

I was about to ask if both fathers had died during the

war when she added, 'My father died before I was born. He was in a work camp in Germany. He had pneumonia.'

'I'm sorry.' I touched her hand in sympathy.

'One million French men were taken to work in Germany during the war. It was called *Service du Travail Obligatoire*. Obligatory Work Service. In reality, they were like slaves.'

'I never knew that,' I said.

'And those who once knew have forgotten,' said Christine. '*Alors*,' she straightened her shoulders and put on a cheerful smile. She pointed again to the photograph. 'The big man is my grandfather. The small woman beside him is my grandmother. The parents of my mother.' Her voice softened. 'That is my mother, on the left.' Christine stroked the photograph. 'She died five years ago.'

After a pause, Christine began to reminisce about her childhood in the forest of Les Landes. Her paternal grandfather had been a tobacco farmer and timber merchant.

'When he died, my mother sold the farm,' she said. 'We moved to Astignac. But I missed our house in the forest. Sometimes I stop to look at it when I take the road through Hostens to the coast.'

33

I hoped I would bump into Didier Rousseau and get a chance to make up for my recent incivility. I would apologise for seeming rude and offhand, and make the excuse that I had been drinking hot whiskey for a sore throat and had not wanted to inflict him with the same complaint. I planned to tell a small lie. To say I had been drunk and cross about not getting enough work done. I hoped it would be enough to put our friendship back on track. I had my speech rehearsed.

Whenever I cycled into Astignac, I dismounted from the bicycle and wheeled it past the spot where I had seem him working. Third time lucky. On a bright March morning, I saw him digging among the vines.

I called out, '*Bonjour*, Didier.'

He stood up, planted the spade in the ground and walked towards me. I gripped the handlebars of my bike and gathered myself for my speech.

'I thought you were married,' I said. 'I thought you cut me dead in Galeries Lafayette. I didn't know you had a twin.'

'You were rude and ungrateful. Because you thought I was a liar who wanted to be unfaithful to his wife.'

I nodded. We both began to laugh.

Didier clambered over the ditch and joined me on the road.

'I'm not married,' he said. 'I'm divorced. In fact, it is you who is not free. The boot is on the other foot. I think that is the correct expression.'

He stood smiling broadly at me.

'But we can be friends,' I said.

'Of course. Now,' his tone became brisk, 'would you like to see what I am doing?'

I laid my bicycle on the grass verge. Didier jumped back over the ditch and held out his hand to help me scramble across to join him.

I followed him down a corridor of vines towards the planted spade. He crouched beside the hole he had dug, plunged both arms elbow-deep into the soil and, to my amazement, pulled out a cow's horn.

'I filled it with cow manure and buried it at the autumn equinox. Now it is the spring equinox, I dig it up.'

No telltale twitch of Didier's mouth, no glint of humour in his eyes. He was serious.

He took a knife from his pocket and scraped the contents of the cow's horn into a glass jar. He held up the jar for my inspection. It looked as though it was filled with dry soil.

'Smell it,' said Didier. 'Don't worry. It is not unpleasant.'

I sniffed nervously at the jar. It smelled like the bark of a tree.

'I will grind crystals. I will put them into the cow's horn. I will bury it again. I will mix the dried manure with rainwater and sprinkle it on my vines to make them grow.'

He stood up. 'It is all done according to a system devised

by Rudolf Steiner. You have heard of Steiner? He had theories about education also.'

'I know about Steiner schools,' I said.

'He called this method of agriculture biodynamic. It's bizarre. But it works. Come and taste my wines sometime. Judge for yourself.'

We walked back to where I had left my bicycle. I held out my hand, he took it, but also put his other hand on my shoulder.

'We are friends,' he said. 'We can say *au revoir* the French way.'

He planted a light kiss on both my cheeks.

I freewheeled all the way down the hill into Astignac.

About a week later, I got back from an afternoon walk with Atalante to find Hugo and Marc Petit seated at the table in the salon. They were deep in conversation. They each had a pile of documents. A map was spread out on the table. Pushed to one side were a half-finished bottle of Château Le Rossignol and two wine glasses. Hugo jumped up when he saw me.

'I didn't hear you come in, sweetie. Come and meet Monsieur Petit.'

Marc Petit got to his feet to shake my hand. He was as tall as Hugo, and still handsome, despite the deep lines in his face. He had eyes like a bloodhound.

'Monsieur Petit ands I are discussing business.' Hugo began to fold the map, but not before I had noticed it was an Ordnance Survey map of the area around Astignac, with some areas blocked out with a yellow marker pen. I guessed they had been discussing a price for Le Rossignol and its vineyards.

'I was just about to offer Monsieur Petit some coffee,' Hugo said. I took the hint and left them to their negotiations.

When I returned with the coffee, the map and documents had vanished. A briefcase now rested on the table.

Marc Petit was standing by the French windows. He asked me if I liked living in Le Rossignol. When I said I loved the house and the garden, he nodded in a satisfied way.

Hugo said quickly, 'You've liked quite a few of the places we've looked at, haven't you, sweetie?'

I had a moment of panic. Marc Petit was watching my face. I felt sure he knew I had not looked at any properties with Hugo.

I bent my head over the coffee cups. 'This area is full of lovely houses,' I said lightly.

'Are you also interested in wine, Madame?' asked Marc Petit.

'I enjoy drinking it,' I said. 'Hugo is the expert.'

'Perhaps you will become interested, if Monsieur Lancaster becomes a winemaker.' He shook hands with me. 'Au revoir, Madame.'

Hugo showed him out.

'You might have warned me,' I said, when Hugo came back into the room. 'I can't just drum up a lie like that. That man wasn't fooled. Those eyes don't miss much. He knows you're mad keen to buy this place. He knows you haven't looked at anything else.'

'You could have been a bit quicker, sweetie.' Hugo sat down at the table, picked up a pencil, reached for a notepad. 'Either I need to raise more cash or he needs to drop his price.'

'He's not going to be fooled into dropping his price

because he thinks you might buy something else. Either he will sell to you or he won't, Hugo.'

'I wasn't expecting him to call. He took me by surprise. He probably intended to catch me off guard.' Hugo began scribbling calculations on the notepad. 'If the American takes two more bottles, I'll have the deposit. He might even take more.'

'Marc Petit looks the sort of man who does exactly what he wants. I wouldn't like to cross him.' I told Hugo about the black eye and broken arm I had seen in the wedding photograph.

'He was in the Resistance,' said Hugo. 'Rumour is, he killed two German soldiers with his bare hands. Somewhere in the woods around here. He broke their necks. Snap. They made him the mayor after the war. He was only twenty-eight.'

I was suddenly queasy. Butterflies seemed to be trapped in my throat. I went to the kitchen and poured myself a glass of water. Bile erupted into my mouth. I added a teaspoonful of bicarbonate of soda to the water and downed it. The butterflies settled down. I wondered if I had an ulcer.

The following morning, Hugo set off for a formal dinner and wine tasting in Munich. I never went to these events. Partners were rarely included. I didn't mind. I imagined an endless line of men in dinner jackets, dipping their heads in and out of glasses, like penguins around a pool.

I sat down at my desk and picked up *Villette*. Yet another story about the plight of the single woman. I would have preferred to be abridging a book in which penniless heroines had unequivocally happy endings. *Jane Eyre*, or *Shirley*, or *Mansfield Park*. But beggars can't be choosers, I said to myself. I took up my pen and was about to make a start when Christine telephoned and asked if I would like a day at the seaside.

'I've been trapped in the house too long,' she said. 'I would like some sea air. Dominique is going to drive us to Biscarrosse.'

I looked out of the window. The sun shone, fluffy white clouds sailed across a blue sky. In the garden, daffodils swayed in the breeze.

'I'll be with you in five minutes,' I said.

We travelled through the vast marshy fields and forests of Les Landes, past tall black barns, low wide houses and flat fields bisected by long straight roads and narrow lanes. Dominique turned into one of these lanes and parked the car.

'We are going to the house where Christine lived,' she said

We walked a hundred metres down a track to a two-storey timber-framed building with brick infill, half the height of the black barn which rose beside it in the forest clearing.

'That was the tobacco barn,' said Christine. 'Where we put the leaves to dry.'

The house looked uninhabited. A swimming pool was covered with a blue, leaf-strewn tarpaulin. A children's swing dangled listlessly from an iron frame. A basketball hoop was attached to the side of the garage.

'I think it is now a gîte,' said Christine. 'People live here only in the summer.'

We walked right up to it and peered through the front windows. It was dark inside. We could see only the outline of chairs and a table.

'I loved our house,' said Christine. 'Especially when Dominique came to stay. We played with the children in the next farm.'

She sang in a high, light voice,

'Le fermier dans son pré
Le fermier dans son pré
Ohe, ohe, ohe
Le fermier dans son pré.'

'We played that game too,' I said. 'We called it "The Farmer Wants a Wife".'

The three of us marched, humming and singing and swinging our arms, down the track, through the spindly shadows of the pines. Gradually, we fell silent, until the only sounds were the soft crunch of our footsteps, the thin whistle of a bird and the sighing of the wind in the trees. The forest felt empty and peaceful. The bracken was bright green with new growth. The sky above the trees was a brilliant blue.

A deer leapt across the path in front of me. I cried out in shock.

'The forest is full of surprises,' said Christine. Her face shone. 'I like to come here. I feel the presence of my father.'

'Me also,' said Dominique. 'Sometimes I imagine my father hiding here.'

'Was he with the Resistance?' I asked.

'He was an American pilot,' said Dominique.

I halted in surprise.

'Christine has not told you? It is not a secret,' said Dominique. 'His aeroplane was attacked. He fell with a parachute. Maman was collecting wood. She found him in the forest. He had many wounds. My grandmother, my aunt and my mother carried him on a charrette.'

We resumed walking back up the track towards the house.

'What happened to him?' I asked.

'He stayed for three months. Then he escaped to Spain. After that, my mother found that she was pregnant.'

We crossed the shadow of the great black barn.

'For a time he was here.' Dominique indicated the barn. 'After that, he was up there.' She pointed to the roof of the house where there was a tiny skylight.

'Did you ever meet him?' I asked.

She shook her head. 'After the Liberation, Maman and the mayor of Astignac wrote to him by the American Air Force. They said they would attempt to find him. But nothing. He was not found. Perhaps he did not receive the letter. That is what Maman thinks.'

'Did she ever try to contact your father again?'

Dominique shook her head. 'No, Maman is proud. And also I had another father. My Papa.'

'What about you, Dominique? Did you ever think about trying to find him yourself?'

'When Papa died, I thought about it. Yes, I would like that my children know their American grandfather. But I have not an address. That is life, *n'est-ce pas*? In my class at school, there were many children without fathers. Some were the children of German soldiers. My mother was proud that I was the child of an American.' She smiled. 'And I thought for a time I was the child of an angel because Maman told me that my father came down from the sky.'

At Biscarrosse plage, we left the car in a near-empty car park and walked for about a mile along a path above the wide, windswept beach. We had to shout to be heard above the howling wind. I felt as though I was being blown inside out. The sea was too rough for surfing. There was nothing between the beach and the horizon but the ragged blue Atlantic.

We ate lunch at a hotel by the quieter waters of a lagoon a few kilometres from the ocean. The dining room had an out-of-season feel. We shared an enormous platter of oysters, crab, langoustines, cockles, mussels and shrimps. Christine and I toasted Dominique again. The maître d'hôtel, on hearing us cry, '*Bon anniversaire*', presented us with three complimentary glasses of champagne.

Drink loosened my tongue. I forgot my promise to Hugo and confided that he was hoping to buy Le Rossignol.

Dominique put down her glass. 'You are sure? Absolutely sure?'

I was already regretting my indiscretion.

'Not absolutely sure,' I said.

'Didier wants to buy Le Rossignol,' she said. 'But Marc Petit makes an impossible price.' She patted my hand. 'Please don't unquiet yourself, Honor. I will see you living at Le Rossignol with great pleasure. I will visit you.'

'I wasn't supposed to say anything,' I said unhappily.

'You are with friends. We will not say one word.' Christine put a finger to her lips.

'In any case,' said Dominique, 'Marc Petit will not sell to Didier because that would please my mother.'

'I know she jilted him,' I said. 'But after fifty years? He can't still be holding a grudge.'

'Great love turns sometimes to great hate,' said Christine.

'Not true love,' said Dominique. 'If you love someone truly, you want what they want. Even if that gives you pain.'

'How can we know true love? Your mother must have thought she was in love with Marc Petit. She was going to marry him.'

'You know, I asked Maman the same question,' said Dominique.

'What did she say?' I was eager to know.

'She said she was in love with security. She was alone. She had a baby. He was the solution to a problem.'

'A problem of economics,' said Christine.

I felt the now familiar scald of heartburn. I pressed both hands against my breastbone.

'You look pale, what is the matter?' said Christine.

'*Crise de foie*,' said Dominique.

I knew the phrase was an overused French euphemism for indigestion and a hangover. Foie means liver. But for a second, I thought she meant *crise de foi*. A crisis of belief.

34

I went to see the doctor in Astignac and described my symptoms. She examined me, took my blood pressure, asked me a few questions about my life. She insisted on a pregnancy test. It was negative, as I had felt sure it would be.

'*Vous êtes stressée*,' she said.

I was both relieved and puzzled. I hadn't thought my life particularly stressed. But the doctor, who had the calm air of someone who had seen everything and was surprised by nothing, pointed out that by my own account, I had been working on two pieces of work simultaneously and cooking meals in two houses. She added that women also tended to absorb the stress experienced by the men in their lives. She prescribed camomile tea, fresh air and exercise.

I emerged into sunshine. It was the first week of April. The trees in the square were sprouting leaves. There was a patriotic display of red and white tulips and blue hyacinths in the bath-sized stone planters outside the Mairie. I had been getting less exercise because Christine was able to manage Atalante again. I had been working in my tiny office with the electric fan heater blowing. The doctor was right. I needed to feel the wind in my face, refresh my lungs.

I decided to cycle to Chateau de la Lune.

It was signposted from Polignac and easy enough to find. I dismounted at a painted wooden sign with a silver crescent moon and a sprinkling of stars on a dark blue background, and wheeled my bicycle along the gravel track which curved downhill through an untidy-looking vineyard with clover and wild flowers growing between the rows of vines. At the bottom of the slope stood a modern two-storey house with a concrete yard in front and a large shed at one side.

Didier was standing near the entrance to the shed. He was using both hands to stir the contents of an oil drum with a long stick.

'Bonjour, Honor. I cannot greet you properly. I must do this for one hour.'

He smiled at the expression on my face.

'Don't worry. I have only five minutes more. Then this will be prepared and I will stop.'

I watched him vigorously moving the stick in a circle, creating a vortex in the liquid.

'It is the manure from the cow horn diluted in thirteen litres of rainwater.' Didier didn't break his tempo. 'I stir it for thirty minutes clockwise and then for thirty minutes anti-clockwise. I will spray it on my vines at the time of the new moon.'

'Otherwise you are perfectly sane,' I said.

He smiled again. 'I also use camomile flowers in a cow's intestine and yarrow flowers in a stag's bladder in my compost. It's true. But you don't believe me.'

He stopped churning and lifted out the wooden stick.

The liquid continued to swirl round. I watched it, fascinated. Didier leaned the stick against the drum. We exchanged a friendly two-cheek kiss.

'I grow my grapes according to the principles of biodynamics,' he said. 'Perhaps it is simpler to say that I grow them in the old way. The way my grandfather grew them.'

'Did he spray them with manure?'

'No. But he did not spray them with chemicals. He planted when the moon was waxing. He pruned when the moon was waning. That was the old way of farming. My grapes are healthy. Good grapes make good wine. Come, taste it.'

He led the way from the sunlit yard into the cool darkness of the shed. When my eyes adjusted to the light, I saw a line of high, wooden casks and, beyond them, a row of smaller wooden barrels, resting on their sides.

At the front stood a small fridge with half a dozen wine glasses, a laptop and a scattering of leaflets on the top. A poster on the wall – gold lettering superimposed on green and purple grapes – proclaimed:

Domaine de la Lune. En Biodynamie depuis 1993.

Beside it hung a large calendar showing the phases of the moon.

Although I had been in the area for more than six months, I hadn't visited many wine producers. Hugo never took me with him when he was buying. 'Nice to have you around when I'm just doing deliveries, darling. But not when I'm negotiating.' We had gone to a couple of 'Portes Ouvertes' – days when vignerons open their doors to the public and invite them to sample their wines.

Hugo had tutored me in tasting. 'Swirl it around in the glass. Put your nose into the glass. Sniff a few times. Say something like, '*belle arome*' or '*belle robe*'. You can say it in English. Great nose. Good colour. Take a swig. Slosh it around your mouth. Suck in your cheeks. Swill it around a bit more. Look thoughtful. Spit.'

Now I watched Didier take two bottles of red and two bottles of white wine from the fridge. They had already been opened. He splashed a little white wine into a glass and handed it to me.

I glanced nervously at the spittoon.

Didier smiled. 'You don't have to spit. Only if you taste a great many wines. Then you should spit. Not to have *un coup dan le nez*. Be a little bit drunk.'

I dutifully swirled the pale, viscous liquid around the glass. I pushed my nose into it. It smelled of grapefruit and freshly cut grass.

'I don't know much about wine,' I said apologetically. 'I just drink it.'

He laughed. 'But that is exactly what wine is for.'

I sloshed the wine around my mouth. It tasted of lemon and mango and other flavours I could not identify. My mouth watered. I swallowed. The taste lingered on my palate. I put down my empty glass.

'Delicious. Absolutely delicious.'

Didier poured a splash of red wine into my glass. 'Cuvée Amélie.'

It smelled of blackcurrants. It tasted of plums and cherries, and something spicy, like cinnamon or cloves. It made my mouth pucker.

Didier poured a few drops into a glass, sniffed it, tasted it himself. He nodded with satisfaction. 'It will keep for several years. This is a flower day. It will taste even better on a fruit day.'

I checked his expression. No hint of a smile.

'The moon affects the taste of wine,' he said. 'It sounds ridiculous. But I have come to accept that it has a big influence. Remember the mascaret? All that water pulled upriver by the power of the moon?'

Didier put his hand on the small of my back and steered me closer to the calendar. I could now see that under each picture of the moon, from a sliver of white to a round white globe, as it waxed and waned over the month, was either a tiny orange carrot, a yellow rose, a bunch of red grapes or a green leaf.

My back was warm where Didier's hand had rested.

'The lunar month is divided into fruit days, flower days, root days and leaf days,' he said. 'Wine is best on a fruit day. It is strange, but my wines taste better on fruit days.'

He glanced at my face. 'You are sceptical. I was sceptical too. But my wine is good, no?'

'Very good,' I said truthfully.

'Perhaps it is because I do not rely on chemicals to kill weeds and fungus, because I must watch my vines closely, because I must work harder, perhaps that is why my wine is good.' He smiled. 'I don't have to believe everything about the theory. I just know that, for me, it works.'

We strolled between the rows of vines. Didier said he allowed weeds and flowers to grow. 'It is good for the vines to compete. They like stress. I plough close to the vines in autumn. It cuts off the side shoots. The tap root burrows deep into the subsoil.'

Four fat white cows grazed in a field on the other side of the ditch that bordered the vineyard. 'These are my blondes d'Aquitaine,' said Didier. 'Sometimes they graze here, between the vines. They eat the clover and the weeds. I use their manure.'

He looked at his watch. 'It is time for lunch.'

'I must go,' I said.

'But you cannot cycle all the way back to Le Rossignol without eating lunch first,' said Didier. 'I will make something.'

He led me to the back of the house where French windows opened into a large kitchen.

'Please, sit down.'

He pulled out a chair from the long pine table on which sat the remains of breakfast – a half-eaten croissant, a smudge of jam on a plate, a knife smeared with butter, a wide cup without a saucer.

He was entirely unembarrassed. He swept the dishes from the table and put them in the sink. He took a bottle of white wine from the fridge.

The sun flooded through the windows and warmed my face. I relaxed.

Didier waved away my tentative offer to help. He swiftly laid the table with glasses, plates, knives, forks, napkins. He opened a tin and tipped the contents into a shallow bowl. He put the bowl in a microwave oven. So the French took shortcuts as well. The thought made me smile. Didier took a packet of smoked salmon from the fridge, halved and buttered two slices of brown bread with swift, economical movements.

'You see? Lunch is easy.'

The microwave hummed while we ate the smoked salmon. The timer pinged. Didier retrieved the dish from the oven.

'Lampreys,' he announced. 'From the Garonne. In a red wine sauce.' He smiled. 'Naturally.'

'One of the English kings died from a surfeit of lampreys,' I said. 'But I never knew what they were.'

'They are like eels.' Didier set the dish on the table and spooned a portion on to each plate. '*Bon appétit.*'

I took a mouthful. 'Delicious.'

'She has changed the recipe from the last time. I think there is more garlic.'

I looked at him in astonishment. 'You know who made this?'

'Of course,' he said. 'My mother. On her last visit to me.'

I studied his face. He was serious. This was not a joke.

'But it's from a tin,' I said.

'She made it here, in the kitchen. Then we took it to the pharmacie in Astignac. Monsieur Martin has a machine. It seals the tins perfectly. I have a cupboard full of them.'

'Tinned lampreys?'

He nodded. 'And tinned confit of duck, and beef bourguignon, and rabbit stew. Fortunately, Maman likes to cook. I am busy all day. I have no wife to cook for me.'

'Some wives do more than cook,' I said.

'I should hope so,' he said, with a smile that made me blush.

I bent my head to my plate. 'I don't think I could cook like this.' Then, in case he thought I was auditioning for the role of wife, I quickly added, 'I would love to be rich enough to employ a cook.'

'Then you must marry Monsieur Lancaster,' said Didier.

I looked up, startled. 'Hugo isn't rich,' I said. 'Not really, really rich.'

'Rich enough to buy Le Rossignol for cash,' said Didier. 'Rich enough to put down a big *dépôt de garantie.*' He studied my face. 'You should not be surprised. Nothing is secret for long around here.'

I wasn't surprised that everyone seemed to know Hugo's business. I was embarrassed that they knew more than I did.

35

Jerry Giff and Hugo were sitting at the kitchen table drinking champagne, when I got back. They looked up when I came in.

'Hello, sweetie,' said Hugo. 'As you can see, we're celebrating.'

'You didn't tell me you'd paid the deposit,' I said.

'Who told you that?'

'Didier Rousseau.'

'Good news travels fast,' said Hugo.

'I guess everybody around here will know soon enough,' said Jerry. 'Three cheers for the Romanovs.' He lolled back in his chair and raised his glass. He had a smug look on his face.

'I was going to tell you when the deal was completed,' said Hugo. 'I wanted to surprise you.'

'I'm surprised already.' I was shaking. I didn't know if I was nervous or angry, or both.

'We still need to raise some more money,' said Hugo.

'We? I don't have any money.'

'He means me,' said Jerry. 'I'm putting in ten per cent. You get a free ride with Hugo.'

He was drunk. I ignored him and addressed Hugo.

'I heard you were paying cash.'

'I've sold the flat and business in London.' He couldn't stop grinning. I realised he was drunk as well.

'I heard from the agent this afternoon,' he said. 'The sale of the flat will go through in a couple of weeks. I'll complete the deal on the business next week.'

He stood up. His chair clattered to the floor. 'Aw, don't look like that. I was going to tell you.'

'What will happen to Patricia?'

'She'll be all right. She'll be kept on.'

He pulled me to him, held me tight and attempted a sort of tango around the kitchen, out into the hallway, into the sitting room. We both fell on the sofa. Hugo was like a large, excited puppy. He was alternately panting and making a kind of yodelling noise.

Jerry ambled into the room with the champagne and three glasses on a tray. 'Can anybody join in?'

It was impossible to stay angry with them. I sat up and tried to catch my breath.

'You'll be a chatelaine,' said Hugo. 'Lady of the chateau. After the harvest, the happy grape-pickers will bring you flowers. It's a charming custom.'

'I didn't see any grape-pickers last year,' I said. 'Only machines.'

'I will bring you flowers,' Hugo said. He slid off the sofa. He knelt. He took my hand. 'I know I've neglected you,' he said. 'I've been away too much. I've been distracted. Following my dream.' He waved his other hand about in a vague, encompassing way. 'I promise things will be better when I'm here all of the time.' He paused. I thought he was going to propose. Oh no. Not in front of Jerry, please. No. But he just went on grinning foolishly.

'Hugo's a happy man,' said Jerry. 'Lighten up. This place makes money. It's established. It has a reputation. We can build it into a brand. Besides, we've still got the other business. Fine wines for connoisseurs.'

'Three cheers for connoisseurs,' said Hugo. He got up, opened the doors to the terrace and went outside. He flung out his arms, beat them on his chest, did a dance on the spot.

'What about your place in Bergerac, Jerry?' I asked.

'Hey, stay cool, OK? I'm not moving in with you lovebirds. I'm not that kind of sleeping partner. I'm keeping my house and studio.'

He drained his glass. 'I ought to be getting back.'

'You're too drunk to drive,' I said. 'You'd better stay over. I'll make dinner.'

While I was cooking, I heard the familiar sounds of football commentary, shouts and laughter, coming from Hugo's office. After a time, the shouts and laughter stopped. The television droned on. When I went upstairs to call them to the table, they were both fast asleep in their chairs. I switched off the television, closed the door, and went back downstairs.

I was asleep myself when Hugo came to bed. He was asleep when I got up. There was no sign of Jerry. A note on the table said, *Thanks for looking out for me. J.*

I had just finished breakfast when Diarmuid telephoned.

'Do you know that stretch of road going down the glen into Ballybreen?'

'I do.' I could picture the winding black road, the broad,

green flank of the mountain with low white houses scattered on it like buttons on a quilt, the glint of the sea in the distance. 'It's one of my favourite places in the whole world.'

'Mine too,' said Diarmuid. 'I got a bit of money for this film. My financial adviser, that is to say, my mother, thought I should invest in a bit of property. So I bought myself a cottage. It has a red door, a bit of a garden and a view of the sea.'

Envy flared.

'Is the whole world buying property?' I said. 'Hugo is only after buying this place. And the vineyard with it.'

There was a definite pause. 'You'll not be wanting to visit me in my humble cottage, in that case,' said Diarmuid.

'Why wouldn't I visit you? Isn't your cottage in a lovely spot? Are you going to live there permanently?'

'I'm thinking about it,' he said. 'But I'll keep the flat in London.'

'I'm pleased for you, Diarmuid,' I said. 'You're a lucky man. How's Katy?'

'She's on a photo shoot in Bavaria.'

I felt restless after Diarmuid's call. I went upstairs and glanced into the bedroom. Hugo was still quietly snoring. I decided to visit Christine and take Atalante for a walk.

I walked her for miles. I walked her until my feet were sore and we began passing houses I had not seen before. When we got back to Christine's house, we were both exhausted. Atalante lapped up a litre of water at great speed and lay in a panting heap on the grass.

Christine persuaded me to stay for lunch. 'You have walked a lot. Your cheeks should be pink. But you look pale,' she said.

'I didn't feel well last night. I couldn't sleep.'

'Is something worrying you?'

'Work hasn't been easy,' I said. 'Hugo is away all the time.'

'Is everything all right between you?'

'Everything is fine.' I paused. Well, she probably knew already. 'Hugo has paid the deposit on Le Rossignol.'

'But that is wonderful for you,' said Christine.

The room was stuffy. I stood up. I could feel my heart drumming. 'I feel a bit sick. Like I did last night,' I said.

'*Crise de foie*,' said Christine. 'I'm going to get you something.'

I sat on the sofa fighting an urge to run outside and swallow great gulps of air. Christine came back with a bottle of clear yellow liquid. She insisted I take two teaspoonfuls.

'This is absolutely for *crise de foie*. It is made from herbs and buttercups.'

It tasted mostly of alcohol.

Christine looked anxiously at me. 'If you don't feel better after the Hepatoum, you must go to the doctor.'

'I've been to the doctor. She says it's stress.'

'Aha,' said Christine. 'You are over-breathing.' She rummaged in a drawer and took out a paper bag. 'You must inhale and exhale slowly into this.'

I put my face into the bag. After a few breaths, I felt myself grow calmer. My heartbeat slowed. I lifted my head out of the bag.

'I'm not in love with Hugo any more,' I said.

I felt as though a clear wind had just blown through the room.

36

Hugo was in his office when I got back to Le Rossignol. I found him bent over his desk, examining a wine label with a magnifying glass. He spoke without turning to face me.

'I'm busy. Is this important?'

'We need to talk, Hugo.'

He sighed heavily, put down the magnifying glass and swivelled around in his chair.

'Make it quick, sweetie.'

'I will.' I took a deep breath. 'I'm not in love with you any more. I think I should move out. I'm sorry, Hugo.'

He looked startled. Then his expression hardened.

'It's Didier Rousseau, isn't it? I thought you'd got pretty cosy with him.'

I shook my head. 'There's no one else. This has nothing to do with anybody but us. Except there isn't an us. There's you and there's me and we've been moving apart.'

'I haven't had time for little chats,' said Hugo. 'I've been too busy buying this place.'

'I wasn't part of that decision. You talk more to Jerry Giff than to me.'

'You didn't want to know,' said Hugo. 'You never took any interest in my work.'

'I did so,' I said. 'At the beginning. When we went places together. But when we moved here, you were always somewhere else.'

'I won't be away as much when the sale has gone through. I'll be more settled. I can start thinking about having children.'

Not with me. The words formed, but I didn't speak them.

Hugo said, 'This is because I haven't asked you to marry me, isn't it? Because I said I wasn't ready. But that's going to change.'

'This isn't about getting married. It's about the way I feel, or don't feel any more. I'm sorry.'

Hugo stood up. 'Give yourself time to think about this.' He was suddenly boyish, pleading. 'You haven't seen your family for a while. Go back to Ireland for a bit.'

My thoughts were racing. I was already wondering what I would do, where I would go.

'I could even come over and join you,' he said.

'I'm not homesick, Hugo. I'm heartsick. I've been pretending to myself I'm in love with you when I'm not any more. It's as simple as that. I'm sorry.'

'Stop bloody well saying you're sorry,' said Hugo. 'It doesn't help.' He flapped his hand, as though flicking my apology away.

'You never said anything before,' he said. 'You could have said something. We could have talked.'

'You know, this is the longest conversation we've had for

a long time,' I said. 'But we're having it too late. It doesn't matter any more.'

We bartered arguments for a while, but it seemed to me that there was no real anger in either of us. We were both weary. Our exchanges faltered, died away. Eventually we were just standing, looking at each other in exhausted dismay.

If Hugo was hurt, he hid it well. He became cool and brisk. He was meeting a collector in Munich at the end of the week. He would leave early. That would give me time to move out. I could leave the keys with Christine.

'It was good in the beginning,' I said. 'We had fun together. I won't forget that.'

'Neither will I,' said Hugo.

We exchanged the usual platitudes about keeping in touch, wanting to stay friends. But that won't happen, I thought. It had never happened with anyone else I'd fancied myself in love with. Except Diarmuid.

I felt detached. As though I was watching myself from the wings. We stood looking uncertainly at each other. I wasn't sure whether we were going to kiss, hug or shake hands. In the end, we both stepped forward at the same time and achieved an awkward mixture of all three.

I glanced back at Hugo as I left the room. He was already seated again at his desk with his back to me, lifting the magnifying glass.

I made myself a cup of coffee, carried it outside and sat on the wall dividing the garden from the vineyard. I was trembling. I wasn't sure if it was from cold, or from the shock of having so swiftly put a full stop to my life with Hugo.

Hugo came out of the house and walked to the cellar. He didn't even glance in my direction. He emerged with a case of wine. He set it on the ground, locked the cellar, put the key in his pocket, carried the case around the side of the house. I heard a thunk, then a thud, then the growl of the car driving away.

So that was it.

I turned to look at the navy blue line of the horizon. I had to think about what I would do next. Christine had told me I could stay with her while I sorted out my life. I could find somewhere to rent in Astignac, she said. I could do my abridgements, perhaps give English lessons. I imagined myself in a small apartment by the river, walking to the post office with my manuscripts, organising a bank account, a telephone account, eating well, but eating alone. Having friends, but being far from my family. With Hugo, I had always felt I still had one foot in London. I realised that was where I now wanted both feet to be.

It was dusk when I went back into the house, picked up the telephone and spoke to Eddie Nugent. I was coming back to London. I needed a job. I didn't care how small it was, or where it was.

'Oh dear,' said Eddie. 'I hope you didn't get a dog.'

'No custody battles,' I said. 'It's a clean break.'

'I've another abridgement for you, Honor. *Persuasion*.'

'At least it has a happy ending,' I said. 'Thanks, Eddie. I'll do it, of course. But they're slow payers. I need something now, while I reorganise my life.'

'How do you feel about out of town?'

'Timbuktu would be fine, Eddie. What have you got?'

'Basingstoke. The Haymarket Theatre. It's a small part, I'm afraid. The maid in *She Stoops to Conquer*. I had someone new on my books playing it but she took the injunction to break a leg rather too seriously and did just that. It's a two-week run. Rehearsals next week. Equity rates. Digs in Basingstoke.'

Back to porridge.

'You're an angel, Eddie.'

'Diarmuid has bought a house in Wicklow. Roses around the door, that kind of thing. I think he wants to exchange the hurly-burly of the chaise longue for the deep peace of the double bed.'

With Katy, I assumed. I felt a stab of envy again. Diarmuid and I had always done things in tandem. Hadn't we? We even fell in and out of love at the same time. Well, not this time. I was alone, and it seemed Diarmuid was getting ready to settle down.

He telephoned not long after I had spoken to Eddie.

'I heard about you and Hugo,' he said.

'That was quick.'

'Good news travels fast,' said Diarmuid. 'Ah no. I didn't mean that. Are you all right, Honor?'

I put an end to his embarrassment by saying briskly, 'Indeed it is good news for me, Diarmuid. I've come to my senses. I was living some kind of fantasy. I think it's called the Cinderella syndrome. Well, I'm not Cinderella any longer. There is no magic wand. I'm in charge of my own life.'

'That's some speech,' said Diarmuid. 'Are you sure you're OK?'

'Of course I'm sure,' I said. 'Why wouldn't I be OK? And how come you knew about me and Hugo so quickly?'

'I saw Eddie after you telephoned him,' he said. 'Break a leg in Basingstoke.'

I telephoned Mum and told her I was going back to

England to be in a play for a couple of weeks. I could come home for a few days before I started rehearsals, I said.

'It didn't work out with Hugo. We're not right for each other.'

Mum didn't say anything. I imagined her soft sigh. Her anxious face. I suddenly wanted to be in Ballybreen, making tea in the kitchen.

'Ah well,' Mum said eventually. 'Better to find out sooner rather than later. Are you all right, Honor? Is your heart broken?'

'It's not,' I said. 'And I don't think Hugo's heart is broken either.'

I booked a flight from Paris to Dublin and went upstairs to begin packing. My clothes went back into the red suitcases. I felt as though I was rewinding eight months of my life.

The bedclothes were still rumpled. Hurly-burly. It was the other way around for me, I thought. I was exchanging the hurly-burly of the double bed for the deep peace of doing the right thing.

I didn't want to stay another night in the bed I had shared with Hugo. I pulled off the sheets and carried them downstairs to the washing machine. I could hear it rumbling and tumbling while I tidied my office into a briefcase, stacked my books into boxes. I picked up *The Odd Women*, it flopped open. My eye fell on a sentence.

'Thirty-one or fifty-one is much the same for a woman who has made up her mind to live alone and work steadily for a definite object.'

My object would be self-reliance. I was not waiting for a prince to turn up. I was not a Victorian spinster doomed to penury. I was an independent woman in the twentieth century and I could take care of myself.

Christine drove over. She loaded my cases and boxes into her car. I hesitated over the pink bicycle.

'Hugo gave it to you. You should take it,' said Christine.

But there wasn't space for it in the car and I didn't feel like cycling to her house in the dark. In the end, we decided I could collect it another time.

'Because you will return,' said Christine. 'You must promise to visit me. There will always be a welcome for you at my house.'

I bequeathed her most of my books. I knew she would give them a good home.

We had dinner in a restaurant on the banks of the Garonne. It was still too cold to sit outside, but we got a table by the window and watched people go by at the same leisurely pace as the brown river.

'I will miss all this,' I said.

'And I will miss you,' Christine replied. 'We will all miss you.'

I stayed at Christine's house that night. In the morning, I took Atalante for a farewell walk. We took Christine's usual route past Le Rossignol. Two men in dark glasses sat in an estate car at the entrance. I thought they were Hugo and Marc Petit. I raised my hand in an embarrassed wave as I walked towards them. The car jerked into life, reversed speedily, and roared away in the opposite direction. So much for me, I thought.

I paused for a minute at the small gate into the garden. Pink blossom on the plum trees, white blossom on the apple trees, creamy blossom on the chestnut tree. Atalante didn't drag me away. She seemed to know that I was silently saying goodbye.

I stopped again at the wrought-iron gates and gazed at

the house. I had closed all the shutters before I left. Le Rossignol was exactly as I had first seen it. Silent, imposing, full of false promise.

I was carrying my suitcases down the stairs in Christine's house when I heard a car pull up, the door slam, Atalante barking, Didier's voice. He came hurrying into the house, took the cases from me, put them on the floor, grasped both my hands.

'Christine told me you are leaving. I am sorry. You must give me your address and telephone number. I hope I will see you when I am in London.'

He handed me his address book. I wrote down Mum's telephone number in Ballybreen. 'I'm not sure where I'll be living, but Mum will know where I am.'

He took both my hands again. 'Hugo Lancaster was not the right person for you. He is too,' he paused, 'closed. He is not open, like you are open.'

He kissed me gently on both cheeks. '*Au revoir*, Honor. Good luck.'

Christine drove me to Gare St Jean in Bordeaux. I got a train to Paris, took the RER to Charles de Gaulle airport, and flew to Dublin.

Tommy and Nessa met me at the arrivals gate. Their gentle chat flowed around me like a warm airstream. You've had a long journey; are you tired, Honor? You'll feel better when you've had a rest; sure didn't every one of us make a mistake; or more than one mistake; the heart is a resilient muscle, isn't that so? You've done the right thing, Honor.

It was early May. The days were lengthening. It was still light when we drove into the mountains. A shower had washed the landscape. The gorse shone bright gold on the hillsides; white hawthorn blossoms were heaped like snow on the hedgerows that lined the neat green fields.

I rolled down the window and drew the air into my nose. The coconut smell of gorse blossom, the yeasty smell of hawthorn, the sharp, acidic smell of cut grass. The smell of home.

37

Melanie

At the end of February, Mom and Ivor came to Carmel for a charity pro-am golf tournament played over three days at three different golf courses on the Monterey peninsula. For the game at Pebble Beach, Ivor was drawn with one of the top professionals in the United States. I took a day off to walk around the golf course with Mom and watch them play.

Ivor stood on the first tee, gripping and re-gripping his club, trying not to look at the photographers hopping and clicking like crickets.

'He's nervous,' I said to Mom.

'Why are you surprised?'

'I've never seen Ivor nervous.'

'All his nerves are in his stomach,' Mom said. 'He takes antacids.'

Poppa taught me how to hold a club and swing when I was seven years old. I played good golf until I was thirteen. After that, I discovered boys. Golf wasn't cool any more. But I still watched it on television with Poppa, and that afternoon, when the sun shone on the Pacific and a strong wind stiffened the flags and made the pines sing, I almost wanted to take it up again.

We moved around the golf course in a small bunch of spectators. The big crowds followed the celebrities, singers, sports stars and Hollywood actors, who, like Ivor, had paid big money to play alongside the professionals. From time to time, we heard roars from the throng following the movie stars on the other fairways.

I couldn't remember the last time I had spent five whole hours alone with Mom. Probably when I was a baby, before Mom went to Washington, I decided. It was a good feeling, walking down the fairways, the sea breeze on my face, Mom's arm tucked into mine.

The seventh hole at Pebble Beach is a short par three. It plays to just over one hundred yards. The green is the size of a postage stamp. From the elevated tee, it looks like it's surrounded by the Pacific Ocean. The bunker at the front is a yawning mouth waiting to swallow your ball.

The professional, then ranked twelfth in the United States, waggled the club, swung it, hit the ball. It flew high into the air, seemed to hover for a moment, drifted left and dropped into the sea. There was a collective intake of breath.

Ivor stooped to place his ball on the tee peg. I was close enough to see the sweat on his forehead. He stood up, addressed the ball, swung the club. Once more the ball flew towards the ocean. Mom gasped. The ball seemed to stop in the air. It dropped like a stone, landed on the green and rolled to within three inches of the hole.

The spectators applauded. Ivor turned to Mom and blew her a kiss.

'He's good.' I tried not to sound surprised.

'Ivor works hard at everything,' said Mom. 'He wants to be a winner.'

Ivor was not so successful with his shot to the green on the eighth. His ball made it over the ocean but landed six feet short of the green. He chipped on, missed the putt. Double bogey. It was his only truly bad hole. He and his partner finished tenth overall.

In the evening, Mom and Ivor stopped by my apartment on their way to the gala dinner. Mom was in a long black silk dress with mink straps. She had a mink stole around her shoulders. Ivor wore a white tuxedo. He was carrying a black leather briefcase.

I gave them a guided tour. It didn't last long. I only had two rooms and a bathroom.

'This is nice, Melanie.' Mom sat on the edge of the sofa because she didn't want to crease her dress. I perched on a stool at the breakfast bar. Ivor stayed on his feet. He was slim and not especially tall, but he was the kind of man who always took up a lot of space.

'Your mom and I spoke to a realtor yesterday. He was playing in the tournament. We had a look in his window on our way over here. The mortgage on a one-bedroom condo is only a few dollars more than you're paying here in rent.'

'I'd like you to have some security,' Mom said. 'To have a place of your own.'

'You need to think ahead,' Ivor said. 'Plan your life.'

'I know that's hard,' Mom said. 'When you're young, you don't always know where you're going. You only see the signposts when you look back.'

'I already told you, Mom. I don't know if that's what I want right now.'

'You ought to give it some thought,' said Ivor. 'You ought to decide what you want to be in ten, fifteen years.'

'When you were my age, did you plan your life?'

'Absolutely,' said Ivor. 'I planned my life when I was ten years old. I planned to get a scholarship, go to college, become a lawyer. I aimed to be partner, then senior partner, and then take over the firm. And that's exactly what I did.'

'You planned all that when you were ten years old?'

'Not the last bit,' said Ivor. 'I worked out that strategy when I was at law school.'

I looked at Mom.

'Women are different,' she said. 'We don't plan with exactitude. We have hopes, dreams. Maybe we should plan more and dream less.'

'My dream is to be a winemaker,' I said.

I waited for Ivor to burst my bubble with a disparaging remark.

'You'd better get into property so you'll have collateral when you need it,' was all he said.

I let my breath out.

'I don't want to rain on your parade,' Ivor continued. 'But you know what they say. The quickest way to earn a small fortune making wine is to start with a big one.'

'I don't want to make a small fortune. I just want to earn my living doing something I love.'

Ivor put his hands up. 'OK, OK. Nobody wants to stop you. I'm just saying it's not a way to get rich.'

'I don't want to get rich.'

'That kind of thinking is why people stay poor.'

'Money doesn't make you happy,' I said.

'Maybe not,' said Ivor. 'But it sure helps.'

'Why are we arguing?' said Mom.

'We're not arguing,' said Ivor. 'We're discussing Melanie's future.'

'Sounds a lot like arguing to me.' Mom stood up and straightened her dress. 'We should be getting along.' She kissed me. 'We think you should at least consider buying something. We can help you.'

'Thanks,' I said. 'I'll think about it.'

'I'm going to help you with something else,' said Ivor. 'Ingrid tells me you're interested in Bordeaux. I'm going to give you one of the great wines to taste.'

'Ivor has donated a rare bottle of wine to the charity auction tonight,' Mom said.

'A premier cru classé,' said Ivor. 'Nineteen forty-five. A legendary year in Bordeaux.'

'It came from the cellar of a French aristocrat,' Mom said. 'He's selling his wines because he needs money. Isn't that what that nice dealer said, honey?'

Ivor nodded. 'Wines like that don't come on the market often. It was a real find.'

'Ivor is giving you a bottle as well,' said Mom.

'Not a premier classé,' said Ivor quickly. 'But it's the second wine from the same chateau.' He opened his briefcase, took out a bottle and presented it to me. 'Treat your palate, Melanie. Get acquainted with a great Bordeaux. You can learn a lot from a wine like this.'

'Thank you. You're very generous, Ivor.' That was true. I didn't add that I was tasting wines all the time. That the oenology department in UC Davis was the best in the United States. That I was also learning from the best winemaker in the Carmel Valley. That I didn't need Ivor to teach me.

'It's one of the bottles that was hidden from the Germans,' Mom said.

'Nineteen thirty-seven vintage,' said Ivor. 'A good year in Bordeaux.'

I went outside with them. The chauffeur got out of the limousine and stood with his hands behind his back, ready to spring forward and open the car door as soon as we said our goodbyes.

'We hope to see you again real soon,' said Ivor.

Mom hugged me. 'It won't be too long,' she said. 'We're planning a big party for Ivor's sixtieth birthday.'

When I went back inside, I put the bottle at the back of the kitchen cupboard. I figured it could stay hidden for another while.

38

The bottle might have remained at the back of the cupboard for some time had I not accidentally bumped into Fred Voss on campus. I was coming out of the Shields Library rearranging books in my backpack when I walked right into him. The books tumbled to the ground. I stumbled over Fred's feet. He caught my arm before I fell flat on my face.

'Melanie Millar,' he said. 'I might have guessed. How are you, Melanie?'

'Still bumping into things,' I said.

'You were daydreaming,' said Fred. 'Right?'

He had a Texan drawl and a dry manner. He had taught the introduction course at Davis. I had enjoyed his lectures. He liked to remind us that a Californian wine had won first prize at the Paris exhibition in eighteen eighty-nine. I particularly remembered him telling us about the Judgement of Paris – a blind tasting in the nineteen seventies – at which mostly French judges had ranked wines from California as better than top-rated wines from

Bordeaux. Fred believed anything produced in France could be at least matched, and probably bettered, in California. 'Heck, we have wines in Texas that are better.' I hadn't been surprised when he left the college to take up a job with The Wine Institute.

Now he helped me pick up the books and replaced them in my backpack. He'd been to a meeting with faculty about internships with the wineries he represented at the institute. He suggested strolling over to the Silo Pub for a beer or a glass of wine, 'If you're not doing anything else right now.'

It was the first week of spring quarter. Thin clouds drifted like smoke in a blue sky, the oak trees along the avenue were bursting into leaf.

'My Alma Mater,' said Fred. 'It hasn't changed much. Even the graffiti is still the same.'

I walked quickly to keep up with Fred's long stride and conversation.

'You finish this summer, Melanie, right? How's the job? You're way over in the Carmel Valley, right? Vincent Briamonte at Cottontail, right?'

The Silo Pub in the student union building was the only place on campus that served alcohol. I had worked a few shifts there. It was after lunch and before classes ended. The pub was quiet. We found a table near the patio. Fred ordered a couple of beers.

I asked him if he knew anything about the wine collection of the last Tsar of Russia.

'Not much,' he said. 'Only that he liked Bordeaux and his favourite wine was Château d'Yquem. Why are you asking?'

'I know somebody who is planning to buy a bottle of d'Yquem that belonged to the Tsar. It's got his name and crest engraved on it.'

Fred whistled. 'I bet that's costing some bucks. A bottle of d'Yquem that belonged to Thomas Jefferson sold for near enough two hundred and sixty thousand dollars. Do you know who's selling this bottle? What's its provenance?'

'A British wine dealer is selling it. My stepfather says he's reputable.'

'Your stepfather is the buyer?'

'He collects Russian memorabilia. Any trinket touched by the hand of a Russian royal,' I said. 'And fine wines. He's got a thousand bottles in his cellar. This plays to both his obsessions.'

'That's neat,' said Fred.

'He's sure the bottle is genuine. I wondered how anyone could tell.'

Fred grinned. 'You know what they say. There's more Lafite in Las Vegas than ever left the chateau.'

He took a long swallow of beer, smacked his lips, put down his glass and grinned. 'They don't fake *this* stuff. Not that I know anyway.'

'Is there a lot of faking in the industry?'

'Oh Lordy yes,' said Fred. 'Goes back a long way. Even the Romans complained about it. It's done for all kinds of reasons. To upgrade the wine; to make it more alcoholic; to make it sweeter. Always, but always, to make it more expensive.' He was suddenly serious. 'It can be dangerous, Melanie. In eighty-six, an Italian added wood alcohol to his wine to make it stronger. Twenty-three people died.'

'That's horrible,' I said.

'Doesn't often happen that it kills people,' said Fred. 'Mostly it's people blending an expensive wine with a lower-quality wine. Stretching it. Making bigger quantities.

Bigger bucks. Sometimes they stick a more expensive label on a cheaper wine. That's happened. You can take a simple burgundy, label it Romanée-Conti, and abracadabra, it's top dollar.'

'What about faking old wines?'

'That's a piece of cake,' said Fred. 'All you need is a few genuine old bottles, a scanner and a high-quality colour printer. Copy the label. Add a bit of dust and a few stains. Hey presto. You've made a thousand bucks. Plus, a lot of rare wines are never drunk. They're traded like paintings or antiques. Even if they're opened, some owners wouldn't know the difference between Romanée-Conti and a two-buck bottle from Trader Joe's.'

'Isn't the chateau name on the cork?'

'Some fancy chateaux didn't have their names on the corks. Some of them recorked their old wines for collectors. Can you believe it? So a fake wine with an old cork and no name gets a new cork with the chateau name on it.' Fred shook his head and rolled his eyes

'How much fake stuff is out there?'

'Nobody knows,' said Fred. 'But six hundred bottles of Romanée-Conti, the most expensive burgundy on the market, were produced in nineteen forty-five.' He paused. 'Thousands have appeared on the market. Literally thousands.'

He sat back and watched my reaction. 'Surprised, huh?'

'Aren't there records? Vincent's partner was able to tell me how many magnums of Lafite were bottled in nineteen thirty-eight.'

'Sure there are records. Some of the top French properties have good records,' said Fred. 'But Saint-Émilion wasn't added to the rankings until nineteen fifty-five. Pétrus isn't classified. It doesn't even have a chateau. But it's one of the most expensive wines in the world. And it has hardly any records before the nineteen sixties.'

He grinned. 'I learned this stuff because I got called in on a fraud investigation a couple of months back. I can't tell you too much about it. But there's a collector out there who's hopping mad because he thinks he's been swindled. His lawyers got in touch with me. I started looking at scientific ways we might prove it one way or the other.' He paused. 'And here's a thing. It looks like it might be possible with carbon dating.'

Fred was enthused, animated, like I remembered him in the lecture theatre.

'Grapes absorb carbon dioxide. Most carbon dioxide in the atmosphere has six neutrons and six protons in the nucleus. After the atomic bomb, two extra neutrons were released, making carbon fourteen. Some geek worked out they could date wine by measuring the amount of carbon fourteen. Neat, huh?'

I thought about the bottle in the cupboard.

'Is it an expensive process?'

'A hundred and fifty, maybe two hundred dollars per test,' Fred said. 'But worth it. The bottle I'm going to get verified cost the owner two hundred thousand dollars.'

He finished his beer and stood up. 'Nice talking to you, Melanie.' He took a business card from his wallet. 'I'm based in the San Francisco office. Give me a call sometime.'

An idea was already forming in my head. 'I have a bottle I've got some questions about,' I said. 'Do you think you could get it carbon dated for me?'

'Sure,' said Fred. 'If you've got a couple of hundred dollars to spare. I'm at the Holiday Inn. If you can drop it off this evening, I'll take it back with me in the morning.'

Two hundred dollars for the prospect, however remote, of proving Ivor wrong about something.

'Thanks, Fred. I've learned a lot from you,' I said.

39

The weeks before Easter were busy at Cottontail winery. Because there was a rabbit on the label and Vincent did some fancy marketing involving an Easter bunny, we sold a lot of gift bottles of Cuvée Carolina. When the rush was over, Vincent gave me time off to go up to Portland and help Poppa clear the house. It had sold pretty quickly. He and May Louise had bought a home in Oregon City, equidistant from her son, Bute, and Lone Oak golf course. May Louise said it made sense to be near both. She and Poppa were planning to move into their new home two days before their wedding.

I left Monterey while it was still dark and got to the exit for Sacramento as the sun was rising. I thought about driving north on 101, stopping for a while in Mendocino, trying to find where Mom and Dad had pitched their tepee, but common sense won out over sentiment. I took the shortest route to Highway 5 and kept going. The journey took me a whole day. I listened to country music stations, sang along with Dolly, Wayne and Emmy Lou. Songs about love and heartbreak, mostly. About an unfaithful lover, a motherless child. They had crude but affecting lyrics. When I wasn't singing, I was wondering where my life was heading. At one point on the highway, somewhere south of Redding, the landscape stretched wide and flat on either side and, for about a mile or so, there was no other car, no human being, not a house in sight, not even a sign to remind me of the speed limit or the number of miles to Portland. I felt totally alone.

Some people like being rootless: Jesse, my dad, Brendan maybe, though I guessed he was headed back home to settle down. Mom had been rootless until she married Ivor, I supposed. I wanted to put down roots. I just didn't know where.

It rained all the way from Oregon City to the outskirts of Portland. Mount Hood was blanketed in cloud. But as I drove up Western Boulevard, the sun came out and brightened the houses. I pulled into the driveway, got out of the car and took a photograph to hang on the wall of my apartment. Then I went inside.

I found Poppa in the basement, surrounded by boxes.

'I sorted everything into stuff to keep, stuff I might keep, stuff I can throw out or give away. Then I resorted the stuff I thought I might hold on to. The thrift box is in the hallway. This is what I'm keeping.'

He sat down on one of the boxes and mopped his brow.

'The older I get, the younger my memories,' he said. 'It seems like only yesterday I was helping in Dad's drugstore. I remember my first day at high school. I had a slice of bread and honey and an apple in my lunch box. I remember your grandmother coming into the store for an ice-cream sundae.'

He stood up. 'I took the desk. It's going in the den. May Louise says I have to have a den in our new house. She's going to have a walk-in closet. I'm leaving the pool table.'

The tin box containing the letters and photographs from France sat on the green baize. Poppa picked it up, held it in both hands, as though weighing it.

'Do you think you'll ever see him?' I asked quietly.

Poppa closed his eyes. He brought the box close to his chest. I could hear his slow, steady breathing.

Poppa opened his eyes. 'It would be nice to shake hands with him before I die,' he said.

We went upstairs and sat on stools at the breakfast counter. Most of the furniture was gone. The house felt desolate and smaller somehow.

'I might go to France to work the harvest this summer,' I said. 'In the Bordeaux area.'

Poppa didn't say anything. The tin box sat between us. 'I won't try to find Dominique or anything,' I said. 'I might take a few photographs.'

'I can still see it all in my mind's eye,' Poppa said. 'The farm, the forest, the track through the trees, the flat roads we cycled along. A photograph would be good.'

'I'm going to miss this house,' I said.

'Me too,' said Poppa. 'But we take our memories with us.'

I turned down an invitation to join him and May Louise for a restaurant dinner. I was so exhausted, I could hardly stay on my feet when I got down from the stool. I fell into bed and slept dreamlessly for nine hours. In the morning, I folded the curtains and the bedcover and put them in my suitcase along with my teddy bear and my school certificates. I retired my framed Muppets poster and the books I felt I could part with. They went into the box for the thrift shop.

I packed up the doll's house, cushioning each tiny piece of furniture, each clay figure in bubble wrap. I wrote a card for Alex – 'I hope you have as much fun with this house as I did.' I wanted to wave goodbye when the Fed-Ex van drove away with my childhood.

I threw my suitcase into the trunk of my car, kissed Poppa and May Louise, wished them luck on their wedding day, and set off again for Monterey.

Two days later, Poppa and May Louise married without fuss in the Episcopalian Church in Spokane that May Louise had attended for some twenty years. It was not the church in which she had been married the first time. Their witnesses were the couple who had introduced them on the golf course. After the ceremony, they went straight to the airport and flew to Buenos Aires where they spent a week learning to tango. It struck me as a fine way to get married.

40

I didn't date anyone after what I mentally dubbed my lost weekend with Brendan. I went to a wine dinner, a couple of campus parties, danced a little, talked about exams and getting jobs, listened half-heartedly to my classmates planning a monster end-of-term barbecue. I hoped I would be on my way to France as soon as the exams were over. I only had to shut my eyes to see again the trestle tables, the grape-pickers singing, the dancing in the chateau courtyard that Brendan had described.

Linda telephoned to talk about her wedding. 'We've picked a date in June. You have to put it in your diary.'

'That's soon,' I said. 'I need to check right away about taking holidays.'

Linda laughed. 'It's June next year. It takes that long to plan a wedding. You can't imagine all the stuff that has to be decided. You and Stephanie are going to be in fuchsia pink silk. I thought maybe you could find a weekend between now and December to come to New York for a fitting?'

'If I'm going to France,' I said, 'I would fly via Kennedy. We could meet up then.'

'You're going to France? That's cool. Pete and I have decided on Paris for our honeymoon.'

A few days later, my course adviser Alicia Shaker stopped me outside the laboratory after a class.

'I have frustrating news for you, Melanie. They have strict labour laws in France. You have to be a citizen of the European Union to work the harvest. You could study some aspect of oenology or get an internship, but it looks like it's too late to set something up for this summer. Maybe next year?'

Next year I would be finished at Davis and working full-time at Cottontail. I hid my disappointment and thanked Alicia for her trouble. I was thinking maybe I could go on vacation to France instead. Maybe after the crush at Cottontail. But I was in low spirits when Mom telephoned to check if I was coming to Ivor's sixtieth birthday party.

'Didn't you get the invitation card? RSVP. That means *répondez s'il vous plaît*. A telephone call would have been thoughtful, Melanie. I need to know the exact numbers for the caterers.'

The whole world seemed to be planning celebrations. I didn't much feel like going to any of them, least of all Ivor's birthday party.

'Sorry, Mom. I've been meaning to call. I can't ask Vincent for another day off.'

'The party's on a weekend, Melanie.'

'I work weekends. It's our busiest time.'

'Can't you swap with someone?'

'There isn't anyone.'

'What did they do Easter weekend? Weren't you in Portland then?'

'Vincent made an exception.'

'I don't know what's gotten into you, Melanie. You sound like you don't want to come. Do you need money for the fare? Is that it?'

'No, Mom. I can pay my fare.' I didn't say I could barely afford it because I'd spent two hundred dollars on carbon dating Ivor's wine.

'Ivor will be real disappointed if you don't come.'

I thought that unlikely, but didn't say. There was a silence. Then I heard Mom call out, 'Come and say hello to Melanie, honey. You can ask her when she's arriving.'

Mom had played an ace. Alex came on the telephone.

'Hi, Melanie. Thank you for the doll's house. I can't wait for you to see it in my room. I've made a new figure for it.' The words bubbled out of her. 'Can you guess who it is?'

'No idea.'

'It's you, Melanie.' She squealed with delight. 'It's bigger than the other figures. I made your curls with real soft embroidery thread. I hope you like it. What day are you arriving, Melanie?' She sounded like she was on her toes with excitement.

'I haven't booked my flight yet,' I said.

'Dad says the longer you leave it the more expensive it gets. He says that's true about a lot of things.'

She chatted happily about the party. 'Mom says Nicky and me can stay up until midnight. It's so we can all sing "Happy Birthday" for Dad.'

I know when I'm beaten. I said I would book my flight straightaway.

I half-hoped I wouldn't know the verdict on Ivor's wine before I left for Atlanta. I was already regretting my impulse to have it tested. I told myself that Fred Voss's talk about fraud had planted a suspicion in my mind and I had a duty to the industry to check it out. But a tiny voice of conscience told me my impulse had been baser than that. I decided that if carbon dating proved the wine had been made before nineteen forty-five, I didn't need to say anything. If the test showed it was later than that . . . Well . . . I put the idea at the back of my mind as something I probably didn't need to worry about.

The day before I flew to Atlanta, Fred Voss was back in Davis for a meeting with the dean. He loped across the lawn towards me waving an envelope. He didn't give it to me straightaway.

'Let me ask you, what made you think there was something suspicious about the bottle?'

I hesitated. 'Just an instinct, I guess.'

'I tried it before I gave it to the geeks,' said Fred. 'It was good. It had structure, acidity, balance. It's a well-made wine.'

I felt a load lifting off my shoulders.

'About seven or eight years old, they reckon. I was surprised they could be that accurate, but apparently levels of carbon fourteen began falling again when they stopped atomic testing.'

He went on talking but, after my initial shock, I wasn't really listening.

'It's all in here.' Fred handed me the envelope. 'Good call, Melanie. I'm impressed. You have all the instincts of a good sleuth. If you're interested, there might be a job for you in a bureau I'm setting up to combat wine fraud. You'd have a steep learning curve, but I reckon you've got what it takes.'

I was too flabbergasted to reply.

41

Mom literally pushed the boat out for Ivor's birthday. I arrived on the afternoon of the party to find her supervising the tying of lanterns to a gondola floating on the long pool between the rows of Greek statues. Her hands were busy with ribbons and balloons. She offered me her cheek. 'I'm much too busy to talk,' she said. 'The guests will start arriving at six.'

I rehearsed what I would say to Ivor should he ask if I had tried the wine. It would be just like him, I thought, to announce in front of an audience that he had given me a rare wine, and then pronounce the verdict on it himself. Well, if he asked my opinion, I would say one of my old college professors judged it a well-made wine with structure and I couldn't disagree with him. And that was the truth, if not the whole truth, so help me God.

Three long tables, each seating thirty, and a top table, seating nine, were set up on the velvet lawn beneath an open-sided, green-striped canvas tent. Ivor and Mom were going to be in the middle of the top table, with the twins on either side of them. I would be at one end, beside Christos and Catherine, now his fiancée. Poppa and May Louise would be at the other end. During the meal – 'I guess it's more of a banquet really' – the Atlanta Community Orchestra was going to play Mussorgsky's 'Night on the Bare Mountain'.

I thought that might be a little strange given the opulence of the garden, the warm, rose-scented air, the party atmosphere. But Mom said it was one of Ivor's favourite pieces. They'd heard it at a concert on their first date.

She was right about it being a banquet. We sat down to caviar with blinis and sour cream, a choice of chilled borscht or vichyssoise, followed by lobster cocktail. Six chefs carved ribs of beef from Texas and a whole roasted hog with an apple in its mouth. There were roast potatoes and sweetcorn, zucchini fritters and four different salads. Afterwards there were ice creams with jello, egg custards and cherry pies. When I got up from the table, I could hardly move.

At nightfall, lanterns glimmered throughout the garden as well as on the gondola. A six-man band played music by the Eagles, the Beatles and Bob Dylan. Ivor led Mom up the steps from the lawn to begin the dancing. With the exception of Christos, Catherine, the twins and me, the guests were all at least Mom's age or older. They danced energetically, sixties style, with lots of swaying and hand-waving.

Mom flitted about, stopping to chat at all the tables. Ivor was almost always in the middle of a group of men, gesticulating, smoking a cigar.

Harvey Kolber, whom I had met at Thanksgiving, danced with me. Then I danced with Christos, and with nine-year-old Nicky who was all awkward politeness and had clearly been to classes.

When the band took a break, Poppa and May Louise tangoed by the pool, moving with surprising agility and humming all the while. *Tarum tum tum tum, tarum tum tum tum, Trum tum tum tum.* They danced off into the night.

I wandered into the house and heard Ivor's voice booming from the gallery. I looked up. He was showing a group of guests around his Romanov collection. I could hear him boasting about the Romanov bottle and how it had been saved from the Bolsheviks. I slipped outside again and sat for a time by the gondola, watching the reflected lanterns quivering on the water.

Sometime after midnight, I found Poppa and Ivor in the conservatory, talking politics. Most of the guests had gone by this time. Mom was sitting on a sofa. She patted an empty seat beside her. I sat down and was about to make some remark about the party when she put her finger to her mouth to silence me because Ivor was in the middle of a tirade against the Democrats. I tried to interject. Ivor swatted away my remark with a dismissive flick of his cigar. I got up again and went back outside. Mom followed me.

'Ivor doesn't like arguing with women.'

'You mean you never have arguments?'

'Of course we have arguments. But not about politics. I already told you. Ivor has strong opinions. You may not like them, Melanie, but it seems to me they're backed up by evidence. He knows what he's talking about.' She nodded approvingly.

'He's not right about everything,' I said.

I heard Poppa call out, 'Goodnight, Ingrid, goodnight Melanie.'

I replied automatically.

'Dad has given up,' said Mom. 'Ivor's too smart for him.'

'Oh, Ivor knows everything,' I said sarcastically. 'He knows all about wine too.'

'Well, yes, he does, Melanie.'

'That bottle he gave me is a fake,' I said.

I immediately wanted to take back my words but Mom pounced on them.

'What are you talking about? What do you mean?'

'It's supposed to be a nineteen thirty-seven Bordeaux,' I said. 'I had it tested. It's definitely not nineteen thirty-seven. I don't even know if it's Bordeaux.'

Mom stared at me.

'I'll tell you about it another time,' I said. 'It's late. I'm sorry I spoke.'

'Honestly, Melanie, a person would think you wanted to spoil things for Ivor. You did the same thing at Christmas,' Mom said angrily.

'I wasn't trying to spoil things then,' I cried. 'I was trying to help and I got no thanks for it.'

'You were interfering. And you're interfering and ungrateful now. Ivor paid five hundred dollars for that bottle he gave you.'

I was silenced for a moment. I had no idea Ivor had given me such an expensive gift.

'Money isn't everything,' I said tiredly.

'You try living without it,' snapped Mom.

Something flew past me in the darkness. I caught its pungent scent as it landed on the stone flags, flared briefly red, and died. Ivor's cigar.

His voice behind me said, 'How much did it cost you to have it tested?'

Oh, no! I felt like I'd turned to stone.

'You could at least look at me,' Ivor said.

I pulled myself round to face him. He had his back to the light from the conservatory. I couldn't see his expression.

'How much did it cost, Melanie? I can lift the telephone in the morning and find out, but I think you should tell me yourself. You owe me that much. Or, in fact, I owe you.' He took a wallet from the inside pocket of his tuxedo. That was just like him, I thought. Taking his wallet to his own party.

'Well,' said Ivor in an even voice. 'How much, exactly?'

'Two hundred dollars,' I said quietly.

'Did I hear right? Did you pay two hundred dollars to prove my wine a fake?'

I was stuck to the spot. I could barely nod my head.

'You must really hate me, Melanie,' he said.

My mouth dried. I couldn't speak.

'Two hundred dollars,' said Ivor. 'That's a big sum to you. You didn't come to me with your suspicions. You acted behind my back. You wanted to make a fool out of me. Yep. You really hate me.'

'I don't hate you,' I cried. 'I just hate the way you put me down, and ignore my opinions and patronise me. I hate the way you think you're right about everything. You think I don't know anything. But I know stuff. I may even know stuff you don't know.'

Ivor retreated from me. Only one or two steps, but enough for me to see the hurt in his eyes. He blinked. Suddenly I saw the boy behind the man.

Mom shouted, 'Please, stop this, both of you.'

Ivor turned and walked quickly towards the house.

Mom said, 'That's some birthday present. I hope you're satisfied, Melanie.' She hurried after him.

After that, my memory is a series of blurred images.

Mom crying in the kitchen. Ivor repeating over and over again he had no idea I hated him so much. Alex appearing in the doorway, rubbing her eyes, running to Ivor, putting her arms around him. Mom ushering Alex back upstairs, but not before I took in her hurt glance at me.

Ivor stood up. 'I can't talk about this right now,' he said in a tired voice. 'Goodnight, Melanie.'

Alex came into my room in the morning. Her hands were little fists at her side. 'Why were you horrible to my daddy?'

I sat up in bed. 'Sometimes people argue,' I said. 'They say things they don't mean. I was cross with your daddy.'

'Why were you cross?'

'Because I think he sometimes doesn't listen to my opinions about stuff. Because he thinks only peasants make wine.'

'He only says that because he wants Nicky to be a judge,' said Alex. 'He's always talking about you. He calls you his clever stepdaughter. He says if I work hard, I can go to college like you.'

I felt tears welling up in my eyes. 'I'm just not a very nice person, sometimes,' I said. 'I'm sorry.'

She looked at me solemnly. 'You need to say sorry to Daddy.'

I went down to breakfast. Poppa and May Louise were chatting with Christos and Catherine. They chorused a cheery 'Good morning, Melanie'.

May Louise whispered to me, 'Isn't it just wonderful to see all the family together? Just one person missing. I can't help hoping Bill will get a call from Dominique one of these days.'

Mom silently put a cup of coffee in front of me and indicated the hot dishes on the sideboard. The others were laughing, smiling. They were talking about weddings. They seemed oblivious of any tension between me and Mom, who had disappeared into the kitchen. I could hear her talking to Mylene and Nicky. I served myself some bacon and pancakes. They smelled delicious but they tasted like ashes. I couldn't eat more than a mouthful. I muttered some excuse, got up from the table and went to find Ivor.

The door of his study was closed. I knocked, heard him call out, 'Enter.'

I went in and closed the door behind me.

'I want to apologise. Explain,' I said.

Ivor looked up from his desk. 'You explained already,' he said. 'You think I'm patronising, narrow-minded and misogynistic.'

I took a deep breath. 'Yes. And I think it was cheap of you to give May Louise a bottle of wine you knew was a fake.'

Ivor was silent for a moment. 'I bought two bottles of that nineteen thirty Sauternes, so-called,' he said. 'I drank one. It tasted good. I was surprised to find out later that it was a fake. I paid good money for it. But I accept it was wrong to give the other bottle to May Louise. Wrong.' The faintest shadow of a smile crossed his eyes. 'Wrong, but not cheap. It cost me four hundred dollars.'

'I know you also paid a lot for the bottle you gave me,' I said. 'The one I had tested.' I gathered my breath again. 'I'm sorry. That was wrong of me. I'm grateful for your generosity, and your hospitality, and I'm sorry I have abused both.'

'It's not a question of hospitality,' said Ivor. 'As far as your mother and I are concerned, this is your home, Melanie. You will always be welcome here.'

At which point, I burst into tears.

I sat down on the nearest chair. Ivor stood up. He came out from behind the desk flapping a large, white handkerchief.

'Truce,' he said. 'But you can blow your nose on it.'

He pulled up a chair beside me.

'You and I are going to make a deal, Melanie,' he said. 'I'm a lawyer. I make deals. I make deals that allow people to get along. That's what we're going to do now. Make a deal that allows us to get along.'

'We get along fine,' I said. 'Most of the time.'

'No we don't,' Ivor said. 'You don't like me. You don't like my politics. You don't like that I'm married to your mom.'

'Mom's happy with you. I'm glad she's happy.'

I blew my nose.

Ivor said, 'Sometimes it's good to say what we really think.' He paused. 'You had your say last night. Now it's my turn. I think you're too wrapped up in yourself. I think you've never forgiven your mother for leaving you when you were a baby. I think you resent all the happy family stuff we do here.' I opened my mouth to protest. No words came out.

'Did you ever try to imagine what it was like being nineteen, living in a tent, having no money, married to a husband who never got off his ass all day? The answer is no.' Ivor sighed. 'You hide your resentment, even from yourself. A lot of people do. I see it all the time. I practise family law. Divorce, family disputes, custody cases. You've never asked me about my work, Melanie. Do you know that? You've never shown the slightest interest. You just think, fat-cat lawyer. You think I'm stupid and pretentious. Well, maybe I exaggerate the Romanov connection a little, but holy mother Russia is in my soul. You think I'm stupid to buy wine I might never drink. But people buy gold bars and paintings and rare books they never read. These bottles are investments too. And I don't care to be swindled.'

He went back to his desk and uncapped a fountain pen. 'Tell me exactly what two hundred dollars buys in the way of proof.'

I told him about carbon twelve and carbon fourteen and comparative levels after the atomic bomb. Ivor took notes. When I'd finished, he capped his pen, sat back in his chair and rubbed his chin.

'Either the dealer who sold it to me is a crook or he's been swindled himself.'

He opened a drawer, took out a sheaf of invoices held together with a bulldog clip, put on his reading glasses.

'I know he sells to other collectors as well. A couple of them were sniffing around the Romanov bottle. Russians. I outbid them.'

He scanned the invoices, one by one.

'Altogether, counting the Romanov bottle, and three cases of rare wines, I have paid Mr Lancaster half a million dollars.'

It was an almost unimaginable sum to me. I was shaken.

Ivor flicked through the Rolodex on his desk. He tapped out a number on the telephone, sat with the receiver to his ear for a couple of minutes.

I hardly dared breathe.

'Answering machine,' said Ivor. 'I'll try again Monday.'

He pushed a business card over the desk to me.

'Engraved, not printed,' he said. 'The guy looks good. Expensive cards. Expensive suits. Expensive girlfriend with an expensive watch.'

I ran my finger over the embossed letters on the card. 'C. H. L. Fine Wines.' There was a telephone number and an address in London.

'Keep it. I already got six. One for every time we met or did business,' said Ivor. 'I thought he ran a legitimate operation. Maybe he does. Or maybe he has suckered a lot of other dumb chucks. Either way we have to find out.'

I took a moment to reply. 'You said "we", Ivor? "We have to find out?" Are you including me in this?'

'Sure,' said Ivor. 'You're the expert, aren't you?' He let out a sudden crack of laughter. 'Hoo, hay. That's shaken your preconceptions.'

'I think I just lost them,' I said.

The door opened and Mom came in. 'I heard a shout,' she said.

'Everything's cool,' said Ivor. He was smiling.

I realised I was smiling too.

'Let's go look at the Romanov bottle,' said Ivor.

We went up to the gallery. The bottle was displayed beside the crystal decanter with the ruby stopper. Ivor pointed out the crest and initials engraved on the green glass.

'The label is yellowed with age. There are a couple of tears around the edges but not so you'd notice. It's in pretty good condition.'

He unlocked the case and lifted out the bottle. He held it as proudly as a baby.

'This has an historical value, never mind it cost me one hundred fifty thousand dollars. I don't want to break the seal to have it tested.'

'Maybe you could get a glass expert to look at it,' I said.

'I've seen a lot of bottles,' said Ivor. 'This bottle is old glass. And special. You can tell it was hand blown.'

'We should maybe talk to an engraver,' said Mom.

'The design is correct. Everything about it looks right.'

'It's beautiful,' said Mom. 'Leave it. Why do you have to know?'

'Because I don't want to be a sucker,' said Ivor.

'Truth matters,' I said.

'That too.' Ivor replaced the bottle tenderly on its stand and locked the case. 'If you'll excuse me, I have some letters to write.'

He patted me on the shoulder. 'You can keep the hanky.'

Mom and I stood for a while in the gallery but we weren't really looking at anything.

'You're right,' Mom said. 'About truth being important.'

'Ivor thinks I resent the family you've got here,' I said. 'That I blame you for leaving me.'

'I think that too,' said Mom.

I felt as though a whole skin just slid off me.

'I'm OK about that now,' I said. 'I don't blame you. I never thought enough about what it was like for you.'

'It was like losing a part of me,' said Mom. 'It nearly broke my heart. I only wanted to do what was best for you. I wanted you to come live with us when I married Hank. But Mom said you should finish your term in pre-school first, and then Hank got posted to Singapore and I thought it wouldn't be fair to take you all that way when Hank was only going to be there for one year. And then it was longer than a year and you were so settled and Mom said you would miss your friends and feel strange in a foreign country and I wouldn't get as good a job back in the States. Sometimes you want to do things,' she said sadly, 'but life gets in the way.'

We went out into the garden. The men from the rental company were dismantling the tent. We sat on a low wall in the rose arbour and watched them untying ropes, unscrewing poles, folding the canvas in sections so it looked like giant squares of mint candy.

'I guess it was a lot easier taking down a tepee,' I said.

'I never took it down,' said Mom. 'I left it there. I left all the cushions and the hanging mirrors and the rag rugs I made when I was expecting you. I figured somebody else in the commune could have them all. I knew I wouldn't be going back. I knew that part of my life was over.'

'You left with nothing,' I said.

'I left with all that mattered,' she said. 'I left with you.'

42

'You look cheerful,' said Vincent when I went with him on his morning walk through the vines on my next Saturday at Cottontail. 'Are you in love again, Melanie? Did you meet someone at the party?'

'Only myself,' I said.

Vincent nodded like he understood.

'I talked a lot to my mom,' I said. 'That was good. We don't get a whole lot of time together.'

'Sometimes I think you talk to the vines,' said Vincent. He examined a leaf. 'This is new growth. They must recognise your footsteps, Melanie.'

'I think it's the compost you got from that farmer up the valley,' I said. 'Didn't you tell me he was biodynamic? I've read a book about that recently. There's a lot of crazy stuff about the moon and cow horns, but it's kind of interesting. I'm going to read some more.'

'Back to the future,' said Vincent. 'A lot of it is the sort of farming my grandfather did. He always sowed when the moon was waxing.'

'That's what Grammy did too. She used to say the way to keep the lawn tidy was to cut the grass after the full moon.'

We walked back up the hill to the winery.

'We should talk about when you're going to start full time at Cottontail,' said Vincent.

'Maybe after the summer,' I said. 'Would you be cool with that, Vincent? I'm kind of disappointed I won't be able to work the harvest in France this year. But I thought maybe I would go to Europe for my summer vacation. I got my passport this week.'

'That's good,' said Vincent. 'Because Louis and I are thinking of sending you to England at the end of the month.'

I stopped right there.

'Are you serious?'

'Sure, Melanie. If you don't have anything else. It's four days, not counting travel. The California Wine Institute is showing our wines in London. Louis set up some meetings with buyers in four British supermarkets plus six big importers. Turns out his mom is getting a new hip at that time and he'd like to go see her.'

I was so excited I almost could not get the words out to thank him. I practically danced all the way to the tasting-room door.

I telephoned just about every person I knew to tell them about my trip.

Mom said, 'Ivor has been to London a lot. You should talk to him.'

Some things don't change. We just change the way we react to them.

'That would be good,' I said. 'Is he home?'

Ivor took the telephone. He told me to visit the National Gallery, the Victoria and Albert Museum and the Elgin

Marbles in the British Museum if I had the time. 'But I guess you'll be too busy.'

He said I should take buses or cabs instead of the subway, so I could see more of the city.

I asked him if he had found out anything more about the bogus wine.

'I'm done leaving messages on Mr Lancaster's answer-phone,' he said. 'I've written him, laying out the facts. I'm asking for an explanation. How come a bottle of wine dated nineteen thirty-seven turns out to have contents made more than fifty years later? I sent the letter by courier. That usually makes people jump.'

He told me he had sent the putative Romanov bottle to an engraver.

'The guy is a master craftsman. Trust me. He hand-engraves shotguns, trophies, glass. He learned from his grandfather in Italy. He gave evidence in a fraud case about an antique gun, alleged to have belonged to General Custer. Hooey. I'll let you know his verdict on the Romanov bottle.'

I didn't drive up to Davis that week because I was flying to London. Which is why I happened to be in a grocery store on Jefferson on a Monday evening and just happened to see Jesse Arguello right in the next aisle, studying the back of a cereal packet.

I moved quickly towards the check-out, but my basket knocked against a shelf and dislodged a can of chickpeas. It rolled across the floor. Jesse looked up. I looked away. He managed to get ahead of me in the line and was waiting outside the store when I emerged.

'Hi, Melanie,' he said. 'I was kinda hoping I would bump into you.'

'You know where I live,' I said.

'I figured if I called I would not get a warm welcome.' He flashed a smile. 'You still got my baseball cap?'

'Some other bum is wearing it,' I said. 'I took it to the thrift shop.'

He put his hands up. 'You have every right to be mad at me. I did a dumb thing, Melanie. I've been beating myself up about it ever since.'

He told me he'd been back in Monterey since February. He was renting an apartment. He was fundraising for an attorney who was running for Congress.

'The Republicans are riding high on the gains they made last year. There's a real drive to get more funds for the Democrats.'

The attorney had helped him get a job with a law firm.

'It's a good job,' Jesse said. 'It's making me think about settling down.'

'With whatshername? Connie from Kansas?'

'That didn't last,' he said. 'It was just a summer thing.'

'You never called,' I said. 'You never even tried to give an explanation.'

We were still standing in the car park.

'Why don't we go talk somewhere?' Jesse fixed me with his dark eyes. He didn't try to touch me. But he came with me to my car. I opened the door and put my groceries on the passenger seat.

'C'mon, Melanie. Can't we be friends? I'm playing guitar tonight. That's regular too. At least come and hear me.'

I followed his motorbike to a bar on the wharf. It was not yet time for Jesse's set. We sat at a table outside. There was a breeze coming off the water. I shivered. Jesse put his arm around me. It felt good. I let it stay there.

He talked softly into my ear. He said he was sorry he had hurt me. That he hadn't contacted me because he was ashamed and he figured I would throw things at him.

'I would have deserved that. I still deserve it.' He was penitent, almost mournful.

I knew what he was going to say next.

'Do you think we could get together again?'

'You haven't asked me if I'm seeing anyone,' I said.

'You'd have told me right away,' he said. 'I know you. We were together for nearly two years. Remember?'

'I've got to go,' I said. 'I'm going to London tomorrow.'

'On vacation?'

'It's work. Vincent is sending me to talk to buyers,' I said. 'I'm also going to spend a day promoting Cottontail at the London Wine Fair.'

I moved to stand up. Jesse tugged me back into the curve of his arm.

'Don't go yet. I mean it. Like, I really, really want to be with you again.'

He turned his head so he was looking right into my eyes. His own dark eyes were moist. 'Will you think about it? Can we at least talk about it?'

One of the bartenders came out and said, 'You ready, Jesse?'

'Be right there.'

Jesse was still holding my gaze. 'How long are you going to be in London?'

'I'll be back Saturday,' I said.

'Can I see you Sunday evening? We could maybe have dinner, go to a movie?'

I hesitated. I had been in love with Jesse. It had been fun most of the time. It would be good to be in someone's arms again. Maybe he had changed.

'I'll come by at seven o'clock.'

'I'll think about it,' I said. 'Now I really have to go.'

'At least stay and listen to one song.' He picked up his guitar case.

I let him take my hand and lead me into the bar. I took a seat at the back so I could leave unnoticed. Jesse seemed to know where I was, even though he was looking from the spotlight into the dark. He took the Gibson out of its case and tuned it. His eyes never left my face as he sang, 'I Threw It All Away'.

It's one of my favourite Bob Dylan numbers. Every man who thinks about cheating on his partner should listen to it first.

When the last plangent chord died away, I raised my hand in silent farewell and slipped out of the bar.

43

Honor

I had three lazy days in Ballybreen. I went to bed early and got up late. Mum didn't ask any direct questions about Hugo. She simply said she was glad to have me at home for a while and wasn't it grand that the weather was so good?

In the mornings, I lay in bed listening to the sounds of the town waking up. There was no clink of milk bottles – Mum now bought cartons from the supermarket – but I could still hear the clanking of a gate and the skittering of horses' hooves above the noise of the traffic.

In the afternoons, I went on little excursions with Mum. She had recently bought a new car that had a swivel seat and easier controls than her old one. It made her more independent, she said.

'I hear Diarmuid Keenan has bought a cottage,' she announced on the afternoon before I was due to leave. 'I met his cousin's wife after Mass a few Sundays ago. She told me where it is.'

'I know where it is,' I said.

'You didn't tell me,' said Mum reproachfully. 'I suppose you had other things on your mind. I gather it's in a grand spot. He'll have a great view. Do you want to take a look at it? We can go there this afternoon.'

'I know the view,' I said.

'I mean take a look at the cottage,' said Mum. 'Then I can tell Eileen I've seen it. It belonged to the nephew of Senator Walshe who married a girl from New York. She didn't like living in the country.'

I looked at Mum's eager, interested face. This was her life, I thought. Innocent gossip, the business of the parish. For a moment, but only for a moment, I wished I wasn't going back to London, but settling instead into the life I had known when I was a child. I envied Diarmuid who was now able to keep a foot in both worlds.

I envied him all the more when I saw the cottage. It was so picture postcard perfect, I almost hated him. Whitewashed walls, a red door, a golden thatch, red pelargoniums in green window boxes.

Mum insisted on getting out of the car to get a better look even though it meant unloading her wheelchair. 'Diarmuid won't mind,' she said.

She bowled along the path that ran around the cottage to a small lawn at the back. From here, a rough field descended to a rushing brown river, bordered with gorse and hawthorn, all in bloom. A kestrel circled slowly overhead.

We peered through the cottage windows. There was a long pine table in the kitchen. Apart from that, the house was empty of furniture. Diarmuid can make this place his own, I thought. I followed Mum round to the front of the house again. She braked at the front door.

'I wouldn't mind being carried over that threshold,' she said. 'Does he have a girlfriend?'

'He does,' I said. 'She's stick thin. She'll be easy to carry.'

We sat for a few minutes taking in the view down the glen. In the distance, I could see the faint shimmer of the sea. Another wave of envy washed over me. All this for Katy?

'Isn't Diarmuid the lucky one?' said Mum.

'He is,' I said.

'Have you met his girlfriend?'

'I have. She works in advertising. She looks like a model.'

'You sound as if you don't like her,' said Mum.

'I like her well enough,' I said. 'I just don't think she's right for Diarmuid.'

'He hasn't taken her home yet,' said Mum. 'According to Eileen.'

'No,' I said. 'But he's given her a watch.' For some reason, the memory made me smile.

Mum looked curiously at me. 'What's funny about that? It usually means a man is serious.'

'It was a fake watch,' I said. 'She thought it was a great joke.'

'Maybe it was and maybe it wasn't,' said Mum.

She hoisted herself back into the car, folded the wheelchair and stowed it in the space behind her seat. I knew better than to help her. We set off down the road to Ballybreen.

'You've mentioned Eddie a lot,' said Mum. 'What's he like?'

'He's gay, Mum.'

She was silent for a while. Then she said, 'Oh, well. Plenty more fish in the sea.'

The telephone rang just after we got back into the house. Mum reached it first.

'Just one moment, please.' She held the receiver out to me. 'He sounds French,' she whispered.

It was Didier. He wanted to ask me something, he said.

'Ask away.'

Through the kitchen door, I could see Mum busying herself with some small, unnecessary task.

Didier said he was going again to the London Wine Fair at the end of the month with a group of biodynamic producers.

'We found the public relations company too expensive last year,' he said. 'We are not using them this time. We are each going to do our own promotion. I wondered if you would be willing to help.'

'Not if I have to dress as a squirrel,' I said.

Didier laughed. 'No squirrels, I promise. We think perhaps to have the Revolution as our theme because we are promoting a revolutionary way of making wine. We have a small budget. If you could think of anything,' he said, 'I would be grateful.'

'Of course,' I said. 'Leave it with me. I'll get back to you.'

When I went back into the kitchen, Mum was ostentatiously turning the pages of the *Irish Times*.

'He sounded nice.' She didn't look up.

'You only heard him say a few words,' I said. 'He's just a friend. I met him in Astignac.'

'Was he a friend of Hugo's?'

'He was not,' I said firmly. 'He was a friend of mine.'

Mum drove me to the airport the next morning. I lifted the red suitcases out of the boot and walked around to the driver's door. Mum rolled down the window. I set the suitcases on the ground.

'Are you sure I can keep them, Mum?'

'I'm sure,' she said.

'You might want to take them somewhere yourself, now that you're tearing around in the car.'

She shook her head. 'They're yours now.'

She thrust her arms through the open window to hug me. 'What did I say to you before? You might take them on honeymoon yet.'

44

In the first week of *She Stoops to Conquer*, on the days when we didn't have a matinee, I took the train to Waterloo station and went hunting for a flat in London. On my third visit, I signed a three-month lease on a minuscule one-bedroom flat in Soho. It was more than I had budgeted for, but I was optimistic about work. Telltapes, the company for which I had been abridging books, was going to produce radio plays. There was a vacancy for a script editor and producer. I had been asked to apply for the job.

I was walking to Tottenham Court Road tube station, with a skip in my step, when I realised I was only a few streets away from Hugo's flat and office. Some kind of residual curiosity led me to the door. The estate agent's board, fixed to a drainpipe, had a SOLD notice pasted on it but the brass plate was still there. I pressed the bell, not expecting an answer, but I heard a squawk from the small speaker at the side of the door.

'Is that you, Patricia?'

Another squawk. The door buzzed. I pushed it open and

went upstairs. The office was almost empty of furniture, but Patricia was at her desk, fingers leaping over the typewriter keys. She smiled when she saw me.

'Nice of you to drop by,' she said. 'Thank you for your card.'

'I wasn't sure I'd find you in. I knew the business had been sold.'

'My last day,' Patricia said. 'I'm just here for an hour or so to tidy up a few things. I've had a good run. I'm ready to retire.'

'Retire? I thought you were being kept on by the new owners.'

She shook her head. 'He's keeping Jason and Freddy. I'm being let go.'

'I'm sorry,' I said. 'What will you do? Will you be all right?' I realised I knew almost nothing about her life.

'I got some redundancy money. I qualify for my bus pass in September.' She brightened. 'And Hugo gave me a bottle of wine as a farewell present. He said it came from the cellar of a French lord. I don't know much about fancy wines and neither does my friend. I didn't have much to do with that side of Hugo's business. My friend said why don't I take it to Sotheby's like Mr Lancaster does? So I put it in the auction and guess what?' She clapped her hands and squealed. 'I got two thousand pounds.'

'Isn't that wonderful, Patricia.'

'We're going on a cruise. I can't wait.'

She produced two tea bags from her handbag, two mugs and a carton of long-life milk from a drawer, an electric kettle from a cardboard box.

'You're just in time. The water's being turned off tomorrow.'

I sat on the only other chair in the office. It was only

four months since I had last been in Hugo's flat, but it felt like a lifetime.

'I was here at Christmas,' I said.

'On your way back from Val d'Isère?'

I shook my head. 'I went home to Ireland.'

Patricia looked surprised. 'Hugo must have been disappointed,' she said. 'He was very insistent on a double room when I made the booking. No twin beds, he said. Make sure it's a double.' She winked.

'We're not together any more.'

Patricia's hand flew to her mouth. She was silent for a moment. Then she said, 'Who did the booting out, you or him?'

'I did,' I said. 'And no regrets.'

She looked pleased. 'You still lasted longer than any of them.'

I helped her carry the last boxes down to the street. I hailed a taxi. Patricia pulled the door shut behind her.

'That's one chapter of my life closed.'

'Me too,' I said.

We didn't exchange telephone numbers or addresses. We both knew we would not see each other again. But there was real warmth in our farewell.

45

Diarmuid came to see me during the second week of the run. He drove down from London and got to the theatre in time to put his head around the stage door before curtain up.

'Break a leg. I'll be in the bar after the show.'

We had a near full house. The play was on the GCSE syllabus. We took three curtain calls. Afterwards, I changed out of my costume as quickly as I could, plastered my face with cold cream to wipe off the artificially red cheeks and hurried upstairs to meet Diarmuid.

'You were good, Honor,' he said. 'You weren't stiff at all.' He banged his hand against his forehead. 'There I go saying the wrong thing again.'

'It's all right. I know I won't make my name on the stage.'

I could hear the low, excited buzz of the audience filing out. They were mostly schoolchildren with their parents and teachers. Hardly anybody came into the bar.

'You've changed,' said Diarmuid. 'It's like you've let go of something. Loosened up. You'll get work.'

I felt suddenly self-conscious.

'I can make a living doing other stuff. Abridgements, script-reading. Even trade shows.' I smiled. 'Remember the squirrels?'

Diarmuid shuddered.

'You owe me one for that, Diarmuid. You promised me. Remember?'

He grinned. 'All right. What's the favour?'

'I've a French friend who needs someone to promote his wines at the International Fair next week,' I said. 'He's coming over with a group of small producers. Same idea as last year. Fancy dress, rollerblades, handing out drinks. The theme is the French Revolution. There's not much money in it. Half of what we got last year.'

'This French friend,' said Diarmuid. 'Is he important to you? Is this the new man in your life? Is he the reason you're looking so well?'

I thought about Didier's smile, the way his hand had warmed the small of my back.

'He's not,' I said. 'But he could be.'

There was a pause.

'If you did it on your own you'd get more money,' said Diarmuid.

I nodded acknowledgement. 'But it wouldn't be as much fun. I'd rather get half the money, and twice the crack. Ah, go on, Diarmuid. Say yes.'

Why was he being so reluctant?

'You gave me your word, Diarmuid. You said cross my heart and hope to die.'

'OK. You win. I'll do it.' He sounded sulky.

'If you're not going to do it with a good grace,' I snapped. 'Don't bother.'

'All right. I won't bother, so. You can do your own favours.'

We stood looking angrily at each other. Oh, no. Here we go again, I thought. We were sailing along nicely and suddenly our little boat is going to capsize. Tears sprang to my eyes.

Diarmuid put his hand out. 'I didn't mean that, Honor. Don't cry. Please. I couldn't stand it when I was ten and I can't stand it now. Here.' He dug in his pocket and produced a crumpled paper handkerchief. 'It's clean. I haven't used it.'

I took the tissue and dabbed my eyes. 'It's all right. I'm a bit drained. That's all.'

'Breaking up is hard,' said Diarmuid. 'It's only been a few weeks. Of course you're emotional.'

'I'm not emotional,' I said crossly. 'I didn't say I was emotional. I said I was drained. Tired.'

'And why can't Honor be both tired AND emotional?' Diarmuid ducked his head and broke into a little tap dance, finishing like a vaudeville comedian – feet planted, head up, hands out. 'Because she hasn't had a drink yet!' He beamed. 'Ta dah!'

He had coaxed a smile from me.

'So sit down,' said Diarmuid. 'I'll go to the bar.'

He came back with two glasses of champagne. 'The cure for everything. Wounded pride, bad temper, broken hearts.'

'And capsized boats,' I said.

'What?'

I was about to explain when the other actors streamed into the bar. Roy Spriggs, the actor playing Tony Lumpkin, tapped Diarmuid on the shoulder and reminded him that they had appeared briefly together in an episode of the short-lived television series *Eldorado*.

They groaned in unison.

Roy said, 'Do you remember the gag? What happens to actors when they die? They go to Eldorado.'

'Or,' Diarmuid's mouth was still open when I kicked him on the ankle to stop him adding, 'Basingstoke.'

'They turn into successful stage actors,' he continued. The pause was hardly noticeable.

Other members of the cast wandered over to join us. Roy ordered a bottle of champagne, 'Since that seems to be the order of day.'

'Count me out,' said Diarmuid. 'I have to drive back to London.'

He kissed me lightly on the cheek.

'I'll do it. But no squirrels, OK?'

I got up to accompany him downstairs to the door.

'Stay where you are,' he said. 'I'll see you next week. Have fun.'

It didn't feel so much like fun when he'd gone. I made my excuses, put on my coat and slipped away.

46

Melanie

Louis drove me to the airport in San Francisco, all the time rehearsing me for my London meetings.

'Calmness and confidence equals composure,' he said. 'You're not on your own. You can call up Vincent anytime. Bottom line, we want to break into the British market. We're willing to sacrifice up to ninety per cent of margin if we get the right volume sales. Stay cool. Try to look like you can walk away from the deal.' He handed me my plane ticket. 'I'm sure you'll do a fine job, Melanie.'

I could not sleep on the airplane, even though it was not full and I had a whole centre row of four seats to myself. I had too many thoughts in my head. Most, but not all, about Jesse. He had looked different. More serious. Maybe he wasn't really a drifter at heart. I thought about the good times we'd had. The way he used to tuck himself around me and kiss the back of my neck. My skin tingled at the memory. Had there been other girls since Connie from Kansas? Probably. No. For sure. Did I want to risk my heart again? The in-flight movie was *Sense and Sensibility*.

It seemed to me it was all about people making the wrong choices in love and finally getting real.

I wondered if I should follow the advice of Mom and Ivor and think about buying a condo in Monterey or Carmel Valley Village.

I read a book about Rudolf Steiner and biodynamic agriculture. Some of his theories were a little wacky, but I liked the idea of returning to a more natural way of farming. Maybe that was something I could talk some more about to Vincent. He was open to ideas. I wanted to do a good job for him. I was going to spend a day handing out flyers at the London Wine Fair. I tried to think of a better way to promote Cottontail Wines. I was going to have a bigger stake in it when I started working there full time. But not until I had been to France. Seen Hostens and Astignac. Taken photographs. Suppose I walked past my uncle Dominique in the street without knowing it? Would he ever get in touch with Poppa?

I lay across the empty seats and dozed on and off until I became aware of a general bustle in the cabin and realised breakfast was being served. We were going to land soon. I moved across the aisle to a window seat and pushed up the blind.

Green fields moved below me. They had the kind of glow the dawn creates when the air is full of moisture. I could see the dark ribbon of a three-lane highway, the white lights of automobiles streaming in both directions. Then houses and more houses until we were over the River Thames and the pilot was telling us that we were now flying over Windsor Great Park. It seemed like only a minute or two later we were on the ground.

I travelled into London on the subway and emerged into a damp, grey street. It was still early in the morning and people were walking fast with their heads down. I had an impression of old buildings darkened by rain, black cabs and grey, waddling pigeons. But as I wheeled my suitcase along the sidewalk, the sky cleared, the sun came out, two pigeons fluttered into the sky like doves and I suddenly noticed the pink cherry blossom in a little park beside the hotel.

A bellhop emerged, took my suitcase, held open the big glass door and said, 'Good morning, Miss. It's going to be a nice day.'

My spirits lifted. 'It surely is,' I said.

Most of the meetings were at the hotel. I only once had to excuse myself and go call Vincent for advice. 'Can I come down thirty cents a bottle on Cuvée Carolina?'

'You decide, Melanie,' he said.

I re-entered the room, shaking my head in surprise at Vincent's confidence in me. I guess the buyer thought the answer was no. She offered to take another five hundred cases if I reduced the cost price by twenty-five cents. Done. Whoopee!

I felt like celebrating, but I had no one to jump around with me and share my triumph. There was no one to listen to my little observations. That was the real downside of travelling alone, I decided. I could not turn to someone and say, have you noticed how small the cars are? And how the doors in the restrooms come all the way to the floor? And have you ever seen so many pigeons? Or so many flavours for potato chips?

It's not very fun to eat alone. On my first evening, I had dinner in my room and went to bed early. The second evening, I ate in a pizza parlour and went to the cinema. I was fumbling in my purse for some change to tip the cab driver, when I realised I still had the business card of C. H. L. Fine Wines. I showed it to the bell captain at my hotel.

'Do you know where this is, please? And how I might get there?'

He checked his London street guide. 'Take the tube to Oxford Circus. You can walk from there.' He drew me a map.

As soon as my morning meetings finished the next day, I followed his directions to the address on the card. It wasn't hard to see why no one was taking Ivor's calls. There was a realtor's SOLD notice on the building. I rang the doorbell anyway. Nobody came. There was a small brass plate on the door. 'Lancaster Direct Wines Limited'. Below it was a mailbox. I pushed it open and squinted into a narrow hallway. A scattering of white envelopes lay on the floor. Beyond them, stairs rose into darkness. The metal flap snapped shut. It had not been polished in a while.

I went into the adjacent deli and joined a queue of people at the counter. I bought a cheddar cheese and chutney sandwich and a takeout coffee. There was a small playground nearby. Two young mothers were pushing two small children on a slow merry-go-round. I sat on a bench, ate my lunch, drank my coffee and waited until I figured the lunchtime rush was over and the harassed-looking man behind the deli counter might have time to talk to me.

He told me he knew nothing about C. H. Lancaster or Lancaster Direct Wines. A lady who worked there came into his shop occasionally, but he had not seen her in a while.

'Now you mention it,' he said, 'I used to hear her typing above me.' He pointed to the ceiling. 'But it's been quiet for at least a week.'

'If she comes in, could you contact this person, please? You can call collect.'

I gave him Ivor's business card.

He looked at it, then handed it right back to me.

'It's none of my business,' he said. 'Lawyers. Whatever this is about, I don't want to get involved.'

When I got back to the hotel, I faxed all this information to Ivor. He called me right back.

'It figures. He didn't reply to my letter.'

'There was a brass plate on the door,' I said. 'Lancaster Direct Wines.'

'So he has another business. That's interesting.'

'Lancaster Direct Wines Limited,' I said.

'Limited?' There was a pause. Then I heard a whoop and a holler. 'Whey hey! Gimme ten minutes.' Ivor hung up.

I didn't mind waiting. I had no meetings that afternoon. I had been planning to go to Harrods. To tell the truth, I preferred playing detective. Maybe Fred Voss was right and I had a talent for it. Or maybe I had read too many Nancy Drew stories.

'The British have a register for limited companies,' Ivor told me when he called back. 'Every British company director has to file a home address someplace called Companies House. I checked with a lawyer I know in London. All you need is the name or the company number. He was able to look that up for me. He said he could send someone over there maybe next week.'

'Let me do that,' I said. 'I've got the time. I can do it.' I was already reaching for the pad and pencil on the bedside table.

I wrote down the address and the company number.

'Take a cab,' said Ivor. 'Get a receipt.'

I walked to the convenience store at the street corner and bought a notebook. Then I hailed a black London cab.

'Companies House, please.'

I didn't have to give the address to the driver. He knew it right away. That was something else different from cities back home.

He dropped me at a grey, anonymous building on the edge of the financial district. Four assistants stood behind a long counter in the lobby. Three of them were already dealing with enquiries. I approached the fourth, a young man with a floppy black fringe not really hiding a spotty forehead.

'Could I please see the documents for Lancaster Direct Wines Limited? I have the company number. Is there a charge for this?'

He pushed a form across the desk to me. 'Cost you a pound. Stick it all down here. Do you need a pen?'

I already had a ballpoint in my hand. I completed the form. I gave him a pound coin from my change purse.

He dropped the coin into a drawer. 'Take a seat.' He jerked his head towards a bench running along the opposite wall. 'This'll take about twenty minutes to half an hour. There's a café round the corner.' He jerked his head again, in much the same direction.

The café had a few tables on the sidewalk. I ordered a cup of coffee, carried it outside, and sat watching people coming in and out of a costume hire shop on the opposite side of the street, amusing myself by trying to guess what costumes would suit them. The shop window displayed tall furry animals – a brown bear, a white bear, a grey and black badger, a pink rabbit and a brown rabbit – in a painted fantasy landscape of meadows, winding rivers and Disney castles. Twenty minutes slid easily by.

When I went back to the desk in Companies House, the young man gave me an envelope containing three microfiches, and escorted me to a viewing booth. I sat at the machine for magnifying the images and peered through the viewer at photos of the original documents. A lot of them were handwritten and there was a heap of stuff to scroll through. Date of Incorporation; Articles of Association; Registered Office address.

I could see that Lancaster Direct Wines Limited was fifty years old; the name had never been changed; no bankruptcy suits had been filed against it; the sole director was Charles Hugo Lancaster. I could even tell from the profit and loss accounts filed in consecutive years, that the business made an average profit of around one hundred fifty thousand pounds sterling. Plus Mr Lancaster paid himself a salary. Why would he bother to counterfeit wines? I began to think he had been fooled by whomever sold him the wines in the first instance.

The home address for Charles Hugo Lancaster was the one I had already been to. I wondered if he had sold his business along with the building. Maybe he had just moved home and business elsewhere?

But here was something. The registered office address was different. I wrote it in my notebook with a feeling of triumph. My detective work was paying off.

I took the microfiches back to the counter. I thanked the clerk. 'By the way,' I said, 'some of the information is out of date. I know that the home address of the director has changed. When does it get updated?'

'Whenever they get around to it,' he said. 'They're

supposed to file changes within two weeks, but sometimes it's more like six months.'

Oh well, I thought with satisfaction. I had the registered office address. I asked the clerk to direct me there.

'Out of the building, first right, turn left into the alley, at the end, turn right, take the second left and it's on your right.' He took one look at my face and added, 'I'll draw you a map.'

The zig-zag lines on his map took me into the heart of the financial district. I was now walking in the shadow of glass towers and skyscrapers. I expected to find the office I was looking for in a small building, like the previous address for Lancaster Direct Wines. Instead, I found myself in the foyer of a tower block, staring at a board with the names of maybe fifty or more companies.

I scanned every inch of it. I read the name of every business or company on the board. They were all law firms, accountancy firms and business consultants. Lancaster Direct Wines Limited was not there.

I walked across the marble foyer to the front desk. A portly man in a pin-striped suit was talking to the blonde receptionist. He stepped back as I approached. The blonde smiled at me. 'Can I help you?'

'I'm looking for Lancaster Direct Wines Limited. This is the registered office but I can't see it on the board.'

The receptionist put on her glasses, picked up a sheaf of papers held together by a clip and ran her forefinger down each page in turn.

'It's not listed here,' she said. 'Is it a small company?'

'One director, I don't know how many employees.'

The man in the pin-striped suit said, 'A lot of small companies list their solicitor or accountant's address as their registered office.'

I pointed at the board. 'You mean it could be any one of those?'

'I'm afraid so,' he said.

'Sorry about that,' said the receptionist.

'Do you have a list of all the companies registered here, with telephone numbers? So I can contact them?'

She tapped the sheaf of papers. 'This is the only list I've got. Sorry.'

A young man wheeling a metal trolley loaded with envelopes and parcels emerged from a door near the desk. He set off towards the elevator.

The blonde took off her glasses, stood up and called to him, 'Jimmy? Anybody in the post room know a company called Lancaster Direct Wines?'

He stopped. He shook his head. 'It doesn't have a pigeonhole,' he said. 'I don't remember seeing anything addressed to it.' He pressed the elevator call button.

'What would happen to a letter that came here addressed to a company that didn't have a pigeonhole?' I asked him quickly.

The elevator doors opened. 'It would go round all the offices,' he said, 'until somebody claimed it.'

He wheeled the trolley into the elevator.

'How long might that take?' I called to him.

'Months,' he said. 'Maybe years.'

The elevator doors closed behind him.

The receptionist and the man in the pin-striped suit regarded me sympathetically.

'I guess I'll just have to write down all the names,' I said. 'Then call up every one of them.'

'You'd better be quick,' said the receptionist. 'It's after half past five. The building will be locked at six.'

The man in the pin-striped suit had gone, the elevator doors had opened and closed a dozen times and scores of folk had walked swiftly past me to the exit before I had written down the last name on the board. My wrist ached. Being a detective didn't seem very fun after all.

47

Honor

My former flatmates, Mona and Sinead, came to London on a one-day shopping trip. I was delighted. The three of us hadn't spent time together since I left Dublin for London.

Mona wanted to buy clothes to take on honeymoon. She and David were going to Amalfi.

'We've been taking holidays at home for the last couple of years, to save money,' she said. 'You never need real summer clothes in Ireland. Not lovely floaty things to wear over bikinis, anyway.'

Sinead and I spent most of the day sitting on faux Chippendale chairs outside fitting rooms, chatting, while Mona tried on silk caftans, bikinis with matching chiffon over-shirts, and lacy negligees. From time to time she emerged from behind the curtains.

'A friend's eye is a good mirror. What do you think?'

By four o'clock, we were worn out. We had not followed Madame Rousseau's injunction to '*manger chaud*' in the middle of the day and had skipped lunch. I suggested afternoon tea at Fortnum's. A great treat. We took a moment to admire the wafer-thin sandwiches, the fat scones, the delicate eclairs, before falling on them like wolves.

Sinead and Mona wanted to know all about Hugo and me.

'There was no big scene. No shouting and throwing things. Hugo didn't fall on his knees and beg me to stay. I think he wanted to end things as well,' I said. 'It was nice while it lasted and I wish him well.'

They looked at me long and hard.

'I mean that. Honestly. I was with him for the wrong reasons. I was discontented in London. My flat was the size of a hen house. I didn't have enough work. I was too proud to go back to Ireland. Falling for Hugo was my escape.'

'But you're happy in London now, Honor?'

'I'm happy in myself, Mona. And when you're happy in yourself you can be happy anywhere.'

'Do you miss home at all?'

'I do, sometimes,' I said. 'But London is where the work is.'

'I hear Diarmuid is doing well,' said Sinead.

'He is,' I said. 'He has bags of talent. I wish I had a tenth as much. He's just made a film.'

'I heard,' said Mona. 'And I heard he has a gorgeous girlfriend. David bumped into the pair of them in Dublin. What's she like?'

'Skittish,' I said. 'Beautiful. Glossy brown hair. Big eyes.'

'You don't like her,' said Sinead.

'I do like her.' Honesty made me add, 'I mean, I don't exactly dislike her. I just don't think she's right for Diarmuid. She's too cool altogether.'

'You're jealous,' said Mona.

'Don't be ridiculous,' I said.

Mona had a knowing look on her face. I was glad to be distracted by someone signalling from another table. It took me a moment to realise it was Emily, married to Hugo's friend, Duncan.

'Excuse me.' I went over to speak to her.

Emily got up from her table and greeted me exuberantly. She was a little bit drunk.

'Mothers' treat,' she said. 'We get together one afternoon a month.' She glanced back at her friends, now heads together, now heads back, wiping away tears of laughter. 'It keeps us sane.'

'How's Arthur?' I asked. 'And Duncan?'

'Both well and keeping me busy.' Emily lowered her voice. 'I'm frightfully sorry about you and Hugo.'

'No need to feel sorry,' I said briskly. 'No hearts or bones broken.'

'I'm so glad. We all thought you'd last longer than Christmas. Oops!' She giggled.

I smiled. I liked Emily.

'Duncan had a bet on it,' she said.

'He won his money, so.'

'He lost.' Emily flapped her fingers. 'Goodbye twenty pounds.'

'But he should have won,' I said.

Emily looked confused. 'What do you mean?'

'I was still with Hugo at Christmas.'

'You didn't come to Val d'Isère.'

'I went home to Ireland. Hugo wanted to go skiing. But we were still a couple. We were together until last month.'

Emily shook her head, as though to clear it. 'When he arrived in the hotel with Katy,' she said slowly, 'we all thought you had split up.'

'Katy?'

'Katy Irvine.' The name hung in the air between us. Emily saw my face change. 'Omigod. You didn't know. I'm sorry.'

'Please don't feel bad,' I said quickly. 'It doesn't matter any more. It feels like a long time ago.' I attempted a smile. 'You can take bets on Katy now. If she's still seeing Hugo.'

'They were at the Caledonian Ball,' said Emily. 'Katy's Scottish.'

We chatted for a few minutes, but my responses were automatic. My memory was busily retrieving missed clues. Hugo's hand on Katy's arm at Cap Ferret. Diarmuid saying Katy was in Bavaria. Hugo saying he was going to Munich. They were probably together now. How dare they. How dare they make a fool of Diarmuid like that. Me as well. I burned with rage.

Emily and I exchanged a quick hug. I blundered back to the table.

Mona had a chocolate eclair halfway to her mouth. 'My last indulgence. I'll be on a diet until August.' She put down the eclair. 'What's wrong?'

'Your hands are like fists and you're shaking,' said Sinead.

I was conscious of two people at the next table turning their heads. I stared fiercely at them. They looked away. I sat down.

'Hugo is having an affair with Diarmuid's girlfriend.' I could hardly get the words out.

'Diarmuid doesn't know about it.' I shivered, although it was hot in the restaurant.

Mona poured tea into my cup, added milk and a sugar lump, pushed the cup towards me. 'Drink this. It's good for shock.'

'Are you sure he doesn't know?' asked Sinead.

'Of course I'm sure. I know him as well as I know myself.' I banged my fists together. 'I wish she hadn't told me. What am I supposed to do?'

'What a creep,' said Sinead. 'You were right to give him the heave-ho.'

'But what's the right thing to do about Diarmuid? Do I tell him, or do I not tell him?'

'I used to work with a girl, a big, friendly girl, from Athlone,' said Sinead. 'She got engaged to an accountant who used to come into the branch all the time. She went home for a funeral. I saw him at a party, pawing all over another girl. I saw him leave with this girl. I saw him come back to the party about an hour later.'

'What did you do?' I could imagine Sinead tackling him, or swinging a golf club at him.

'I didn't do anything. But I nearly went mad worrying about it. I saw him at the same caper with the same woman in a pub one night, about a month later. I felt I had to say something to my colleague. "You're just jealous," she said. She never spoke to me again. She asked for a transfer to another branch.'

Mona said, 'If you tell Diarmuid and he knows already, he'll be embarrassed. If you tell him and he doesn't know, it's you who'll be embarrassed. If he breaks off with her, and he's miserable, he'll blame you. If he stays with her, you'll wonder why you bothered. Sinead is right. Stay out of it.'

'I gave no advice,' said Sinead. 'I just told my story. But I think I did the right thing.'

I signalled for the bill. Mona and Sinead gathered up the ribbon-handled carrier bags. I exchanged a goodbye wave with Emily.

We emerged into the rush hour. Mona and Sinead were already discussing whether to take a taxi from the airport in Dublin or ask David to meet them. We worked our way along the crowded pavement. We halted at the entrance to the crowd-swallowing tube station. Mona and Sinead embraced me in turn.

'Supposing I don't tell Diarmuid,' I said, 'but he finds out anyway, and he also finds out that I knew all along and didn't tell him?'

'You'll have to make up your own mind,' said Mona. 'But every way you look at it, you can't win.'

48

I couldn't sleep that night. I got out of bed and unpacked boxes of books. I drank a mug of hot milk. I divided the books into fiction, non-fiction, poetry. I heated more milk and added a slug of whiskey. No matter how much distraction or sedation I gave my brain, it returned, like a dog to a bone, to the same question. Should I tell Diarmuid about Katy and Hugo?

I was still in a state of exhausted indecision when I arrived at the Wine Fair in the morning. I stood outside the exhibition centre with two big black plastic bags by my side. I waved my entrance pass at the attendants, 'Just waiting for someone.' I exchanged smiles and small talk. I tried to look nonchalant. Inside, I was all trepidation. Supposing I was with Diarmuid and we met Hugo? Then I remembered with relief that Hugo had sold his wine importing business. But supposing Katy turned up with Diarmuid? I wished for the hundredth time that I hadn't suggested Fortnum's for tea; that I hadn't gone over to speak to Emily; that she hadn't mentioned Hugo and Katy. Those two suited each other, I thought. They both skimmed along the surface of life like flat stones across water. Diarmuid was a rock.

Taxis drew up, dropped people, drove away. No Diarmuid. Would I feel better or worse if he didn't turn up? At least my brain had another bone to chase for a while.

Just when I had decided that Diarmuid wasn't coming, he jumped out of a taxi and jogged towards me.

'Sorry, Honor. I had a late night. I slept in. I haven't had time to shave. Do you mind?'

'Not at all,' I said brightly. 'You're a sans-culotte. You ought to look a bit rough. Our costumes and rollerblades are in the bags.'

I had rented the rollerblades from a shop near Hyde Park and borrowed clothes from *She Stoops to Conquer*. Diggory's costume – red breeches, coarse linen shirt, leather jacket and a musket – for Diarmuid; taffeta gown, panniers, silk petticoats, corset and powdered wig, as worn by Mrs Hardcastle, for me.

We emerged from our respective cloakrooms and surveyed each other.

'I wasn't sure if Diggory's gear would fit you,' I said.

'He's an unmannerly sort of character altogether,' said Diarmuid. 'I suppose you think I'm well suited to his clothes?'

'They fit you anyway.'

'I'm the same size I was fifteen years ago,' Diarmuid said insouciantly. 'I dare say you remembered.'

I was already blushing from the heat generated by the twelve-inch powdered wig. I was almost as pink as my rose-coloured taffeta frock with the hooped skirt and plunging neckline. I was laced into a corset so tight I could hardly breathe.

'You're like a painting by Fragonard,' said Diarmuid. 'The one in the Wallace Collection. *The Swing*. All pink frills, white stockings, and peeping cupids.'

I instinctively tugged at the white lace trim on my décolletage. I imagined Mum's voice, edged with disapproval. 'You need a lily for your valley.'

We skated to where Didier was standing on a chair, straightening the banner – *Chateau de la Lune, biodynamique depuis 1993* – over his stand. He jumped down and swept a bow worthy of the court of Louis the Sixteenth. He took my hand and kissed it.

Diarmuid tugged my other hand. 'Let's go.'

We picked up our trays of plastic goblets filled with red and white wine and skated away.

The Grand Hall was arranged in blocks, exactly like the year before. Diarmuid and I followed the same routine. We glided up and down the avenues of stalls, handing out the goblets. At each intersection, we swirled around each other in a graceful figure of eight. We worked our way back to Didier's stand where he refilled the goblets, smiled encouragement and promised it would not be long before we stopped for lunch.

Diarmuid and I swapped terrible jokes in cod French. We dubbed each other Citizen Bidet and Countess Pommesfrites. I began to relax.

Skate, figure of eight, skate, stop, offer a glass, smile, skate, figure of eight, stop for a refill. By the end of the day, I was on autopilot and freewheeling towards Didier, when a five-and-a-half-foot-tall brown rabbit in a top hat stepped into my path.

I tried to stop. Tried to turn. Too late! Tray and goblets flew through the air. The rabbit and I fell to the ground in a flurry of brown velour and pink taffeta.

I couldn't move. I couldn't breathe. I lay blinking at the blue-white dazzle of the arc lights in the roof of the arena.

A small voice came from somewhere inside the giant, goofy head that rested on my corset. 'Gee, sorry.'

49

Melanie

My fault. I turned to look at a banner advertising bio-dynamic wine. Wham-bam! Next thing, I felt like I was lying on some kind of bolster with drapes.

I was totally winded. My right arm was trapped underneath me. Out of my right eye-hole I saw a flyer for Cottontail Winery flutter to the ground and a plastic goblet roll to a stop.

I struggled to get up. My left foot was trapped in yards of cloth. I panicked. Then strong hands grasped me, lifted me and hauled me sideways. I kicked myself free and rolled on to my back. I seemed to be lying beside a mountain of pink ruffles. I squeaked an apology.

A man's concerned face appeared above me. I raised two grubby paws. He pulled me to my feet and held my arm for a moment to steady me.

'Thank you. Oh, thank you. I'm so sorry. My fault. Always is.' My voice sounded funny inside the rabbit head. I took it off and shook out my hair. 'Did I hurt anybody?'

I thought maybe I'd crashed into someone carrying a roll

of cloth. I looked around. A small, murmuring crowd had gathered. Some of them were picking up Cottontail flyers from the floor. There was no sign of my top hat with the Cottontail Winery stick-on. There was no pile of fabric on the floor. But a man with two-days' stubble on his face and a musket on his back was steadying a girl in a pink frock with a stiff bodice and enormous frilly skirt. A powdered wig sat at an angle on her head. She looked dazed.

Omigod! She was the bolster.

The musketeer had both hands on her waist. She stood, bosom heaving, one hand on his shoulder, trying to regain her balance. They looked like they were about to waltz. He guided her to a chair. I heard him ask her if she was hurt. She shook her head. 'My corset's like a suit of armour. I'll be all right.'

I almost cried with relief.

'And you, Mademoiselle? Are you hurt?' asked a voice in a French accent.

I turned and looked into a pair of worried blue eyes.

'I'm OK, I guess. So long as nobody's injured. Thank you for helping me.'

The bystanders began moving away.

The man with the musket called out, 'How's the rabbit?'

The blue-eyed Frenchman considered me. 'I think the rabbit is fine also.'

I felt suddenly very shy. Like I had arrived too early at a party where I didn't know anybody.

He bowed and said, in a more formal tone, 'Didier Rousseau. Enchanted to meet you, Mademoiselle.'

'Melanie Millar.' We shook hands.

The man with the musket began to pick up flyers and plastic goblets from the floor.

'Excuse me.' The Frenchman crouched to help him.

I was too bruised to stoop. I limped to the empty chair beside the girl in the big pink frock. Her wig lay on the floor like a crushed meringue. I blazed with shame. 'I'm so sorry,' I blurted. 'It was my fault.'

'I should have seen you. It was my fault as well.' She gave me a tired smile. 'Why the bunny suit?'

I tucked my bobtail to one side and sat down carefully. 'I work for Cottontail Winery, in the Carmel Valley, in California. Our logo is a cottontail rabbit.'

'At least it makes sense,' she said. 'We were squirrels last year. No connection with French wine at all.'

The man with the musket materialised with a tiny paper cup in each hand. 'One for the rabbit,' he said. 'And one for Marie Antoinette.'

He reminded me a lot of Brendan. He was taller. His features weren't so regular. But he had the same laid-back charm.

'Thank you.' I put my nose in the cup and sniffed. 'Rum or Cognac?'

'Cognac. Compliments of the Hennessy stand. That'll take the soreness out of you.'

'I'm Honor,' said Marie Antoinette. 'And this big ragamuffin is Diarmuid.' She smiled at him and raised her paper cup. '*Sláinte*.'

'Cheers. I'm Melanie. You're both from Ireland?'

'Everybody is from Ireland in the sight of God,' said Diarmuid. 'Even the French.'

Honor made a face at him. They acted like they'd known each other a long time.

The Frenchman stowed a case of wine under the table and retrieved my top hat. It must have rolled underneath when I fell. He put the hat on the table. He tidied a whole heap of Cottontail handbills he'd picked up off the floor. I thought maybe I should put on the hat and go distribute them. But even as I thought about it, I realised the arena was emptying.

'I guess I'm too late to hand out any more flyers today,' I said.

'There's always tomorrow,' said Honor.

'I fly back to California tomorrow.'

'I can give them out for you,' she said. 'No bother.'

She called out, 'We can hand out leaflets for Melanie tomorrow, can't we, Didier? She's flying back to the States.'

He picked up the top hat and came over to where we were sitting.

'Of course,' he said. 'But in return, she must dine with us tonight.'

He held the hat with both hands and peered into it.

'I have seen a rabbit appear from a hat,' he said. '*Quelle surprise! Voilà!*'

He seemed to smile with his whole body. 'But I have never seen a surprise appear from a rabbit.'

50

Honor

Melanie and I went together to the Ladies cloakroom to change. We were both moving gingerly. I offered to unzip her bunny suit. She helped me out of my corset and hooped petticoat. In the atmosphere of intimacy thus created she said, in too casual a tone, 'So you're doing this promotion for Didier. Are you dating him?'

I liked her directness.

'I'm not. He's just a friend.'

'I just adore his accent,' she said. 'I guess he's married.'

'He was. But he's divorced.'

'So are you dating Diarmuid?'

'He's just a friend as well.'

'It's real nice of him to take my rabbit suit back to the shop.'

'He lives near there. It's no problem to him.'

'It's a long way from my hotel.' She hesitated. 'I had some business in the financial district. But it's finished. I don't have to go back there.'

'Did your business go well?'

'Not really. But I still have hopes.'

The wire hoop on the frilly petticoat was bent. Melanie obligingly stood on it while I twisted it back into shape.

If only life were as easy, I thought.

Didier had booked a table in a recently opened restaurant in Soho. He ordered champagne. We stood at the bar, studying the menu, exchanging the usual polite enquiries about our jobs and our families.

Didier told Melanie he had been a banker. 'But I put the key in the door five years ago and became a winemaker, like my grandfather.'

Melanie said she didn't come from a winemaking family. Her grandfather had worked in shipping. She grew up in Portland but now lived in Monterey and took classes at UC Davis.

'That's a long commute,' said Diarmuid.

'You know California?'

Diarmuid told her he'd been there recently. He was too modest to say he'd been making a film.

I told Diarmuid about Mum's new car. 'She took me for a drive. We stopped to look at your cottage.'

'I heard.'

'It was really Mum who wanted to see it.'

'You weren't interested?'

There was no good answer to that.

'How's Katy?' My voice didn't croak the way it sometimes did when I was nervous.

'She's at a conference in Paris. She's coming back tonight on Eurostar to St Pancras around half past ten.'

I was glad to be distracted by the arrival of a waiter to show us to our table.

The sommelier stood ready with a wine bottle.

'Mademoiselle will taste it.' Didier indicated Melanie's glass.

Melanie went pink. She put her nose into the glass and sniffed. She swirled the wine around her mouth. She swallowed. Nodded her approval. 'You chose a Californian Cabernet? I am so happy. That is such a compliment from a French winemaker. Thank you.'

The dining area had high ceilings, long windows and a wooden floor. The sound bounced between the floor and the ceiling and reverberated around the walls. The table centrepiece was an abstract arrangement of dried grasses and geometric shapes in steel and alabaster. I found I was moving my neck from side to side like a Balinese dancer to speak to Melanie and Didier. Diarmuid pretended to be interested in what Didier was saying about wildflowers and white moons, but I could tell he would rather be somewhere else.

'All our talk about wine must be boring you,' said Didier.

'Ah, no,' said Diarmuid. 'You're all right.' He raised his glass. 'Carry on.'

There was an odd tone in his voice. I looked at him sharply.

Melanie said, 'No. Didier is right. I'm sorry. It's just that I'm finding it all so interesting.'

'Melanie is a winemaker,' I said.

'I wish,' she said. 'Right now I'm still studying.'

The noise level rose. After a time, we were almost shouting across the table. Eventually, we split into two conversations. Didier and Melanie on one side of the table; Diarmuid and me on the other. From time to time a drop in the ambient sound level allowed me to hear Didier and Melanie talking about 'malolactic fermentation' and 'carbonic maceration'.

Didier was gesticulating a lot. Melanie looked enraptured. Their heads were close together.

'Those two fancy each other,' said Diarmuid.

He was in an strange mood. He seemed preoccupied. He asked me about my new job but hardly listened to my answers.

I asked him about the cottage.

'*Is folamh, fuar teach gan bean*,' he said. 'It's an empty cold house without a woman.'

We had barely pushed away our pudding plates when he looked at his watch and announced he would have to leave.

He ignored the pleading in my eyes. 'I can't stay. I have a train to meet.'

He shook hands with Didier and thanked him for dinner. He kissed Melanie on both cheeks and wished her a safe journey home. He gave me a quick hug and left the restaurant without looking back.

'I ought to be going as well,' I said. 'Thank you for a lovely dinner, Didier. Please, don't get up.'

'Let me call you a taxi.'

'I'll get one easily in the street.'

I exchanged kisses with him and Melanie. They looked good together, I thought.

51

Melanie

I didn't mention my French uncle at dinner. A big noisy party sat down at the next table. Didier and I had to talk real loud to hear each other. I didn't want to broadcast something so personal to the entire world. It was something to speak about in a quiet way. We talked mostly about wine. I told him I was keen to visit France.

'I asked my tutor about going to Bordeaux to work the harvest, pick grapes. But I don't think there's time to arrange it for this year.'

'You can come to Chateau de la Lune,' said Didier. 'I cannot employ you. But you can pick my grapes *le gîte et le couvert*.'

'What does that mean?'

'I think the English expression is bed and board. I cannot afford to pay anyone. My grapes are picked by my sister's children and their student friends. They stay in my house or camp in my field for three days. They get plenty to eat and drink.'

'Sounds like fun.'

Didier ordered a half-bottle of Sauternes to drink with dessert. The sommelier poured a thimbleful for me to taste. It was like a slow explosion in my mouth. It had an endless finish. I put down my glass.

'What do you think?' Didier touched the back of my hand with his fingers.

A shock ran up my arm. I nearly jumped.

'I guess it's what my boss calls a different kind of wow,' I said.

Diarmuid and Honor refused coffee. Diarmuid said he had to meet someone. He said goodbye and left the restaurant. Honor looked exhausted. She left soon after him.

I didn't feel tired at all.

'It was too difficult to talk in here,' said Didier.

'But the food was good,' I said. 'My duck was delicious.'

'You like duck? That's good.'

'Really?' My voice came out in a squeak.

He drummed his fingers on the table. 'I've been inside all day. I'm like a lion in a cage. I need fresh air. Could I escort you at least part of the way to your hotel?'

'Sure,' I said.

He must have been holding his breath. I heard a puff as it escaped.

'I don't like being indoors all day either,' I said. 'I prefer working in the vineyard to working in the classroom or the laboratory. The tasting room isn't too bad. I have a nice view.'

'Would you like to go somewhere with a nice view?'

'That would be good.'

Didier marshalled me into a black cab. He asked the driver to take us to Primrose Hill. We walked through tall iron gates into a park. The sky was grey-blue and streaked with pink vapour trails like tiny comets. The street lamps along the paths were like the old gas lamps you see in movies. The air smelled of lilac and cut grass. The couple walking ahead of us up the steep hill had their arms wrapped around each other. They weren't walking fast. But neither were we. We walked side by side, in a step with each other. We didn't talk much. I was conscious of Didier glancing at me from time to time.

When we got to the top I gasped with delight. London glittered in the dusk as far as the red rim of the horizon.

'I used to come here to watch the sunset,' said Didier.

'With your wife?' The words shot out.

'Actually, not,' said Didier. 'I came alone when I wanted to think.'

'I hope my being here doesn't stop you thinking,' I said.

He looked at me with a kind of desperation. Then he took my face in his hands and kissed my mouth.

It was like all the sweetness in the world concentrated in one spot.

He released my face and stepped back.

'I'm thinking that we live on opposite sides of the world. I'm thinking that I am too old for you.'

My heart felt like it was on some kind of trapeze.

'So what age are you, Didier?'

'I'm forty.'

'That's not old. My grandfather is seventy-five. That's old.'

'What age are you, Melanie?'

'I was twenty-six last month,' I said. 'That's plenty old enough for kissing.'

Didier was very still. Then put his arms around me and kissed me again. We kissed like we never wanted to stop.

52

Honor

I decided to walk to my flat. I wanted to tire myself so I would fall asleep. I felt happy for Didier, in a melancholy way. At one time the possibility of a relationship had quickened the air between us. We had both rejected it without ever needing to discuss it. But for the first time since I left Hugo, I felt bereft.

The air was soft and smoky. In Soho Square, the leaves on the trees shimmered in the persistent twilight. I threaded my way through the drinkers shouting and laughing outside a bar.

Diarmuid was probably on the platform at St Pancras station by now, I thought. I imagined him smiling as Katy came through the barrier towards him. Anger rose in me. I quickened my step. Diarmuid was holding out his arms. No. I didn't want to see that. Picture something else. Like Hugo also arriving to meet Katy. Yes. That's better. Hugo was walking under the archway into the station. Katy was running past Diarmuid. She was jumping into Hugo's arms. Diarmuid was spinning around. He was staring at them.

Hugo was hugging Katy. They were laughing. Diarmuid was unbelieving, thunderstruck. That was a satisfying plot development. I stopped. Some residual road sense reminded me to look right before crossing Dean Street. The scene at St Pancras station became a freeze-frame in my head. I reached the opposite pavement. My brain began rolling the film again. Hugo was carrying Katy out of the station. I was enjoying this. I strode up St Anne's Court. Hugo and Katy were getting into a taxi. It disappeared into the night. I reached the block where I lived. I tapped on the keypad to open the front door. Now, where was Diarmuid? My camera eye searched the crowd. There he was, still where I had stranded him. He looked distressed. I wanted to comfort him. Don't feel bad, Diarmuid. The film was speeding up. I was writing the dialogue as I bounded upstairs to my flat. Listen to me, Diarmuid. They've been carrying on for months. Making a fool of you. I was in the scene and not in the scene at the same time. Can't you see she's all wrong for you? I put my key in the lock. You need someone who truly loves you, Diarmuid. I opened the door. I switched on the light. You need me.

It hit me like a guided missile straight to the heart. I was in love with my best friend.

The door swung closed behind me. I leaned my back against it and said out loud, 'Honor Brady, you are stupid, stupid, stupid.'

53

Melanie

Didier came to the hotel to have breakfast with me. We were almost bashful with each other. He didn't say much. He just kept reaching across the table to hold my hand.

'I woke up this morning with a smile on my face,' I said.

'Me too.'

'I wanted to open the window and yell, "Hey, London, listen up. I'm in love."'

'I have already told my friends about you. They said I could invite you for breakfast at their house. But I wanted you all to myself.'

'I'm glad about that,' I said.

'We will stay with them when we visit London together.' Didier spoke with total assurance. 'I will go to America in August. You will come to France in September.'

'We have June and July to get through,' I said. But I already knew we would write each other and speak on the telephone most days.

'Miss Millar?' The bellhop handed me a sheet of paper. 'This fax came through for you yesterday evening.

I didn't see you when you came in last night. Sorry about that.'

It was from Ivor. His handwriting covered the page.

I just spoke to the expert. It's an antique bottle but the engraving is modern. Hand engraving, no matter how good, always has tiny flaws. This has no flaws at all. Ergo it was done with some kind of high-precision tool. He thinks maybe a dentist's drill.

He'd signed it, *Ivor the Sucker.*

'Oh, no,' I cried.

'What's wrong?' Didier went pale.

'It's OK. Nobody died. It's not that kind of bad news. My stepfather bought a premier cru classé presented to the Tsar on a state visit to France. It looked the real deal. The bottle was engraved with the Romanov crest. Turns out it was done with a dental drill.'

Didier started to laugh.

'It seems kind of funny, I know. But Ivor paid over a hundred thousand dollars. This is serious fraud. The same dealer sold him other fake wines as well. We already knew about those. We thought maybe he'd been swindled himself. Ivor wrote him, called him up.' I took the business card for C. H. L. Fine Wines from my purse and gave it to Didier. 'But he got no reply. Mr Lancaster seems to have vanished. We don't have a home address.'

Didier stared at the card. He lifted his briefcase from the floor.

'I went there Tuesday,' I said. 'There's a sold sign on the building.'

Didier flicked through documents. He pulled out an invoice and waved it triumphantly. 'Lancaster Direct Wines. I recognised the address. C. H. Lancaster is Hugo Lancaster. He imports my wines. I know him. I know where he lives.'

'I already went there,' I repeated. 'He sold the building. I went to Companies House. I saw the documents filed for Lancaster Direct Wines. I checked his home address. It's the same. I have a bad feeling he's not going to register a new one. The bird has flown.'

'He lives in France,' said Didier.

It took me a beat to catch up. 'You're kidding.'

'I know the exact address.'

I hunted in my purse for my pen and notebook. My hands shook with excitement. 'I don't believe it. This is fantastic. I can't wait to tell Ivor.'

Didier was already scribbling the address on the back of the breakfast menu. 'He lives in Chateau Le Rossignol. Eight kilometres from me. Near Astignac.'

'Astignac?' I spoke so loud the waiter almost dropped a tray.

Didier was startled. 'Do you know it?'

I put down my pen. I was trembling so much I could hardly speak. 'I have a French uncle,' I said. 'I think he lives in Astignac.'

We stared at each other.

'But you are not sure?' Didier was clearly astonished that I didn't know where my uncle lived.

'It's a long story,' I said. 'And I didn't know any of it until last summer.' I took a deep breath. 'It goes back to World War Two, nineteen forty-four. My grandfather was in the US Air Force. His plane was shot down near Bordeaux. He was badly injured. He was found by a girl. She took him home and hid him from the Germans. She nursed him until he was well enough to escape. I think they fell in love.'

'I can guess what happened next,' said Didier. 'She got pregnant?'

'You guessed right,' I said. 'But Poppa didn't know about it until he was back home. He got a letter from a man who said he was going to marry this girl and adopt the boy. Poppa was married. He already had Uncle Bobby. My grandmother was expecting my mom.'

Didier was frowning. I didn't want him to think badly of Poppa.

'My grandfather sent all his savings. Twenty-five thousand dollars. It was a lot of money in those days. The man wrote back and thanked him. He said it would be better for everybody if Poppa didn't contact them again.'

'So he has never met his son,' said Didier. 'That is sad. And you have never met your uncle.'

'I only know about him because Poppa had a cardiac arrest and nearly died. He decided to tell us in case his son turned up one day looking for him.'

'Do you know his name?'

I hesitated.

'I'm curious,' said Didier.

'Poppa promised not to get in touch,' I said. 'That was the deal.'

'I was born near Astignac. Perhaps I know him.'

My heart began to thump. 'Dominique Petit, that's his name. You might know the man who adopted him. He was the mayor of Astignac after the war. Marc Petit.'

Didier spilled his coffee. He turned pale.

I almost cried out in shock. I put both hands on my breast to calm myself.

'I know Monsieur Petit,' Didier said slowly. 'And I know his son. But he cannot be your uncle. He was born in Algeria. He is the same age as me. And his name is Claude-Henri. It's impossible.'

'He must have an older brother,' I said. 'Who maybe stayed in Algeria?'

'I never heard him mention a brother,' said Didier. 'I think he is the only son. His father wanted him to be a vigneron. But Claude-Henri wasn't interested. He's an optometrist in Cap Ferret. He's a nice man.'

'Maybe he never knew about his brother? Maybe his father got divorced in Algeria and married again?'

'Perhaps,' said Didier.

A waitress had noticed the spilled coffee. She brought a fresh cup for Didier. He smiled his apologies. I was grateful for the interruption. It gave me time to compose myself.

I wrote Mr Lancaster's name and French address on the fax. 'I'll send this to Ivor. He'll be very thrilled.'

54

Honor

A sweet intensity that develops into a long finish.

I was at the Wine Fair handing out mugs of hot milk. A security guard stopped me. 'It's not milk,' I shouted. 'Look, it's wine.' I had a glass in each hand. But they were filled with pink rose petals. The guard turned into Diarmuid. He laughed like Santa Claus. Ho Ho Ho. 'I don't know how it happened,' I said. Mum opened the oven door and pulled out yards and yards of white silk. 'Listen,' she said. 'Your dad is singing my favourite song.' I couldn't hear it. Someone was drilling into the wall. Bzzzz. Bzzzz. I tried to walk away from the noise. The corridor went on forever. Bzzzz. Bzzzzz.

I wakened with a jolt. Bzzz. Bzzzz. I blinked at the beside clock. 0630. The milkman? Nobody delivered milk in central London. Somebody locked out? There was a keypad to open the front door. Bzzzz. Bzzzz. Some drunk staggering along the street thought it funny to ring my doorbell. I pulled the duvet over my head. Go away.

Bzzzz. Bzzzz.

I gave up, groped my way to the window and raised the blind. Sunlight flooded into the room. I opened the window and looked down into the street. Diarmuid was thumping his fist into his hand and bouncing up and down in an agitated way.

I shushed him. 'Stop ringing the bell. You'll waken the whole house.'

I pressed the buzzer to open the street door. A slam echoed through the building. I heard Diarmuid's footsteps on the wooden stairs. I opened the door to my flat.

'I thought you were a passing drunk,' I said.

'You're not far wrong.'

'What's happened? You look a mess.'

'Thanks, old friend. It's usually me who says the wrong thing.'

I led the way into the sitting room and pulled back the curtains.

'What is it, Diarmuid? What's wrong?'

'I saw Katy last night.'

A jealous rage rose in me. I turned away and pretended to straighten the curtains.

'Good God, Diarmuid, I thought somebody had died, or had an accident.'

'I have to talk to you. I couldn't wait.'

Love means having to listen even when you don't feel like it. I sat down on the sofa.

'You're always falling for the wrong man,' said Diarmuid. 'I can't stand seeing you being hurt. Please. Tell me you're not in love with Didier.'

His words took me by surprise. I looked at his face. He was earnest, serious. A thought crept into my mind. Was it possible?

'I'm not in love with Didier,' I said as steadily as I could.

Diarmuid dropped to his knees. His eyes were level with mine.

'I thought you were in love with him. I thought he was the new man.'

'Didn't I just tell you he wasn't?'

'No need to bite my face off.' Diarmuid had a crazy smile on his face.

My heart jumped.

'I've split up with Katy,' he said. 'I told her last night. I'm not in love with her. I know that because I was sick with jealousy when I saw you with Didier.'

There was a sound like rushing water in my ears. I was drenched with happiness. I was performing a kind of interior dance, like a dolphin, leaping through water, pirouetting, plunging, coming up for air.

Diarmuid took my hand. 'I've loved you for years, Honor. I can say that now. I'm a free man.'

He held my hand against his cheek. He moved his mouth to kiss my palm.

'It's an empty cold house without a woman, Honor. Tell me, do I have any chance at all?'

55

Melanie

I left Didier at the breakfast table while I went to the front desk to settle my bill.

'Could you send this for me, please?' I gave the receptionist the fax for Ivor.

I floated back to the restaurant on a cloud of satisfaction. Didier was buttering a piece of toast. He looked like he was miles away. I dropped a kiss on his head and slid on to the banquette opposite him.

'Penny for them?'

Didier smiled, but I could tell he was thinking hard about something.

'You know, before he went to Algeria, Marc Petit wanted to marry my mother. She also had a child by an American. My half-sister Dominique.'

I was punch drunk with surprises. 'That's amazing,' I croaked.

Didier shrugged. 'Not so amazing. After the war there were thousands of French children with American fathers. At least your grandfather sent money. A lot of money.

Doudou was not so lucky. Her father never sent a letter, or a sou.'

It was a sobering thought.

'It's possible he never knew about her,' I said. 'Poppa nearly didn't know about his son. It took two years for the letter to reach him.'

'What was the name of the girl who found your grandfather?'

'Amélie. Poppa was never told her family name. In case he got picked up and interrogated by the Gestapo.'

Didier put down his knife. 'My mother's name is Amélie.'

'It's a pretty name.' I reached cheerfully for the marmalade.

Didier said, in a careful voice, 'What is the name of your grandfather?'

'Bill,' I said. 'Bill McKitterick.'

Didier said, 'My sister's name is Dominique. Her father was an American airman. My mother found him in the woods after his plane was shot down. His name was Bill.'

'Hey, what a coincidence.' The words were hardly out of my mouth when it seemed like they jumped right back in again and swam around in the space I made when my jaw dropped.

'This is hard to believe,' Didier spoke very slowly. 'But I think my sister's father is your grandfather.'

At first I could not take in what he said. Then I felt like I was in one of those loopy daytime TV shows where people discover things like, Oh no! They've been given the wrong baby in the hospital! And they're actually married to their uncle! Didier was speaking but I could not hear what he was saying. My thoughts were sliding away from me. My heart was pounding. I was totally confused. Names raced around my head. Dominique. Doudou. Didier. Dominique. If Amélie was his mother then Didier was? What?

'Oh, no,' I cried. 'You can't be my uncle. That's gross.' I almost gagged.

People turned to stare at us. Didier grabbed my sleeve.

'It's all right, Melanie. Stop. Think about it. I am not your uncle. That is impossible. I wasn't born until nineteen fifty-four. Long after your grandfather left France.'

He shook my arm. 'Look at me.' He held my gaze. 'Listen to me. Dominique is my half-sister. We have the same mother but different fathers. You are not related to my mother. You are not related to my father. We are not related by blood.'

His words got through to me at last. I calmed down enough to ask, 'So who is Doudou?'

'That's the silly name I call my sister,' said Didier. 'She hates it. She prefers Dominique.' He stroked my face. 'My sister is your aunt. But you and I are not at all related by blood, Melanie. It is perfectly as it should be.'

The people at the next table resumed eating.

My heartbeat had slowed but my brain was racing again.

'You know, like, this is impossible, Didier? It's hard to believe. You tell me you know where Hugo Lancaster lives. Then you tell me you know all about Poppa. Also you tell me he has a daughter, not a son. It's all too much. It's too heavy. I think maybe I'm hallucinating. Or I'm going to wake up in Monterey and discover I've dreamed it all. Like Bobby in *Dallas*.'

Didier laughed. 'I watched that show when I lived in London. But *la réalité dépasse la fiction*. Truth is stranger than fiction. Isn't that what you say in English?' He moved to sit beside me on the banquette. He put his arm around me. 'It seems very strange, but it is easy to explain. Hugo Lancaster lives in the house where my mother was born. Le Rossignol. I was born there also. That is why I know these things.' He kissed my cheek. '*C'est simple.*'

I leaned my head against his shoulder. My brain began to make sense of it all.

Didier suddenly stiffened. 'You said that your grandfather sent money.'

'Yep,' I said. 'Twenty-five thousand dollars.'

Didier took his arm from my shoulder. He stared at the wall. He tapped his fingers on the table. 'My mother never received any money. I am certain of that.' Even in profile I could see the angry twist of his mouth.

I pulled him round to face me. 'She must have gotten the money. I saw the receipt from Western Union. I saw the letter that thanked Poppa. I remember it.' I could see it as clearly as though it were in front of me. '*Thank you for the money and the letter*,' I quoted. '*Please not to contact. That is better for all. Signed Marc Petit*.'

Didier was stony faced.

'Now I come to think about it, he got his pronouns mixed up,' I added. 'That's probably why Poppa thought he had a son.'

'Bastard,' said Didier.

'Don't you dare say that about my Poppa.'

'Marc Petit is a bastard. *Un salopard*. He never gave the money to Maman.' Didier banged his fist on the table. The plates jumped. The room fell silent. A waiter hurried over.

'Everything all right, sir?'

Didier put his hands up. 'Of course. Sorry. Everything is all right.'

I started to laugh. I was a little hysterical. People began to stare at us again.

Didier made a gesture that was apologetic, explanatory and utterly French.

'It is shock,' he announced to the restaurant. 'She has just discovered that her uncle is her aunt.'

56

Honor

On midsummer's evening, Diarmuid and I built a sandcastle together on the beach at Brittas Bay. It had four towers, crenellations, a moat and a piece of driftwood for a bridge.

We retreated to the tartan rug we had spread near the dunes and lay propped on our elbows, admiring our creation.

'It's like the one you kicked over,' said Diarmuid.

'Why did I kick it over? I can't remember.'

'Because I said girls couldn't build sandcastles and your effort wasn't any good.'

Pink clouds drifted across the sky. Waves flopped on the shore. Beyond the white breakers, the sea was calm. Fishing boats sat steady on the horizon.

'We built a good one together,' I said.

Mum did laps around the sitting room in her wheelchair when Diarmuid and I announced we were going to get married.

'I knew it,' she crowed. 'It was in the air when the two of you walked through the door yesterday.'

Tommy shook Diarmuid's hand and thumped him on the back. Kathleen said it was about time. Mum wheeled herself to the piano and began to play and sing.

'Drink to me only with thine eyes
And I will pledge with mine.'

We all joined in. Diarmuid too.

'Or leave one kiss within the cup
And I'll not ask for wine.'

Christine telephoned me in London as soon as she got the wedding invitation. 'I am so happy for you, Honor. I will send a formal reply, but of course I will come.'

After all the congratulations and recapitulations, she said, 'I have news for you as well. All of Astignac is talking about it.' Her voice was alive with excitement.

'Last week, the alarm went off at Le Rossignol. It made a great noise. I ran outside. Atalante was completely frenetic. You know she thinks it is her territory ever since she stayed with you. Then all the dogs in the commune began to bark. The police came. There were cars everywhere. There was even a helicopter like a big lighthouse in the sky. There was a car chase. Like a film *policier.* The thieves took a wrong turning in Astignac and drove into the river.'

I suddenly remembered the men in dark glasses I had seen sitting in a car outside Le Rossignol on my farewell walk with Atalante.

'What happened to them? Did they drown?'

'The police rescued them. But the wine they stole is in the mud at the bottom of the Garonne. Madame Lanot told me they were Russians. Her daughter is married to a policeman.' Christine paused for breath.

'Where was Hugo? Is he all right?'

'He was not there,' said Christine. 'And some days later, one of my neighbours saw two *déménageurs* with a lorry at Le Rossignol. I went there. The house was empty. I looked through the windows. No furniture. But I found your pink bicycle at the back.'

'The robbery must have shaken him,' I said. 'But it's strange. He paid the deposit to buy Le Rossignol.'

'And that is another very interesting thing. I heard he did not go to the notaire's office to complete the purchase. He has lost the deposit. And now there is a possibility that Didier will buy Le Rossignol.'

'But that's wonderful.'

'And there is something even more wonderful,' said Christine. 'Dominique has found her father.'

57

Melanie

A bin of wine, a spice of wit,
A house with lawns enclosing it,
A living river by the door,
A nightingale in the sycamore!

Poppa was silent for most of the descent into Merignac airport. The plane broke through some high cloud. We saw a wide brown river. The city of Bordeaux fanned out on both sides. Now we saw fields and low, white factory buildings shining in the sun.

'We dropped bombs here in nineteen forty-three,' Poppa said. 'I never saw it in daylight.'

The plane swooped towards the runway.

Didier was waiting outside the baggage hall. He held out his arms and I walked right into them.

I introduced him to Poppa.

'Melanie has told me all about you,' said Didier.

'Mostly good, I hope. I'm real pleased to meet you.' Poppa looked around hesitantly.

'Maman and Dominique are at Chateau de la Lune,' Didier said.

Poppa was silent in the car. I guess he was in the memory tunnel.

We bumped down a grassy track through a vineyard and there they were, standing in the shadow of the house. Amélie, hair like a silver helmet, a rope of pearls around her neck. Dominique, taller, with bright red hair.

Poppa got out of the car. 'I don't know whom to greet first,' he said hoarsely.

I have them in my mind's eye still. Poppa, arms half-outstretched; Amélie watchful; Dominique gripping her mother's arm. Then it was like everybody moved at the same time and it was all handshaking and cheek kissing, like the French do.

Didier pushed me forward. 'This is Melanie,' he said.

Amélie looked at me in a considered way. She took my hand. She kissed me on both cheeks.

I glanced at Didier. He winked at me. He was smiling. I relaxed.

Dominique took both my hands in hers. 'It is a great pleasure to meet you.' She turned to Didier. 'You said she was pretty. You didn't say she was beautiful.'

A man with cropped grey hair and a big nose came out of the house and said to Poppa, 'Do you remember me? I came to interrogate you at Hostens. Jean-Jacques Marly.' He stuck out his hand.

Then a whole lot of other people arrived. Didier's twin brother, Philippe, with his wife and six-year-old daughter; Dominique's husband, Michel-Henri, and their two grown-up daughters; Amélie's new stepson, his wife and baby; several cousins with both young and grown-up children. It seemed like everybody, except the baby, was carrying food.

Amélie and Dominique took Poppa by the hand. The three of them led a procession to the back of the house. There was a long table on the grass under a fig tree. A blue and white checked cloth covered one end. A plain white cloth covered the other. Within minutes, the whole table was covered with bowls of tomatoes, green salads, fruit tarts, cheeses, baskets of peaches and apricots, plates, flatware, glasses, bottles of wine.

Didier carried bunches of vine prunings to the brick-built barbecue on the terrace. He lit a match. A column of sweet white smoke ascended into a blue sky.

I thought about a puff of white silk descending from the sky all those years earlier.

Lunch lasted most of the afternoon. Many hands cleared the table and carried the chairs into patches of shade among apple trees. The baby slept. The children played hide and seek. Poppa and Dominique sat side by side, still at the table, the edges of their sun hats touching each other, talking.

When the sun was low in the sky, people began to leave. A mystifying number of adults and children kissed me goodbye. A convoy of cars trundled back up the track to the road. Only Poppa, Amélie and Jean-Jacques remained with us. They dozed on the terrace, occasionally waking to exchange a few phrases in a mixture of French and English accompanied by looping, explanatory gestures.

'Jean-Jacques was magnificent when we went to see Marc Petit,' said Didier. 'He stayed calm, and that made me calm also, although I was very angry. He negotiated a good agreement. It is better that we did not need to use the law. Also the law is very expensive.'

'I spoke to Ivor before I came over,' I said. 'He's hired a detective. That's expensive too. Mom thinks Hugo Lancaster will simply vanish again. Like he did as soon as he knew Ivor had gotten his address. Why waste another half million dollars? I think Mom might persuade Ivor to give up.'

It was one of those summer nights when it seemed like the light would never fade from the sky. Didier took me for a drive along an undulating road above the wide, flat valley of the Garonne. The slopes on either side were covered with vines. We dropped down to a narrower road and turned right on to a track that ran through a grove of oak trees and emerged in a vineyard.

Didier stopped the car. We got out. Rows of vines marched uphill. At the top of the hill was a wall. Beyond the wall was a garden of fruit trees. At the top of the garden, a handsome house with a single turret, glowed pink and gold in the last rays of the sun.

EPILOGUE

1996

Bright night. The moon is a white globe. The sky glimmers with stars. Yellow lanterns hang from the trees. The air is filled with laughter at this traditional end-of-vendange party – the acabeilles – at Le Rossignol.

The students who have picked grapes and carried baskets until their backs hurt, now lie on the grass, exhausted, happy, replete. Melanie buries her face in the bouquet, the gerbaude, which they presented to her. She smells roses, carnations, vine leaves, violets. She lifts her face for Didier's kiss.

A rocket sizzles through the air and explodes in a million tiny stars. Melanie and Didier break apart. They applaud. A second rocket shoots into the night sky.

In the woods beside them, a bird begins to sing. A run of notes. An ornamented trill. The sound is richer, deeper, more substantial than any birdsong Melanie has heard before. More urgent than a whistle. Sweet. Insistent. Strong.

They turn to each other again.

ACKNOWLEDGEMENTS

My thanks to the following winemakers and experts who gave me their time and patiently answered my questions:

Jane Anson, Bordeaux correspondent, *Decanter Magazine*;
Venla Freeman, California Wine Institute;
Véronique Jean, Château Chadenne, Fronsac;
Tamara McIntosh, MSc UC Davis, viticulturist;
Olympe and Yvon Minvielle, Château Lagarette, Camblanes;
Anne Néel, Château Lamothe de Haux, Haux;
Franck de Pape, La Cave du Marmandais, Cocumont;
Nigel Reay-Jones, Preignac, Sauternes;
Andrew Shaw, Buying Manager, wines, Waitrose;
Colin Sheriffs, Château de l'Orangerie, St Félix de Foncaude.

My thanks also to Gérard Peltier, Antoine de Pins and

Marie-Claude Gillespie for advice about all things French; to Pamela Watts for advice about writing, and to Marilyn Hocking and Clive Lewis for telling me their father's intriguing story.